Apparition

GAIL GALLANT

Appa

rition

DOUBLEDAY CANADA

Doubleday Canada and colophon are registered trademarks of Random House of Canada Limited

LIBRARY AND ARCHIVES CANADA CATALOGUING IN PUBLICATION
Gallant, Gail
      Apparition / Gail Gallant.
Issued also in electronic format.
ISBN 978-0-385-67962-6
      I. Title.
PS8613.A459376A66 2013   jC813'.6   C2012-906597-8

This book is a work of fiction. Names, characters, places and incidents are products of the author's imagination or are used fictitiously. Any resemblance to actual events or locales or persons, living or dead, is entirely coincidental.

Cover image: (girl) © solominviktor/shutterstock; (boy) © Fuse/Getty Images; (barn) © Soundsnaps/Dreamstime.com
Cover design: Terri Nimmo
Printed and bound in the USA

Published in Canada by Doubleday Canada,
a division of Random House of Canada Limited

www.randomhouse.ca

10 9 8 7 6 5 4 3 2 1

For my dearly departed friend,
Fran Hunnicutt

1

I pull open the curtains on my bedroom window and see the neighbour's tabby cat creeping through the remains of our once-loved garden like it's walking a tightrope. *Don't fall, kitty.* I look a little closer and there she is: my mother in her heavy blue sweater, down on her hands and knees by one of the old flower beds, carefully picking at weeds. I knew it was going to be one of *those* days.

My mother died three years ago.

I lean my forehead against the cold glass and watch her. As always, she seems worried. I take a deep breath, pull myself away from the window and check my face in the dresser mirror. I look like a witch, and not the sexy Halloween-costume kind. Before I leave my bedroom, I take one last look out into the garden, knowing that, this time, she probably won't be there. Yeah, she's gone. It's been two years since I lied and told my grandmother I don't see her anymore. It's only my imagination, apparently, so what's the point of more time in stupid psychotherapy?

I walk into the kitchen, head down, hair hiding my face, and Joyce gives me a double take.

"Well, you've looked better. What's up?" My grandmother doesn't believe in "mincing words"—that's her phrase.

"Not much," I say. "I think I might be getting a cold or something. Nothing serious."

I grab a box of cereal from the cupboard and a bowl from the dish rack and sit down at the far end of the table, hoping the cereal box will block me from her hawk eyes. I can still feel them on me, though, from where she's perched against the counter. Time for a distraction.

"But no problem getting started on the packing today. Just let me know what you want me to do." I try to sound sincere.

That works. She's eager to get us packing for the move. I live with my two brothers, Ethan and Jack, and my grandmother, Joyce. She prefers "Joyce" to being called Grandma or anything. We're moving to a new house next month, outside of town. Totally her decision.

"Well, the boys have their assignment—to tackle the garage. How would you feel about starting on the basement?"

How would I feel? Like slitting my throat. "Uh, sure. I mean, do you want me to pack *everything* down there? Are there boxes?" Ugh.

"Lots of boxes, and tape and markers to label them. All downstairs."

"Okay. I'll get started after breakfast." Could anything be worse than spending the day in the basement, packing stuff I'd rather set on fire?

Ethan bounds down the stairs, heading straight for the living room to flick on the TV. He's fourteen, two years younger than me, but he acts like a little kid. Watching TV and playing video games, that's Ethan's whole life since Mom died. I can't even remember what he used to be like.

The phone rings. Joyce calls for Ethan to turn down the volume, answers it and immediately assures whoever's on the line that this isn't a bad time to call. She listens. "Oh dear," she says. "Well, Amelia is sitting right here." She walks across the kitchen and holds the receiver out to me. "It's Mrs. Sorenson," she whispers.

Matthew's mother? What does she want? And it's Sunday morning. Why isn't she in church?

"Hello, Mrs. Sorenson?" I say into the phone, and as soon as I speak, the hurt comes flooding back.

"Amelia, do you know where Matthew is? He never came home last night." She sounds upset.

I hesitate, trying to imagine Matthew pulling an all-nighter.

"No . . . no, I don't know where he is." I try to concentrate. "Did . . . did he say where he was going when he left the house?" I'm not sure I want to admit I saw him.

"He was in a strange mood last evening. He left without telling us and took his father's truck. I'm sorry to bother you, but I didn't know whom else to ask. You are his closest friend."

Hearing that makes the pain even worse. I'm thinking, *Yeah, that's what I thought too.*

Just then Ethan walks into the kitchen, and I can hear Joyce telling him that Matthew is missing.

"Well, he was with Amelia last night," Ethan blurts out, blinking hard, his mouth twitching. Ethan has nervous facial tics, but Joyce doesn't want us to talk about it. Now she turns her death-ray eyes on me. Mrs. Sorenson just said something, but I'm not sure what it was. I turn my back to Joyce so she won't read my face.

"If I hear anything at all, I promise to call right away," I say. I can't wait to hang up. I'm not about to tell Mrs. Sorenson that Matthew's probably spent the night with some strange girl. She won't like that one bit. Serves him right if he's in deep trouble. He'll have to dig himself out. As I put down the phone, my grandmother jumps on me.

"Ethan says you were with Matthew last night. I thought you were over at Morgan's." Joyce is pretty scary when she's interrogating. "Do you know where Matthew is or not?"

"No, I don't." I give Ethan the evil eye. "Matthew just passed me on the road when I was walking home from Morgan's and gave me a lift the rest of the way. I was with him for, like, five minutes, and I don't know where he went from there."

"Well, you seemed a little odd when you came in last night."

Damn. She must have managed to clock me in that split second as I passed the kitchen door. I have to admit that my grandmother is pretty sharp most of the time. For her age, I mean. Compared with a lot of the parents in Owen Sound, she's Einstein. She doesn't miss much. That's why I try to stay outside her radar range.

"We didn't have a fight. Nothing like that. I was a little irritated at him, but it was nothing major." She's listening intently now, and I know I'm caught. "It was just something he said." I pause, looking down at the cereal getting soggy in the bowl. The sight of it makes me want to hurl.

"Well, if it has anything to do with why he didn't go home last night, you should tell his parents."

I know that not saying anything will only make this an even bigger drama, so I force myself to explain.

"He told me he was off to hook up with a girl, that's all. I was just pissed because he was all so secretive, and we're supposed to be such good friends. So I felt a bit . . . betrayed. No big deal. But you know, it's none of *my* business."

Joyce sees through me, I can tell. It's pretty bad when even your grandmother knows you are secretly in love with your best friend. I suddenly feel like I'm going to start crying again—as if I didn't do enough of that last night—so I grab my cereal bowl and leave the kitchen, mumbling that I'll start work on the packing in a minute.

Back in my room, I put the bowl of mushy cereal on my dresser and crash down on my bed, quietly crying again.

2

*L*ast night, I was taking a shortcut along Industrial Road after spending the evening watching TV with my friend Morgan. The chilly breeze was rustling brown leaves along the edge of the asphalt. There was a line of trees on my left with an empty field beyond, and the shopping mall's rear parking lot on my right. After closing time, the lot was deserted. Not another soul in sight. Just pools of light around lampposts, and the silhouette of an abandoned car.

Somewhere in the distance behind me, I could hear this engine approaching. The noise quickly got louder. *Somebody in a hurry,* I thought. *Where's the freakin' fire?*

An old black pickup truck blew past me. But about a hundred yards up the road its brake lights lit up, which was strange, because there's nothing on that stretch to stop for. A homicidal maniac tracking his next victim, I figured. Wouldn't it just be my luck?

I had a lot on my mind. First of all, it was finally starting to sink in with me that Joyce really *was* going to make us move out of town.

And secondly, I was stressing about Brittany, who was at Morgan's place too. Morgan's my best girlfriend but we're not always that close. She's pretty chummy with Brittany, which I really don't get. Anyway, Brittany let slip that they'd both been invited to a Halloween party that I didn't even know about. With my family moving outside of town, out of the only house I've ever lived in, I knew I was going to get left out of everything from now to forever.

And thirdly, there was Matthew.

Up ahead, the truck had crawled to a stop, like it was waiting for me, and now I was pissed off at myself for taking such a deserted route home. I didn't even have my cellphone on me. But I kept walking, imagining the attention that my gruesome death might bring. My name in the paper. My picture, even. Hopefully a decent picture and not my hideous school photo. That's when I came up alongside the truck, its engine still running and the passenger's window rolled down. Matthew, leaning over from the driver's seat, stuck his head out, grinning at me. What a shock! I'd never seen that truck before, and he doesn't even have a driver's licence. He shouted my name over the engine noise. "Amelia!"

If you'd asked me before last night, I would have said that Matthew was my very best friend and favourite person in the world. Only that would have been lying. The truth is, I've been madly, pathetically in love with him for ages, and trying not to show it. It all began three years ago, I guess, at a real low point in my life, right after my mother died. He started paying attention to me, for no reason. We sat together in math, and then at lunch and in the library, and this year in history class. Mostly we just talk a lot. We're always having these big arguments, but somehow we manage to stay friends. We disagree on everything—TV shows, tattoos, the point of life, whatever. His parents are super-religious Christians and I was raised without any of that, so he's always trying to save my soul. He's got an answer for everything. He gets so enthusiastic about his ideas and opinions it's almost funny. I've never met anyone who can get so intense just talking about ordinary stuff. I've known for ages I was in love with him, but I've been terrified to tell him. He doesn't even suspect.

Things were pretty great between us, even though we didn't really hang out much outside of school on account of his parents. But then he took this job out of town this summer, working for guys in a Mennonite community who are experts at taking down old barns. He had hardly any access to computers or anything, and I only heard from him twice over two months. I found myself missing him more than I could have imagined, and I decided that when he got back, I was going to tell him I loved him, straight out, and hope for the best.

By late August, I was so excited to see him again I could barely stand it. When I finally did, a few days before the new school year started, it was like seeing him clearly for the very first time: his eyes, his smile, his long legs in those narrow black jeans. I couldn't stop thinking, *Wow*. Seriously. The problem was, I was still too chicken to tell him the truth.

The first couple of weeks back at school were total agony. Then on Friday, something weird happened. We were sitting together after school in an empty corner of the library, doing some history homework. But mostly we were having one of our typical arguments. Matthew was saying that everyone believes in things they can't prove, and I was bragging that I only believed in solid things like flesh. I was tapping my fingertips on his chest when I said that, for emphasis. We were laughing. I could feel his breastbone, and all of a sudden I started thinking about his bare skin under his T-shirt. I stopped tapping. The next thing I knew, my whole hand was flat against his chest. I couldn't help it. I don't know what I was thinking, but the words just slipped out. "*Your* solid flesh," I said.

I felt him inhale, and it caught me like the sensation of going over the crest of a roller coaster. I could feel his heart beating. He was looking at me with eyes wide with something like fear, his mouth partly open. And then he looked away and laughed in this nervous way he has. Shifting his attention to his textbook, he said, "I'm sorry. What question were we on?" Like nothing had happened.

That was the moment to say something. But I couldn't. Instead, I pulled my hand away and said I should be heading home. I could barely breathe. I kept my head down and started throwing my books into my bag, grabbing my pens and stuff, shoving things in so fast that my papers got all mixed up. It was too much trouble to put on my jacket, so I just grabbed my school bag and jumped to my feet, my jacket hanging from one arm. But before I could make another move, his hand shot up and grabbed my wrist.

"Don't go," he said.

He held on tight to my wrist, looking down at my hand. And then he said in this quiet voice that it would be great if maybe I could come to a service at his parents' church one of these days. A church service? Are you kidding me?

"Gee, I don't know, Matthew," I said, sarcasm creeping in. "Sounds awfully romantic."

But he didn't smile. Didn't say anything. He just held on, staring at my hand so hard that I thought he was going to either kiss it or bite it. Finally I couldn't stand the tension. I squirmed out of his grasp, told him I'd think about it and practically ran out the door. My heart was pounding. What had just happened?

I think about Matthew all the time. I love his eyes: dark, intense and narrow, like he's always *this close* to figuring something out. Also his grin. And his straight black hair hanging down his forehead, his square shoulders, his long legs. I don't know why, but he makes me laugh. He can crack me up with a sideways glance.

Morgan always says I should take a chance and just fess up. But I'm a pessimist by nature. I figure it would never work out between Matthew and me. He's a religious freak, and I'm just a freak.

Then last night there he was—grinning at the wheel of this pickup truck, looking like the sexiest guy on the planet. He said he could drop me off at my house if I wanted. I hesitated at first because I was a little bit in shock from running into him so unexpectedly. Also, my hair looked lousy. But I said, "Great. Thanks a lot." I wasn't going to turn down a chance to be with him, even for a few minutes.

As soon as I got into the passenger seat, even before I'd done up my seat belt, the truck took off, and that's when I realized he was acting odd. I asked him where he got the truck. "My dad's," he said, kind of distracted. So much for worrying about what I looked like— he wasn't looking at me at all. He said he had been on 12th Line earlier in the day, meeting with an old farmer about taking down his barn. It was going to be a big job, he said, talking even faster than usual and still grinning like crazy. Working after school and on week-ends, it could take a month or more. He thought he could take all the boards down himself, and get help on the frame. Grey County is filled with big old barns that are close to falling down, each one about a hundred years old, the wood weathered grey. The boards are in high demand among people who make reproduction antiques. Every year a few more old barns disappear. Sad, really.

I hadn't told him yet that I was moving—I guess I'd been hoping the deal would fall through—but that seemed as good a moment as any to face reality. "Believe it or not," I said, "my grandmother bought a farmhouse on 12th Line. The blue one on the east side, just past the bridge? For her horses, so she doesn't have to board them anymore. We're . . . we're moving in about four weeks." It was depressing to hear myself say it. "Maybe you can take that barn down too."

He didn't say anything. No sympathy, no reassurance, nothing. That surprised me, but he was acting odd and I thought maybe it had something to do with what had happened on Friday.

"Matthew, about what happened between us in the library yesterday . . ." I was searching for something to say, but when I looked over at him, I swear he wasn't listening at all.

Then he shot a sideways look at me. "It was nothing." He was smiling when he said it, but it was like he was thinking about something else.

After a moment of awkward silence, I asked him where he was off to, because it was almost ten o'clock. He just raised his eyebrows. As he stopped the pickup truck in front of my house, I joked that if he was up to no good, he didn't have to tell me. But as soon as I said that, I got a bad feeling, like I had guessed right. Still grinning that strange grin, he looked out at the dark road and said, "If you must know, I'm meeting a girl."

"Really?" The shock of his answer had almost made me forget how to unbuckle my seat belt. I was struggling with it like the truck was filling up fast with lake water, like I was going to drown. "Well, I hope you two have a nice time," I managed to say, wrestling myself out of the truck and slamming the passenger door. I gave him one last look through the rolled-down window and said, "Isn't it a bit late for church?" It was sarcastic but I couldn't help myself.

"Who said anything about church?" He drove off down the road, leaving me there at the foot of my driveway. I would have been less shocked if he had said, "I'm going off to blow up the post office."

As I walked up my driveway I was burning with a jealous rage, but by the time I got to the front door it had already turned into flat-out heartbreak. The idea that Matthew, having spent all those lunches and spares with me for almost three years, was hot for someone else made me feel like throwing up. Only the day before, I'd thought maybe something was happening between us. I'd felt, well, hopeful. But it had meant nothing. Just my sick imagination again.

A couple of loud sobs slipped out before I told myself to shut up. I was shaking so badly I had trouble getting the key in the front door, and out of the corner of my eye, I saw the window curtains twitch. When I finally got the door open, I sneaked as quietly and quickly as I could past the living room, where Ethan was now back watching TV, and the kitchen, where I saw Joyce look up from emptying the dishwasher, to my bedroom at the back of the house.

I shut the door behind me, dropped onto my bed and pushed my face into a pillow to muffle the sound of my crying, unable to blot out the vision of his grinning face.

I'd thought Matthew and I totally belonged together. How could I have been so wrong?

3

I'm grateful that it was my older brother who broke the news. Jack came home early Sunday evening and walked straight to my bedroom door, his face all white, breathing heavily through his mouth like he'd been running. He didn't want to have to do it, I could tell.

He said they had found Matthew in an old barn on 12th Line. "Murdered. That's what they're saying."

I looked at him. His eyes were red.

"Can you believe it? Less than a mile down the road from our new place," he said.

"Wh-what?"

He started talking slowly, as if in a foreign language. "Run through the middle with some kind of old farm tool." He stopped, watching me like he was afraid. "A pitchfork or something." He made a little motion like a turtle, ducking his head into his shoulders. "Right through his stomach."

He sat down beside me and put a heavy arm around my shoulders.

"God, I'm really sorry, Amelia. I know you two were close." He hugged and rocked me and held the side of his head against mine. Just like he held my hand when Mom was lying dead in her blue hospital gown. I don't remember when he left my room. I just remember hearing him say, "Not again."

I stay in my room through Sunday supper. I want to call Matthew on the phone. *Do you know I hardly slept last night, Matthew? I was so upset with you.* I don't feel like eating. I don't feel like talking to Morgan, even when she calls a third time. I don't feel like dealing with my grandmother, who wants to check on me constantly. Jack knocks gently and asks through the door a couple of times if he can get me anything. He's a good brother. (Though maybe Morgan put him up to that. He's got a crush on her.) But I'm okay. I'm really not feeling anything at all. Everything seems too far away. Even my own body. So far away I can't move my arms or legs. Without turning my head, I study my bedroom wall. I look at cracks I've never noticed before. The pale green lines in the drapes, some thick, some thin. And at some point late in the night, when I can't keep my eyes open any longer, I curl up on my side and go to sleep.

I open my eyes the next morning and it slowly dawns on me that I slept in my jeans and sweater on top of the bedspread, with the light on. Otherwise everything is normal. It's Monday, and that means school.

Joyce knocks on the door and opens it a crack, and then a bit wider. She sticks her head in.

"Amelia, you're going to have to eat something. I know you might not feel like it, but I'm going to bring you a bowl of cereal. Or even better, you can get up and eat it at the kitchen table."

Joyce thinks cereal is the answer to everything. She just waits, looking at me. She's not leaving.

I finally tell her I'll get up. I'll eat some cereal in the kitchen. But I don't think I want to go to school.

She starts to say something, then stops. She nods and says, "No problem," and shuts the door behind her.

Matthew, you'll have to go to history class without me. You'll have to lend me your notes.

It takes me a while to get up off the bed. In the kitchen, Joyce has set a bowl and the carton of milk and the cereal box at one end of the table. She's sitting at the other end, a cup of tea in front of her.

"The boys left already," she offers, like she's looking for something to say.

I sit down and look at the bowl, then pick up the box and pour some cereal. I feel a little hungry, but after only two spoonfuls I've had enough. Joyce asks if I'd like to eat anything else. She asks if I'm okay. I'm thinking that I must remember to ask Matthew why a loving God allows so much pain in the world. *What's his problem, Matthew? Does he love us or not?*

Joyce says she's going to start packing up the dining-room hutch. That's a big job. All the china, the crystal, the silverware—it's all Mom's stuff. Joyce is not really a "fine china" person. I tell her I'll help, even though I feel sick.

We sit at the dining-room table, wrapping the fragile pieces in thin foam sheets and stacking them in empty boxes she got from the liquor store. I'm trying hard not to break anything, though my hands are shaky. Mom loved this pattern, turquoise and blue with delicate little gold scrolls. I keep my eyes on the colours, wrapping each plate and bowl and saucer and teacup in its own tissue, fitting it snugly into a box. *For you, Mom. You have such beautiful china.*

After a while, Joyce wants to take a break for lunch. I follow her into the kitchen and she puts some chicken vegetable soup in front of me. I try a bit, but it tastes weird and I'm not hungry. When the doorbell rings, she leaves the kitchen to answer it while I look down into my soup. I hear her greeting someone, then saying that the timing isn't very good. She's whispering in the hallway.

I get up to see who it is. Maybe it's Matthew? But it's a man in a suit and tie who says he's come for a little chat with me. Joyce stands in the hallway between us.

"Amelia, this is Detective Grierson. He's working on the . . . the case involving Matthew. Detective Grierson, this is Amelia. She's not feeling well today, so we're taking it easy. Doing some packing. We're getting ready to move."

Grierson nods like that's interesting. He looks strong and a little rough, and like he'd rather not be wearing a suit. He leans forward and stretches out a long arm to shake my hand. I focus on the strength of his handshake.

"Do you mind if we have a talk, Amelia? It's very important. I just want to check on a few things. Is there somewhere we can sit down? In the kitchen?"

I nod, but I'm hesitating. Joyce leads the way.

"This is about your friend Matthew," he says.

It's about Matthew.

"Matthew . . ." he begins, then stops. "I think you know we found Matthew's body yesterday. We think he died sometime Saturday night." He pauses like he's expecting me to have something to say about that. Then he goes on. "But we don't know how he died. We don't know the circumstances. We need to find out what happened. And according to some of the kids at school, you were his best friend, and the last known person to see him alive. Is that true? Can you tell me about that?"

Matthew is dead.

Detective Grierson is holding a pen and a notebook. He's got the pen touching the page like he's waiting to write something. After a moment he asks me again. "Can you tell me what you remember about Matthew on Saturday night?"

I try to remember. His eyes. His smile. I try to think.

"I believe he drove you home. Is that right? Picked you up on Industrial Road?"

I nod.

"Can you tell me anything you remember about him that night? Anything at all?"

He waits for me. "He looked good," I say finally.

"Really?" the detective says. "He looked good? What do you mean by that, exactly?"

How can I tell this stranger what I mean? "I don't know." I look over at Joyce.

"Okay." He looks at Joyce too, then back at me. "Anything else? Did he say where he was going? Did he say what his plans were?" He writes something in his notebook.

I remember what Matthew told me. "He said he was meeting a girl. That's all he said."

Grierson nods. "That's very helpful, Amelia. Who was she? Did he say? Or can you guess?"

I stare at the table until I forget the question.

He tries again. "Do you know anyone he might date who lives out that way? On 12th Line?" He pauses. "Has he ever mentioned anyone he knows out there? A friend, an acquaintance? Someone he could possibly have been heading out to visit?"

I remember the farmer. "A farmer. With an old barn."

"Anyone else?"

He keeps looking at me like he's got all day. Finally I manage to shake my head. He writes something else down.

"Did Matthew have any troubles that you know of? Any enemies? Any run-ins or conflicts with anyone in the last while?"

I think hard about nothing and then shake my head.

"Did Matthew use alcohol or drugs?"

I'm still shaking my head.

"One last thing," he says after a long silence. "Do the letters *D-O-T* mean anything to you? His mother found them carved into Matthew's desk, and she's pretty sure the carving was recent. Could it stand for something? Be some kind of code?"

"Dot? You mean like dot-com?" I'm trying to think. *Dot. Period.* "Not really."

Matthew is dead. Period. The end.

4

This morning, my grandmother tells me she wants me to see Dr. Krantz again.

Dr. Krantz is the psychiatrist she made me see every week for a whole year after my mother died. It was to deal with how I was missing Mom, my hallucinations and that. I tell her I really don't need to see Dr. Krantz, and she says that in that case she wants to see me eating more and going back to school. I manage to swallow a few spoonfuls of cereal and get dressed. Not wanting to go to school is hardly a sign of mental illness, I tell her as I leave the house.

On my way to school, I talk to Matthew. *I realize that people die, Matthew. I've always known that. My father died in a car accident when I was four. And even when you know for a long time that someone is going to die—like I did with my mom—it still feels sudden. But this? I was expecting to be hit by an asteroid someday more than I was expecting this.*

When I arrive at school, there are several police cars parked in the lot. I guess they're investigating. Everyone in school—everyone in town—is in a freakin' panic. That's what Ethan says. After all, a murdering psychopath is on the loose in Grey County. The police are refusing to confirm that Matthew's death is a murder, at least until the coroner's report is in, but everyone else has figured it out. People say he was cornered in a dark barn by a pitchfork-waving maniac. I haven't really thought about that part. I can't.

Jack says that the old farmer who owns the barn is a suspect, mainly because he lives alone, and because he has an artificial eye that's pretty creepy. He hasn't exactly acted guilty, though. I heard he was more flipped out by Matthew's death than anyone. Morgan's friend Brad has an uncle who's a cop, and he told Morgan that the old guy was shaking and unable to talk even two days later, it gave him such a bad fright. He's been staying with his daughter and her family ever since. The police must be afraid he'll die of a heart attack before they can get to the bottom of this.

I enter the school's front doors, tracking my way through the crowded hallway with eyes down, weaving between running shoes and baby-doll flats and ankle boots. As I stand at my locker, trying to remember my combination, an arm slips around my shoulders. It's Morgan, giving me a tight squeeze, which feels nice. But she holds me a little too long, and that makes me feel like crying again.

I don't have much to say and neither does she, and that's good. Then she walks me to class. The kids in the hallway seem to be in a state of hysterics or something. They're all talking louder and faster than usual, and a lot of them are looking at me. Kids I hardly know are grabbing my arm and saying they're sorry. It's funny, in a way, how before Matthew I felt invisible at this school. It's as if he made me easier to see.

Everywhere people are hugging, rocking in each other's arms. A few girls are crying. It's like one big emotional meltdown, and it's happening all around me. Was Matthew more popular than I realized? Are they feeling sorry for him? Or are they afraid they might be next? This is crazy. *Are you seeing this, Matthew?*

My first class is history, and my regular place has an empty seat beside it. I think about sitting down, but I can't. Then Brittany calls my name from across the room, and when I look up she gives me a little wave. She points to an empty seat near her. I walk over, feeling eyes following me. The attention is embarrassing, but it's better than sitting in my old seat. Even Brittany looks like she feels sorry for me.

I get through the class by focusing hard on every word the teacher says. *Every. Single. Word.* This could help my grades.

Later, as I try to get through the hall to my next class, I run into Jack. He seems surprised to see me. He gets me in a headlock to amuse his football friends, but he lets me go pretty quickly. I know he's worried about me. Jack is like that. He looks at me now like he's taking a reading.

"I'm okay," I tell him.

With Ethan it's different. I catch his eye from a distance in the cafeteria and he looks guilty. It's because, for him, this is exciting. He's sitting with his posse at the far end of the table and doing most of the talking. Even from across the room I can see him twitching. He's been doing that weird thing with his face ever since Mom died, especially when he's excited or nervous. It's a flinch, like a nurse just jabbed him with a needle. He doesn't seem to notice he's doing it. But he must know, deep down. Joyce talked to the family doctor, but I think they figured it would go away on its own if we ignored it. That's hard, though. It gets on my nerves, like a constant reminder that something's wrong with our family.

The principal announced over the PA system that Matthew's funeral would be Thursday morning at eleven a.m. and that everyone from school was free to attend, with a letter of permission from a parent or guardian. Joyce wrote me a note. Jack insisted I get a ride over with him and his friend Jeremy, who has his own car.

Matthew's family's church is on the east side of town, down the road with the Pizza Hut on the corner. It's a white frame building with a pointy roof and a big front porch. The double doors are open when we get there, and there are dozens of kids standing around in the parking lot and on the steps. You can hear the organ playing inside.

We wade through the crowd and take a seat near the back. The dark wooden casket is already at the front, with small stands of arranged flowers on either side. I can see Matthew's parents, together with his uncles and aunts and cousins, sitting in the front pews. Their heads are bowed low. Even though he never said anything about his parents that sounded appealing to me, I feel sorry for them. Matthew was their only child. And the sad organ music only makes everything seem worse.

Just before the service begins, my grandmother walks in with two of her horse-loving girlfriends and squeezes in behind us. I feel her lightly touch my back. The small church is packed now. *So this is what your funeral looks like.* The pastor talks for a long time, mostly about how we don't know God's plan for us and we can't always understand why he lets some things happen. He talks about heaven and how perfect it is there, and he says that Matthew is looking down on us right now. He says that someday we will join him, and on that day we'll understand why Matthew's life ended the way it did. It reminds me of what Matthew used to say about my mother. How she was happy in heaven. Part of me felt so comforted hearing him say that. The other part of me thought, *Actually, she's hanging out in the back garden.*

During the sermon, Mrs. Sorenson's shoulders begin to shake. And then Mr. Sorenson's shoulders begin to shake. They are both leaning far forward in their seats. There is the sound of sniffling from all corners of the church, and the sniffles turn into sobs. But now I'm sitting beside Matthew in the library and he's doodling on the back of a handout, drawing a picture of a tree. There are birds nesting in the tree. He draws lines in the trunk, making it look strong and real. I grab his pen and draw a noose hanging from one of the branches, just for fun. I'm smirking. Matthew rolls his eyes and pulls the pen from my hand, changing the noose into a tire swing. Now I'm swinging back and forth under the tree, looking up into the branches, looking at the little birds.

Something's happening at the front of the church. A bunch of men are taking up positions around the casket, lifting it off its platform and beginning a slow procession down the aisle. I watch as the casket comes toward me and then goes by. Hard to believe anything is in it. People begin filing out by rows; ours will be one of the last to leave. The church takes forever to empty. I want to say something to Matthew's mother as she shuffles past, but what?

Outside, a crowd surrounds the Sorensons, and on the fringes of the circle there's a television crew pointing their camera this way and that. I'm stuck on the steps with Jack until my grandmother comes up and pulls me by the arm toward her car.

"You don't want to go to the cemetery, Amelia. Come with us."

My grandmother's car gets stuck in a small traffic jam leaving the church parking lot. Rita, her friend, is riding shotgun, and I'm sitting in the back seat, staring out at the crowd huddled at the church steps.

As our car inches toward the exit, I notice a man standing on the sidewalk. His hair is charcoal grey, and a bit long and messy, like an old rock musician's. He's wearing a brown trench coat, his hands pushed deep in its pockets. His face looks sad and tired. He watches me watching him from the back window as we drive by. He takes his right hand out of his pocket, and for a second it looks like he might wave. And as we drive down the street, he's still looking at me. As if I'm the one he came to see.

5

I'm lying on my bed, door closed, curtains drawn, light out. It must be about four o'clock in the afternoon. But it could be four in the morning. Either way it feels the same.

I'm calm and still, flat on my back, legs straight and close, with my hands folded on my chest. The tears are overflowing at the outside corners of my eyes and trickling like little creeks straight toward my ears. I'm wondering whether they'll actually go into my ears, but so far they haven't. I feel the cool lines of their paths.

Ethan arrives home from school with his usual steel-band entrance. "Amelia! Amelia!" he calls at the top of his voice, barrelling down the front hallway. I hear Joyce tell him to hush up. "Amelia?" He's whispering loudly and knocking at my bedroom door.

"What do you want?" I snap.

Having his sister best friends with a gruesome murder victim is the most exciting thing that's happened to him in ages. He opens the door a crack, letting some light cut across my bed.

"You're in for a surprise. Everybody's already talking about it. The report." He must mean the coroner's report. "Why are you just lying there? That's how people lie in their coffins, you know."

"I don't care." I don't want to hear details of how Matthew died.

"But he wasn't murdered! The police are saying he wasn't murdered."

"What do you mean?" I sit up. "It was an accident?" That's unimaginable.

"No, not an accident. Everybody knows that. He did it to himself. On purpose. He committed *su-i-cide*." He draws out the word as long as he can.

"That's a lie!"

"They say he threw himself at the pitchfork or whatever it was. He hurled himself at it. He set it up so it was pointing straight at him, and he ran into it. Full speed!" He says it like he's talking about a superhero.

"That's impossible. Matthew would never kill himself! He would never, ever, *ever* kill himself!" I'm yelling now, and looking for something to throw. "Get *out*!"

"Okay, okay." Ethan closes the door but I can hear him muttering, "Just thought you'd want to know. *Sorrr-y!*"

Matthew would never do that. That much I know. *Do you hear what they're saying, Matthew? How did you let this happen? How could you be so stupid? What kind of ridiculous trouble did you get yourself into? Suicide? Anybody but you.*

The sun's going down. I have a lot of math homework and that's all I'm going to think about right now. I sit in my room at my desk and sharpen a pencil with my steel sharpener. Where did I get this thing? It's so old. Must have been Mom's. Yes, that's why I kept it. Just a little thing that she used for years. That she held in her hand. I flip through the pages of my notebook, looking up my math assignment. I think I can do these questions. I know this stuff pretty well.

About an hour later, my grandmother raps gently on my door. She says there's someone on the phone—my history teacher. That's strange, but I pull myself up from my desk and take the phone from her hand.

"Your dinner's still in the oven," she says, sounding almost friendly, and she walks away.

As soon as I say hello, I know something isn't right.

"Hello, Amelia?" The voice is slow and gravelly and deep, like the voice of a weary old cowboy from a Hollywood movie. It isn't Mr. Chambers.

"Yes?"

"Amelia, I'm sorry I had to lie. I was afraid you wouldn't take a call from a stranger. I was at the funeral earlier today. I . . . I think you saw me."

Somehow I know it's the man on the sidewalk. Should I just hang up?

"My name is Morris Dyson," he continues. "I'm a writer. I write a column for the local paper. Mostly short history pieces."

The name sounds familiar. He pauses and I'm wondering what I should do. I don't want to talk to this guy.

"I just want to ask you a few questions, that's all. It's not for print. It's not for an article." There's a long pause. "I have a personal interest."

"Well, I really can't talk right now. Sorry." And before I know it, I've hung up. I'm totally surprised I did that. It's not like me.

Immediately the phone rings again, and I suddenly realize where I've seen him before. I answer it.

"Amelia?" He starts speaking before I even say hello, talking faster. "I'm sorry but I think something very strange happened to your friend Matthew." He pauses. I'm holding my breath. "And I don't think the police are going to figure out what it was."

"You were at my mother's funeral too. I remember you standing at the back of the church."

He almost stutters. "I . . . yes . . . I knew your mother . . . I did."

"I don't understand why you're calling me."

"If you think about it, you probably do. . . . You know why I'm calling you."

All I can think about is hanging up again, but then he asks me, "Aren't you curious about what *D-O-T* means?"

"Sorry?"

"*D-O-T*. Dot. I saw it in the police report."

"The carving in Matthew's desk? I don't know anything about that."

"But I've heard you and Matthew were close."

"Obviously not *that* close."

"Why do you say that?"

I hesitate. "Because he was off to meet some girl that night."

"Do you really believe that?"

My throat constricts. My eyes sting. No, I don't believe it. I can't believe it. But all I can say is "I don't know."

"Well, did you think he was suicidal? Did he seem depressed?"

Of course not. Not Matthew. "I always thought he was a happy enough person, whatever that means." But what do I know? Not much, it seems.

"You know what I think? I think that if he'd had a secret girl-friend, you'd have been suspicious before Saturday. I think that if he'd been a suicide risk, you might have sensed something was wrong. Amelia, something's not right here, and I want to figure out what really happened."

"Why?"

"Because . . . his isn't the first strange death to take place in that barn."

My stomach sinks. I swear I don't want to know, but I hear myself ask, "Who else?"

"Do you know Hank Telford, the farmer? His son, Paul, was my best friend. Back in March 1980, he died in that barn. He was nineteen years old. They said it was suicide, but I never bought it. So you might say I'm on a personal quest. I think there's something going on in there. Something paranormal."

I feel a sensation like cold water is creeping up the back of my head. "Why are you telling me this? What do you want from me?"

"I know you're afraid, Amelia. I think it's because you know something—maybe more than you realize."

"I don't know anything, and I have to go. I'm sorry."

I hang up, shut the door and sit down on my bed before my shaky legs give way. He doesn't call back, but I can still hear his voice over my pounding heart. *There's something going on in there.*

6

The leaves are red and yellow and orange but soon they'll be gone, leaving black skeleton branches against the grey clouds. The apple orchards look best in fall. All bare, twisted and tortured. Makes you wonder if Tim Burton grew up in Grey County.

The news that the police think Matthew committed suicide was a big relief to a lot of people. At first. That meant there was no insane killer out there. The rest of us were safe. But after a week or so, people began saying it didn't make sense. Not Matthew. He was a pretty cheerful guy. He got on with everyone well enough. He seemed to like his parents. He didn't seem like the type.

But everyone talks about the possibility anyway. In some places teenage suicide is an epidemic, they say. One of the leading causes of death among young men. Some people think that if you talk about one suicide, you'll encourage others to follow suit. Like they do it out of boredom or something. Well, not everyone wants to live all the time. I don't know, but I think adults don't take wanting to be dead very seriously. Not unless it's close to home.

Our school had an assembly on Monday. They brought in a counsellor to talk to us about the dangers of keeping emotional problems bottled up inside until you crack under the pressure and think death is your only escape. She talked for an hour about all the horrible things that can make us want to end our lives. An hour of her and I felt like *I* was going to crack. She encouraged us to open up and talk to a responsible adult about our painful little secrets, like sexual abuse, bullying, domestic violence, drug problems or drinking, and homosexuality.

Sure. Look what happened to me when I told Joyce about seeing Mom's ghost. It only freaked her out.

The counsellor got really pumped talking about kids who commit suicide because they're afraid of being gay. After that, there were rumours that Matthew was gay and was afraid to tell his strict, religious parents. I had a pretty strong hunch that wasn't true, but I kept it to myself. The rumour lasted only a couple of days. Then there was a shift, and kids started wondering if he'd just gone psycho. Maybe he was hearing voices. Maybe he thought the Devil had told him to kill himself. Explains the pitchfork, for sure. But the Matthew I knew didn't kill himself.

A week or so after the assembly, I woke up from a bad night's sleep and decided to visit the town cemetery. It just seemed like something I should do again. It'd been a while.

I walked over after school, to the south end of town, at the top of the hill. There are about a dozen steps up from the sidewalk to the wrought-iron entrance gate. You can see the Sound from the highest point. You can almost see Georgian Bay. It's a beautiful place, really. I could never figure out why the movies make cemeteries look scary. They've always felt sad and beautiful to me. Cemeteries are just there so the people who've been left behind have a nice place to hang out.

The first thing I did was find my mother's grave. It looked fine, but I should have brought flowers. She loved flowers. Sometimes I think it was her flower garden that kept her alive for so long after they told her the cancer was terminal. Even when she was too sick to do anything else, she'd sit on a lawn chair in the back garden, wrapped up in a blanket. Every once in a while, she would get to her feet and shuffle over to the flower bed and pull out a weed that had caught her eye. As if flowers alone could make life worth living. It must piss her off, how we've let the garden go.

There were only two gravesites where the soil looked freshly turned, and one of them had MATTHEW JAMES SORENSON carved into the headstone. There were lots of flowers. Some were already dark and wilted, but some were fresh and colourful. Looking at the darker soil in front of the gravestone, I tried to imagine the casket six feet under me. Then I tried to imagine something inside the casket. I couldn't, so I gave up and took a wander around, heading for an older section of the cemetery where the stones looked much more weather-worn, mossy and even cracked. They're my favourites.

I walked slowly through the rows, reading names and dates. The oldest gravestones were from the late 1800s. Most of the people buried there died in their sixties or seventies, but there were also a number of babies and small children. I looked for teenagers among the stones but I only found one girl. She died in 1932, at sixteen, same age as me. There was a separate area for local soldiers at the other end of the cemetery, and I was willing to bet there were some teenage boys over there. But in this section, where people died upstairs in their beds or suddenly in the cornfield or wrapped in a blanket by the fire in the kitchen, they seem to be either really old or really young.

Dr. Krantz had worried that I was suicidal, just because I was obsessed with dead people and thought I could see ghosts. Like it was my fault I saw my mother checking up on her garden once in a while. It's true that I did think a lot about the whole option of being dead, especially after Mom died. But it was Matthew who talked me out of it, not Dr. Krantz, and without even trying. It was one of our first mega-discussions. He said suicide was just another form of murder. He said life was a gift and only God should decide when to end it. But his best argument was that suicide was the ulti-mate act of hopelessness, which was an irrational position, since there was always hope, no matter how little. In my life, he was walking proof of that. He made life seem hopeful, even by saying nothing at all. I started to see suicide as a "bad mood" thing, and moods don't last forever. They come and go. Besides, even if death isn't the end of life, that doesn't mean it's an improvement.

When Matthew told me Mom was up in heaven, it sounded so sweet. Nicer than the idea of being a ghost. He didn't have a clue about me and ghosts, and I would have died before telling him. He couldn't have handled it. Instead, I started paying more attention to how I dressed for school in the morning. And I started trying to stand straighter when he was around, and not slouch so much. Turns out good posture's not a bad idea after all. One day I got up the nerve to wear diamond-patterned green tights under a short denim skirt, and even though I felt self-conscious all day long, it was worth it. Sitting beside Matthew in class, I saw him checking out my legs from the corner of my eye. The embarrassment on his face when he knew he'd been caught, now *that* was sweet. Of course, I was embarrassed too, knowing I was trying to turn him on. He quickly looked away but he couldn't help grinning, and that was *my* idea of heaven.

I found a bench near the back edge of the cemetery and sat down, facing the oldest gravestones. From there I could see the whole cemetery, and in the distance, Matthew's fresh grave. *I'm wondering,*

Matthew, if anyone could have saved you that night. Me, for instance. What if I had been more honest, sitting in the truck in front of my house? What if I'd screamed and cried and called you names? Smacked you across the head, even? Told you how much I loved you? Could something like that have snapped you out of that awful mood you were in?

Should I have reached over and grabbed the keys out of the ignition? I could have screamed out of the car window until Ethan, spying on us from the front room, came outside to see what the ruckus was about. *Call 911, Ethan!* I could have yelled. *Matthew's not himself tonight!* But that's just it—the Matthew I knew wouldn't have killed himself.

When I finally looked up, I saw I wasn't alone. There was a woman in the distance, over by the war monument. She looked like she was crying, standing there with her head in her hands. A fresh wave of sadness and loss washed over me. I tried to see her more clearly. She was dressed in one of those cool retro jackets, fitted at the waist with a slight flare at the bottom and a stylish little fur collar, like in the 1940s. I wondered vaguely where she'd bought it—not in town. But I wouldn't want that colour. It was brown, like the dead leaves on the ground.

It's getting dark already, Matthew. I'd better go home.

I walked back through the rows of gravestones, thinking about the woman's brown coat again. I remembered how my mother once talked about getting her "colours" done in the city when she was a teenager. It was all the rage, she said. Experts analyzed your skin tone and told you what colours of clothing suited you best. They assigned everyone to a season. My mother said I was like her, a "winter"— pale skin, dark hair. She said I should stay away from earth tones, they'd make me look sick. Of course, colours can only do so much when you really are sick, the way she got sick.

It wasn't until I reached the gate that I looked back at the woman at the war monument. She was still there, half-hidden by a gravestone, camouflaged by autumn colours. But the pain in her face was so fresh that I could practically see her husband face down in a muddy trench, bleeding. I descended the steps from the cemetery two at a time and ran back toward town like there was a German fighter plane overhead, aiming its machine guns at my back. Trouble is, I see things sometimes, and there's nothing I can do to stop it.

I'm pretty sure that the woman in the cemetery wasn't really there.

7

oday is October 21, and that means moving day.

For weeks I've been looking out my bedroom window into the backyard, hoping to see my mother. She hasn't been there since the morning after Matthew died, more than a month ago. I can't imagine her anywhere else but in that garden, so I need to see her one last time, before we're gone for good. *Where are you? Don't you realize we're moving? Don't you care?*

We finished packing last night. We lined the whole front hall with boxes, with Magic Marker labels like *Living Room* and *Kitchen* and *Ethan's Room*. And the dining room was filled with dozens more, in piles three or four high. You could tell Jack's boxes by how none of the tops closed flat. That's because he has so much sports equipment that doesn't quite fit—goalie pads and a couple of hockey and lacrosse sticks and a baseball bat. Jack inherited all the athletic ability in the family. He's probably the best athlete in our entire school. He's not too tall, but he's all muscle—which is why his nickname's "The Hulk." Unfortunately for him, that hasn't been enough to win Morgan over. I don't know what it is. Maybe the broken nose that never healed quite right? Personally, I like Jack's nose.

In the kitchen, we're down to essentials like cutlery and a can opener, a half-dozen dishes and a couple of pots. Everything else is packed. The walls are bare except for faint outlines of whatever used to hang there, spice racks or pictures or shelves, and little holes where nails and screws held them up.

I sit on my mattress on the bedroom floor, waiting for the movers to show up. I have my jeans and toiletries and underwear in a suitcase at the foot of my bed. Everything else is in boxes. Everything I've saved from my childhood. Letters from friends I met at camp. Birthday cards from Mom. My old diaries—always good for a laugh—and a few notes from Matthew, saying things like "Know thyself" and "Do you have my red pencil?"

A loud bang on the front door makes me jump. The movers are here.

The next couple of hours are a sickening blur as all our belongings are carried out of our home for good. As the back door of the moving van is slammed shut and locked, I run to my bedroom one last time. She has to be there. She has to be! *Mom?*

I look out the window. She's at the far corner of the backyard, standing in profile, looking at something. That's different—I've never seen her standing before. She's wearing her old wool cap, like she's going somewhere. *Mom, can you hear me?* Her head lowers and she just stands there, still, like a statue. *For once, can you just look at me?* Nothing. Then her face slowly tilts up. As she turns toward my window, I raise a hand to the glass. I see her smile, nod slightly. But something has changed. Where is that feeling of concern that's always flowed from her before? I just feel love. We hold each other with our eyes until mine blur over. I wipe the tears away but it's too late. She's gone.

By nine p.m. we're sitting among boxes in our "new" kitchen, with its ugly dark wood cupboards and an orange linoleum tile floor, eating lasagna that a friend of my grandmother's brought over. The air was cold and stale when we arrived this afternoon, because the house had been sitting empty for two months. But now the oil furnace is on and the wood stove in the living room is lit. Add to that the smell of baked lasagna, and even I have to admit it's not awful in here. Jack and Ethan take seconds and thirds like they haven't eaten in a week.

I go upstairs to my new bedroom and shut the door behind me. It's at the back north corner of the house. Ethan's and Joyce's bedrooms will be the two at the front of the house and the small extra room is going to be Joyce's office. Jack's claimed the bedroom above the garage. I was tempted, but it's only attached to the house by a covered walkway about six feet wide, so you have to go outside to get from your bedroom to the rest of the house. Forget it.

I check out my bedroom window, the sill littered with a dozen or so dead cluster flies. It's dark out back, but I can see a faint light coming from Jack's window above the garage. Beyond the garage, about thirty feet back, is the beginning of the fenced field, with a small barn and a paddock on one side. It's the whole reason we've moved: for Joyce's two horses. Granddad died of a heart attack long before I was born, and after that, Joyce lived alone on a horse farm in Wellington County. She only sold it and moved in with us in Owen Sound when Mom got too sick, back when I was twelve. Ever since, she's been boarding her two horses, Marley and Ponyboy, at the riding stables where she works. But she missed her old life, so basically we're here in the middle of nowhere because she wants to live with her horses again. I've never been into horses myself. Maybe because when I think of horses, I think of Joyce.

I turn on my computer. We aren't set up for Internet yet but I need to see the desktop picture. Good, it's still the same. Somehow, I'd been afraid it wouldn't be. Me and Matthew, smiling for the camera. It's from last year's math class, a picture Morgan took and e-mailed to me. Without taking my eyes from the photo, I sit on my bed, dead tired and miserable. I think about my mother and start crying, as quietly as I can. She seems gone for good. Like she's decided she's not going to worry about me anymore. I feel like I've fallen down a well and no one even notices I've gone missing.

After a while I dig out my cellphone, even though I try not to use it often because it's expensive. I pull a torn piece of paper from my wallet. I've been carrying it around for weeks. I didn't know why before, but now I do. I dial the number scribbled on it, my heart pounding.

A guy answers on the third ring. "Hello?" He sounds almost my age. That catches me off guard.

"Hello. Is . . . uh, Mr. Morris Dyson there, please?"

"Yup, he is. Hang on." I can tell he's put a loose hand over the mouthpiece because I hear his muffled yell: "Dad, phone." No answer. Louder, "Dad? Phone!"

I wait, my anxiety growing. Is this a mistake? I hear someone else asking something and the guy answers, "Some girl . . . too young." *How rude*, I'm thinking. Then I hear Mr. Dyson clear his throat as he takes the receiver.

"Hello? Morris Dyson speaking."

"Mr. Dyson? It's Amelia Mackenzie."

"Amelia? Yes. Hello."

I hear the hint of surprise in his tired, gravelly voice.

"I've decided I'd like to meet you after all. I was thinking after school tomorrow. Around four?"

"Yes. Of course. We could talk at my house, if that's okay?"

I think about it. "Well, okay. But, Mr. Dyson? Only because you knew my mother. That's the only reason."

"I understand, Amelia, and I appreciate it. I'm at 87 3rd Avenue West. White frame two-storey. Tomorrow, four p.m. I'll be here."

What have I got to lose, Matthew? I write down the address.

8

hen I step inside Morris Dyson's house, I'm so nervous I can barely look up at him. We shake hands, then he invites me to take a seat in the kitchen and offers me a cup of tea. It feels like the hardest thing I've ever done, but I take a deep breath and force myself to get to the point.

"Mr. Dyson, there's something I need to ask you. What did you mean when you said there was something paranormal going on in the barn? When you phoned me after Matthew's funeral, I had this feeling that, that maybe you meant . . . I don't know, like a ghost or something. I just need to know if you believe in ghosts."

At first he simply stands there, like he isn't going to answer me. Then the kettle starts whistling and he unplugs it.

"Please, call me Morris," he says, pouring hot water into two teacups. It seems to take him forever to go on. "Well, mostly I believe in history, and I like telling history stories. Local history, social history, family history. That kind of thing."

That figures, because his furniture is really old-fashioned, like in a pioneer museum. And he fits right in.

"The first European settlers in Grey County were mostly Scots. And I don't know what it is about the Scots, but over the years—and I've been at this for almost twenty—I've run into an awful lot of ghost stories. I haven't published anything about them, but I keep track of them. I research them. I look for patterns." Then he pauses and asks, "How about you, Amelia? Do you believe in ghosts?"

I can't think how to answer that, but I finally say, "I'm not sure."

"Well, do you believe you've ever seen one?"

"I don't know." Why did I even come? Why bother if I can't talk about this? "Maybe," I say, "but I'm pretty sure it was just my imagination."

He nods slowly, saying, "I see." He sets a cup of black tea in front of me and places a small carton of milk and some sugar cubes on the table. "Why do you think that?"

It's time for the truth. "Because that's what I've been told."

He looks at me a little longer, like he's trying to figure me out, then he starts to talk. "I called you last month because I've always wondered about my friend Paul Telford. He killed himself in the same barn as your friend Matthew. He had his whole life ahead of him and he was looking forward to living it. I was sure of that. He was in love with a great gal named Janice. He'd just got accepted into McGill, we both had. On the night it happened, he was in a terrific mood. But there was something strange: he told me he was heading off to meet some mystery girl. That didn't make sense, because of Janice, but he wouldn't tell me anything more." He pauses and I look at his face, so full of sadness and worry. There's a deep line between his brows. He clears his throat, which was sounding pretty raspy, then continues. "His father found him dead in the barn the next day. He'd poisoned himself with something he'd found lying around in there." He clears his throat again. "The thing was, there was always this big bolt on the barn door, and he never used to go in there. He'd forced his way in that night. I don't know why he did that." He stops and stares into his teacup, then takes a sip and continues.

"Paul's parents were devastated. Mrs. Telford never got over it and died not long after. I stayed in touch with his sister, Emily, off and on for years. She told me that Paul and Janice had had a big blow-up the day before he died. Janice had apparently suggested they see other people while he was away at university, and he got really upset. Emily saw him after the fight, crying behind the barn. Then, the very next day, I see him in this euphoric mood, off to hook up with some mystery girl. So like I said, it made no sense."

I'm focusing my eyes on the sugar cubes in their small blue bowl. I start to lift my teacup but my hands are shaking too much. I carefully put the cup back down in the saucer.

"My mother's ghost first showed up in the backyard the day after she died," I say. "I thought I saw her working in the garden a bunch more times after that. Always from my bedroom window. Every time she appeared, I got this terrible strong feeling that she was worried about something." The words are pouring out now. "I ran outside the first few times, but every time I did, she was gone. She never looked up from what she was doing or anything, but I always imagined she knew I was watching. Until Saturday."

"You saw your mother's ghost on Saturday?"

"It was our moving day. We moved out to a farm on 12th Line. About a mile north of the Telford place. That morning, she . . . well, she looked up at me for the first time. I think she was saying goodbye."

"I'm so sorry, Amelia. That must have been painful."

I swallow hard and continue. "When I first started seeing her, I told my grandmother and she got all upset. She made me see a psychiatrist. For a whole year! I guess I'd gone crazy and this was the proof. Anyway, the psychiatrist convinced me that I was only seeing my mom because I missed her so much. That it was my imagination. Only . . . she always looked real to me. She always felt real."

I stop there. The pain is building up in my chest and I'm afraid I'm going to start crying. I try to pull myself together, straightening up in the chair. Morris stands up and starts pacing the kitchen floor.

"What I've never told anyone except my mom is that years before that, I used to see my grade two teacher sitting alone in the schoolyard on Saturdays. But she died in an accident the year after I was in her class. And there were others. God, I don't know why I'm telling you this; I didn't even tell my mom about the others." I turn and look at Morris. He's stopped pacing and is looking at something through the kitchen window, his back to me. "The thing is, I guess deep down I do believe in ghosts, Mr. Dyson. Even if they *are* just my imagination."

"Please, call me Morris."

"All right. Morris. Which is why I'm wondering if maybe there is something wrong with that barn. Something that made Matthew kill himself."

He turns and looks at me for a minute without saying one word. Then, as if he's reached a decision, he says, "Amelia, I need to be honest with you. What you're telling me isn't a surprise. It's the reason I phoned you."

"What? What do you mean?"

"Well, as I told you, I knew your mother. She took a night course I taught at the college. I didn't know her well, or for long, but maybe I knew her in a way no one else did. I knew that she was a clairvoyant. That she had a special awareness. Of ghosts."

Has anyone ever told you something that takes you so by surprise, it practically knocks you over? But then you realize that you've known it all your life, and you want to fall on your knees and thank that person for reminding you of it? It's as if you'd forgotten something so important that it left this big hole, and nothing made sense until you got that memory back.

"Amelia, your mother thought you were clairvoyant too. I think she wasn't sure how much to tell you before she died."

He sits down. Elbows on the table, he clasps his hands and pushes his forehead against his knuckles, almost like he's trying to pray.

My mother in her hospital bed. Oxygen through a plastic tube at her nostrils. Thin, veiny hands, bruised and bandaged, taped to a morphine pump. "Don't be afraid, Amelia." That's what she kept saying. "Don't be afraid."

I finally gasp and let out a painful sob. "She didn't say much."

Like Morris, I've been holding up my head, but now my arms drop, accidentally hitting the saucer and flipping over my cup of tea. Morris and I both jump up and my chair tips backwards, banging to the floor.

Morris grabs some paper towels and starts sopping up the hot tea, telling me all the while how my mother accidentally ran into him at a coffee shop when he was writing about ghost sightings at a vacant lot that had been the site of a house fire about fifty years earlier. Mom said she knew the spot and asked if she could read what he'd written, and when she handed his article back to him she said, "It's his dog. The old man is looking for his dog. It died in the fire with him." When Morris asked how she knew, she said the old guy had told her—the ghost.

I'm trying to pay attention, but it's difficult. I'm back on my chair, legs sprawled out like a boxer between rounds. I feel numb, like I've been punched in the head. Like my brain has short-circuited.

"And for the record," Morris says, having dumped a wad of wet paper towel in the garbage bin, "your mother was one of the sanest people I've ever known."

I force myself to my feet, working to keep my balance. "I have to go."

"Can I show you one thing before you do? It's my own little secret. It's downstairs."

He means the basement. Mysterious and creepy old guy wants to take me down into his basement. I take a deep breath and shrug. What more could happen? "Okay."

He leads me across the kitchen and down some narrow stairs.

This doesn't feel like a typical basement. I like it. There's a wood stove, lots of books and antique stuff, and a very large old desk. Morris runs around the desk and reaches underneath, pulling a long tube from what seems to be a hidden shelf. He takes a sheet from the tube, unfurls it with a loud flourish and flicks on an overhead light.

It's a worn and marked-up map of Grey County, the kind that shows you different colours for farmland and forest and land formations. Some kind of topography map. The roads are marked but not named. He points a finger along a series of red dots, each tagged with a number and a piece of paper with tiny handwritten notes. I lean in for a closer look. The dots run roughly in a line, cutting through the county more or less horizontally.

"What is that?"

"Well, each of those dots represents a ghost story that I've stumbled across over the years, buried in the local records or passed on by word of mouth from elderly folks in the county. I've been gathering research on these stories for ages."

"But why are they all lined up like that?"

"Good question. Among believers in the paranormal there's the idea that spiritual energy runs through the landscape in specific alignments, sometimes called ley lines. That was a phrase first used back in 1921 by a British archeologist, who noticed that geographic and historical landmarks often seemed to occur in alignment with each other, along single tracks over hundreds of miles. For instance, in England there is said to be a ley line connecting Glastonbury, which is believed by some to be the burial place of King Arthur, to Stonehenge and other important ancient sites. He thought of them as ancient trackways or footpaths. 'Ley lines' just means lines cutting through the landscape."

"Okay. But what's the point?"

"Well, what's important is that the alignments are more than pure coincidence. They have a spiritual purpose. And this isn't just Old World folklore. It's universal and timeless. You'd be amazed at how many references there are to special routes or pathways in aboriginal mythology, kind of like migration routes for ghosts. Ancients from Australia, China, South America—even right here in Grey County— believed the souls of the dead travelled along ghost roads to get to the underworld or some other final resting place. The idea is that certain locations have sacred power—the ground is hallowed and the places are haunts."

"But what do these ley lines have to do with ghost sightings?"

"Well, my theory is that when people die they take a journey, an actual journey, only sometimes they get sidetracked on their way, or stuck from the start. And those people are what we think of as ghosts. They haunt the spots where they get stuck, unable to move forward along the line. Call it having unfinished business, or just getting trapped. Emotionally trapped."

Listening to him, looking at his map, I suddenly feel like a door has opened up and the world has doubled in size. It sounds completely crazy, only it kind of makes total sense.

"Interesting, eh? And guess what? Can you find the Telford property on the map?"

I take a closer look at the roads and find Highway 26, and then I figure out which road running south is 12th Line. I find Big Trout River, which cuts through just north of our new place, and run my finger along 12th Line to where I imagine the Telford property must be. It roughly lines up with the other red dots.

"See what I mean?" says Morris. He picks up a red marker and makes a little dot for the Telford property.

"But what about my mom in the backyard of my home in Owen Sound? I mean, our house wouldn't be on that line."

"Not every ghostly apparition I hear about is on that line, just most of them. That's the pattern. But my research isn't just about the pattern. It's everything I've learned along the way about the nature of ghosts. And that's where your mother came in." He takes one last look at his map, lost in some thought. "I learned so much from her." A shadow of sadness passes over his face. "It must have felt like a blessing to see her after she'd died," he says, and he starts rolling up the map. "She might have been worried about you. Maybe, for some reason, she's less worried now." He fits it back in the tube, and he perks up. "So now you know all my secrets."

A voice from the kitchen at the top of the stairs makes me jump. "Not quite. What about the time you killed the Wilsons' dog?"

Morris's eyes roll at that. "Ignore him. A total accident fifteen years ago. That's my son, Kip."

"I'm just saying, someone could get hurt around you," says the voice.

"He's staying with me for a while. Up from Chicago. That's where his mother lives."

"Ah." I nod. "Well, I should really get going."

"Of course," he says. He returns the tube to its hiding place under the desk and follows me back up to the kitchen.

Turning the corner at the top of the stairs, I practically bash into his son. I guess my nerves are bad, because it gives me such a start. Also, he's kind of good-looking and I suddenly feel awkward, and embarrassed that my eyes and nose might still be red from crying.

"Sorry," I mumble, trying to smile politely.

"Don't be," he says, a bit cocky, almost like he's flirting.

Totally not like his dad. More like a son of Brad Pitt.

Morris makes a speedy introduction. "Kip, Amelia. Amelia, Kip."

I mumble again, too self-conscious to look him in the face.

"Hi there," Kip says, with a look of suspicion. "I must say, you two don't look like you're up to anything creepy. Not at all."

He says that like he's teasing us, and it gives me the nerve to glance up at him. He's a head taller than me. His hair is dirty blond, longish like his dad's, shaggy but thicker. He has the shadow of a beard on his chin. Blue, blue eyes, and a wide smile. As if there's some private joke going on. I don't know why, but that bugs me. Nothing about this seems like a joke to me. In fact, how could anything be more serious?

"Excuse me." I have to squeeze past him, and it's all I can think to say.

Morris walks me out onto the porch. I turn to him.

"You can't know how much . . . how much this means to me," I say, struggling to keep myself from getting too emotional again. "It changes absolutely everything. Whatever you plan to do about that barn, count me in. Whatever you're up to, I'm in."

I catch one last glimpse of Kip as Morris and I shake hands goodbye. He's standing in the middle of the kitchen in blue jeans and bare feet, looking at the floor, smiling to himself and slowly shaking his head.

———

Sitting at my desk in my bedroom tonight, I'm feeling so anxious and excited that I can't stand it. Thoughts and memories are exploding in my head like fireworks. The hardest part has been coming home from meeting Morris and trying to act as though nothing's changed when, really, I feel like my life has taken a dramatic turn. It's frightening but it also feels good somehow, like a huge relief. I've been keeping things locked up inside for so long. If only my mother had said more! Did she try, and I just didn't understand? I'm so angry at losing her when she was the only one who ever understood me, and I'm angry at being abandoned to Joyce, of all people.

What must it have been like for Mom, having Joyce for a mother? My mom was warm and gentle, not like Joyce at all. I used to ask myself why Joyce couldn't be more like a proper grandmother. You know, gentle and kind. More like Mrs. Ross, for instance.

It's been ages since I've thought about Mrs. Ross. She lived in the seniors' residence where Mom and Joyce used to volunteer. They had a program called Young Readers for Seniors. Mom said I should sign up, back when I was in grade eight and she was really getting sick, because she thought I was such a good reader. But it was the last thing I wanted to do. Then the next year, after she was gone, something changed my mind. I went for two hours, once a week, for about half a year. In all that time, I only managed to get through one book with one old lady: Mrs. Ross.

Mrs. Ross was tiny but she had great posture. She was like a ninety-pound white-haired gymnast. Always so neat and ladylike. She listened to books on CDs, but she said she liked having a live voice read to her once in a while. She always seemed so happy to see me. Of course she couldn't see me very well. She wasn't blind exactly, but she had an eye disease and her sight was lousy.

Now, she was my idea of a sweet old lady. A real grandmother type, not like Joyce. In fact, Mrs. Ross made Joyce look like a drill sergeant. Joyce means well, I guess, but there's nothing sweet about her. Whereas Mrs. Ross could win contests for that kind of thing.

I read Mrs. Ross a book called *Great Expectations*, by Charles Dickens. It was her choice, not mine. I only know him because of the movies of *A Christmas Carol* and *Oliver Twist*. Reading the book was absolute murder because of the crazy way everybody talks, with those old-fashioned English accents. I think she got a kick out of listening to me try to read the dialogue. She sure looked like she was having fun.

Once she asked me how I felt about the fact that Pip, the main character, is an orphan, and so is Estella, the girl he loves. Pip is raised by his mean old sister and her nice but stupid husband, and Estella is raised by crazy Mrs. Havisham in a big, rundown mansion. I don't know why I hadn't thought of this myself—I guess I was paying more attention to the mystery and romance and buttered bread down poor Pip's pants—but Mrs. Ross said something that totally shocked me.

"I guess you must really identify with those two kids. Because you're an orphan too, like Pip and Estella."

I don't know why that hit me so hard. I know I don't have parents and all—not like most other kids—but it's hard to see yourself as an orphan when you have two brothers and a grandmother, even if she's kind of tough on you. *An orphan.* That sounds pretty harsh.

Just then, Mrs. Ross reached out her hand and was feeling for mine. It was embarrassing but I let her find it, and she held on to it, with her bony bird fingers and soft, loose skin. She held on for ages, and the longer she held on, the more uncomfortable I became, and the more I felt like crying. I didn't feel up to reading much more that day. Especially when she finally gave my hand a squeeze and let go, saying something like "It's hard to lose someone you love." Her eyes got shiny with tears and she talked a bit about her husband, who had died ten years before. She said she still missed him every day. When she said that, I kind of wished we were still holding hands, but I didn't know what to do about it.

That's the only time we ever shared something personal. Normally we'd focus on the book, with me reading and her making little comments on the side.

I'll never forget the way I felt when I came to the end of *Great Expectations*. It was like something important just up and walked out of my life. I felt depressed for a week. But I never went back to see Mrs. Ross again, because by then I was totally into Matthew. Sometimes I think about her and wonder if she's still alive. I think about how I wouldn't mind reading to her again someday. Before she's gone for good.

I turn on my computer and stare at Matthew's face, his dark, smiling eyes.

Matthew, there's this Halloween party at Brad Wilson's next weekend. He never invited me. But Morgan's going and she says I should go too, because she heard Brad say that he's fine with people bringing other friends if they want. So should I go? I just have this feeling that if I don't hold on to this little lifeline that Morgan throws me once in a while, I'll sink. But I'd have to wear a costume. Ugh. A white sheet, maybe?

9

I'm in the back seat of Jack's friend Jeremy's car. Jack's up front in the passenger seat. We're driving to Brad's house, for the big Halloween party that everyone in town seems to be planning to crash. This is my first social event in a long while. I wasn't going to bother with it, partly because coming up with a costume seemed too stressful, but Jack talked me into it. He said he'd be there with a few of his grade twelve buddies and would keep an eye on me.

Not too many brothers are as nice as Jack. But the truth is, he also wants to keep an eye on Morgan. He's got it bad for her, poor guy.

Jack's dressed up as a zombie, with lots of white face paint, green around his eyes and mouth, and fake blood dripping from his ears and nose. He's put red food colouring all over his tongue. Jeremy's a vampire, with spiky bleached hair and a long black trench coat—like Spike from the old TV show *Buffy the Vampire Slayer*. I'm guessing three-quarters of the people at this party will be either zombies or vampires.

Me, I've got my costume in my lap. It's a rubber Bob Marley mask that Joyce picked up in the city last week. It has a dreadlock wig attached. Bob Marley was a Jamaican reggae singer, and Joyce is a big fan. I think he died before I was born. I just looked at the mask and said, "Fine. Whatever." It's not great to breathe through, but I like the fact that no one will ever guess it's me underneath. That's what I'm counting on.

We pull onto Brad's street. The house is a three-storey Victorian on a corner property near the river. I've heard that his parents won't be home, and there are already lots of cars parked in the driveway and along the road in front. There's a big scarecrow sitting on the front porch, made of clothing stuffed with straw and topped with a carved pumpkin head. Another carved pumpkin, lit from the inside by a candle, has been placed near the front door on a bar stool. Fake cobwebs hang from the porch roof.

As Jeremy parks the car, I take a deep breath and put on my mask. I'm trying to screw up the courage just to get out of the car. There's cackling witch laughter coming from a recorder somewhere in the garden as we walk up the driveway. I can't see much out of this mask. *Matthew, what am I doing here?*

We're greeted by a bottleneck at the entrance: vampires and zombies are jamming the front hallway. The lights are low, the music is loud and someone in a platinum-blonde wig and stiletto heels is sitting on the floor, where she's apparently fallen, blocking our way. She's laughing—uncontrollably, it seems. Okay. Jack gives me a glance and steps over her, barely missing her head. He parts the streamers hanging from the ceiling light fixture like he's swimming the breaststroke and moves on down the hallway, edging toward the kitchen at the back of the house. I calculate whether I've got the leg reach to follow him and take a shot, but I knock "Marilyn's" wig half off, exposing part of a brunette head. I'm realizing that there's already been a fair bit of alcohol consumed here this evening, and suddenly, like the girl on the floor, I feel I'm in a little over my head.

I make my way down the crowded hall. It's too loud in here, and I've lost sight of Jack already. On either side there are dimly lit rooms with streamers and bowls of orange-coloured taco chips and Cheezies. There are hordes of kids yelling above the music or hopping up and down to the beat. Some look familiar. I even know the names of a few. But there's no one I know well enough to talk to. Then I catch sight of Jack, already getting comfortable with a beer in hand, flirting with some zombie girl. I don't want to ruin his chances of a good time, so I try to keep my distance. I jump as someone screams and then laughs loudly right next to my ear. A black rubber spider falls at her feet. I'm not up for all this horror. But how am I going to get home if I leave now?

I need to kill time, and I figure the best way to do that is to keep moving from room to room. There's a slow circulation of ghouls going on anyway, and I work my way into it. I pretend I'm on my way somewhere, to get something or talk to someone. I have something to do. Yes, I'm quite engaged in whatever that thing is. *Excuse me. Sorry. You first.* I keep my head low. No one knows who I am. No one is looking at me. No, that's not true—this Bob Marley look isn't exactly blending in. I'm getting some double takes, but that's all. I nod a little as I edge through the crowded rooms, acknowledging people as if I'm one of them. But within ten minutes I've moved around as much as I can without driving myself completely mad. I'm going to have to find somewhere to hide. My best bet is the front living room. I think I saw an unclaimed corner of couch in there.

I'm making my way back through the dining room, squeezing past bodies, when I see a face in the hallway that stops me cold. It's like catching a glimpse of myself in a mirror, only the mirror image doesn't match up. For one thing, this other Bob Marley is a guy. He's pretty tall, and his shoulders are . . . well, guy shoulders.

I'm frozen where I stand as this other Bob Marley saunters toward me. He puts a hand on my shoulder and leans into me, speaking low and close, like we're in on some secret together.

"Wow," he says into my ear. "Bob, I can't believe you'd show up at a party like this not once but twice."

Does he think I'm a guy? I try to be friendly. "Uh, my grandmother bought this for me."

"Yeah, I got this from my stepdad. He's always trying to broaden my cultural range." He pauses and adds, "Eternal optimist."

"Oh," I say, trying to think of a response to that. "Well, my grandmother isn't much of an optimist, eternal or otherwise. Although she does lighten up when she's having a beer and a smoke out back with her horses."

"Sexy." He's nodding. I can tell that amused him, and he's looking intently at my eyes through the holes in my mask. "So, Bob, why *are* you here?"

"Well, I . . . you mean, other than because I get to wear a mask?"

"Ah. That's enough for you?"

"Sometimes, yes." I'm feeling a little bolder now. "Why are *you* here?"

"I've got a thing for Brad's mom." He's looking around. "But I'm not seeing her." His blue eyes are striking, the way they scan left and right behind the Jamaican face. "What do you think? Would she be a vampire or a zombie?" He looks around, then shrugs like he's unimpressed. "Young people today, they're obsessed with vampires."

"You're not from around here, are you?"

He ignores that. "It's a sad reflection of the decline of religious literacy in popular culture. I'd like to see Jesus kick some vampire butt."

That makes me laugh. "What about the zombies?"

"Zombies, they're cool. Jesus was a zombie, for Christ's sake. That's what Easter's all about."

"I never thought of it that way." Holy jeez, he's different!

"Are you kidding? Don't you know about the 'resurrection of the body' stuff in the Bible? The Bible's all about zombies."

"No, I seriously never thought of that."

"Really? What are they teaching in Sunday school these days? Young people are so confused."

I'm starting to wonder if this guy is older than he sounds. "So is that why you're more interested in their mothers?"

"Have you *met* Brad's mother?"

I'm getting an image in my head of a desperate housewife. Whatever. I think I've had enough of this guy. And two Bob Marleys at one party is just too weird. "No, I haven't, but good luck with that. Maybe I'll see ya around."

"You think I'm that easy to find?" He's different, all right.

I'm edging by him with an eye on the hallway when someone pushes him from behind, bumping him against me. He apologizes quickly. It's embarrassing but I'm wearing a mask, so whatever. I manoeuvre past, eyes down, and manage a little backhanded wave as I head toward the hallway and the living room, my original plan. I glance back at him once more and he waves a finger at me. I can just about hear him over the noise.

"I'm warning you, I never forget a face."

His blue eyes flash but something about his body language spells mild disappointment. Maybe he's lonely too.

There's a very vampy vampire in the hall. Brittany—of course. And there's Morgan nearby, dressed as a nurse. A vampy nurse. Lots of blood. They don't recognize me in my reggae getup, and I linger for a minute or so, on the verge of saying something. But they walk past me down the hall, getting sucked into the crowd.

I really can't take much more of this. I change course and make my way to the front door, squeezing between two new zombies who've just arrived and stepping out onto the porch. I didn't want to do this, but I pull out my cell and phone home. Joyce answers.

"Joyce?" I haven't quite thought of what to say. "I . . . I don't feel very well. I don't think I want to stay at this party much longer. You don't need anything in town, do you?" I'm looking at my watch. It's 9:35. "Is there any chance you could swing by and pick me up? I don't want to have to wait for Jack and his friends to bring me back."

She's quick to say that she needs a few things from the convenience store and will come by in about twenty minutes. What a relief. I'll just wait out front, I say. She knows the house.

A group of partiers are standing in the driveway in the dark, laughing and talking, drinking and smoking. Jack is among them. He sees me, breaks from the group and walks over.

"What's wrong? Not having much fun?" He's looking pretty down himself.

"Oh no, it's fine. I'm just not that much in the mood, I guess. Not really feeling like a party tonight after all. I mean, glad I came and all, but I think I'll be taking off soon."

"No way. Already? But how are you going to get home? If you hold out awhile, Jeremy will give you a lift. We're going to move on to another place after this."

"It's okay. I called Joyce." I'm embarrassed to admit it, but he just nods.

"And how are you doing? Everything okay?" I can tell something's wrong with him. Jack's usually pretty cheery.

"Oh, you know. I'm good."

"What's up?" I don't really have to ask what's bothering him. He's been trying to get closer to Morgan for about a year. She keeps sending him mixed messages and jerking him around. Something new must have happened. But Jack just shrugs. "Did you talk to her, at least?"

"Yes, I did. I tried to, anyway. She just kind of walked away. Walked over to some other guy who caught her eye. Right in the middle of . . . well, just embarrassing." He's really upset. "So it's time to give up, that's all."

"I'm sorry, Jack. I know she's my friend, but you can do better." I can tell from the pained look on his face that he doesn't believe me. I guess that's love for you.

"Don't worry, I'm done. I'm throwing in the towel. It's over." He says that with a bitter smile.

Okay, I should change the subject. "Where else are you going tonight?"

He looks at me sideways. "You don't want to know." He pauses but I don't ask. I guess he's right. "A couple of the guys want to check out the Telford barn. On a dare, kind of. You know, just because it'll be spooky."

"Jack . . ." I don't know how to say this. "Not a good idea."

We sit in silence, then he says, "Halloween and all."

I feel like a weight is pushing on me. I sit down heavily on the porch step and Jack sits down beside me. He takes a drink from his bottle of beer.

"Actually, Amelia, I wasn't going to tell you this, but I was talking to Matthew's cousin Richard last week. You know—the guy who works in the hardware store? He told me something and said I should probably keep it to myself. He said that a week before Matthew died, he had a talk with him about you. I didn't know if I should tell you or not."

Oh. I can't breathe. I lift the lower part of my mask away from my mouth and nose to get some fresh air.

"He said Matthew asked his advice about something that was bothering him."

Oh my God!

"Matthew said he was afraid that his parents wouldn't approve of you because you don't go to church or anything, and he was afraid that if he started getting more involved with you, they would freak. Point is, he was really serious about you. That's what he told Richard."

What? My mouth locks open. *What?* My eyes close tight and my throat seizes up. I let the chin of my mask go and Bob Marley is back on. Jack leans hard on my shoulder and pushes himself to his feet. I can't see clearly now, but I try to speak in a normal voice. "What advice did Richard give him?"

Jack shrugs. "I don't think he had any." He looks away, then turns back to me and adds, "But I thought you might want to know." And he slouches, beer in hand, back over to his friends.

"Thank you," I whisper.

10

I'm finally drifting off to sleep after hours of tossing around in bed, images of Halloween in my head, when voices out back wake me up. I get up and go over to my window. In the backyard by the door to the garage are four figures in the moonlight: Jack and his friends, arguing. I check the time on my alarm clock—2:12 a.m.

I open my window, put my face to the screen and whisper as loudly as I can, "Hey, guys! Past two. Time for bed."

"Amelia," someone below answers, "your dumb-ass brother is giving us a hard time. We had to drag him out of that damn barn. Now he says he's going back. You want to try talking some sense into him?"

There's some pushing and shoving going on in the shadows. A few of them have had too much to drink, and I think Jack is one. I hope they don't start fighting. I dress quickly and sneak downstairs, trying not to wake Joyce or Ethan with the closing door.

"What are you guys up to?" I hiss, approaching the four of them from the side of the house.

They're a sorry-looking bunch, all still in traces of Halloween makeup. Jeremy's the designated driver, so he's making the most sense. He tells me they broke into the Telford barn and spent about an hour just hanging out in there. He says it was spooky as hell. But just when they'd all had enough, Jack said he didn't want to leave.

"He started going all weird on us," Jeremy says. "Pacing up and down the barn. He's acting like a jackass."

I study Jack. He's looking everywhere but at me, grinning and preoccupied.

"Well, that's dumb," I say. "Jack? Are you being a jackass?" And it occurs to me to ask, "Did you take something?" Drugs, I'm thinking.

Jack laughs and rolls his eyes. "All right, all right. I give up." He flaps his hands in the air, waving us away. "I've had enough. I'm gonna crash. I'm gonna sleep like a baby tonight." He grins, shaking his head and reaching for the garage side door. He opens it, waves over his head at us and disappears inside.

The other three guys shuffle back to the car parked at the front of the house, muttering among themselves. Jeremy throws me a good-night kiss as they disappear around the corner. I stand where I am for a minute, waiting for Jack's light to come on upstairs above the garage. It finally does. I see a shadow lean against the window, probably looking down at me where I stand in the headlights of Jeremy's car as it reverses out of the driveway. Then it's dark again. Shivering with the cold, I slip back into the house.

In my bedroom again, lights out, I take one last peek at Jack's window. It's dark. I sit down on my bed and think about getting back into my pyjamas, but I've got a chill. Something's bugging me. I get up and check the window again. This time, in the moonlight, I see the side door slowly open. A figure moves in the doorway and steps outside. Jack looks around and up toward my window. I know he can't see me in my dark room, but I lean back from the window just in case and hold my breath for a few seconds. Then I peek down again. He's walking away from the garage, along the back of the house and out of sight. What the hell is he doing? Where does he think he's going? I don't like this. I hurry back downstairs, and this time I grab a heavier coat.

I know he's headed back up the road toward the Telford property. The sky is clear of clouds and full of stars, and the moon is about three-quarters and bright. I run across the front yard to the road and start up the hill. Within a minute or so I can see a silhouette ahead of me, approaching the crest of the 12th Line hill. I call Jack's name, and I see him stop and slowly turn around. He's waiting for me. He's laughing quietly to himself, but he also looks impatient. I'm hurrying, walking as fast as I can, and when I finally reach him I'm winded.

"Jack. What's up? Where are you going?"

"Nowhere, Amelia. You should get back home." Now he sounds irritated.

"I'll go back home if you come with me."

"I can't. Now why don't you take off? It's late and too cold for you, little sis." The tone of his voice is strange. He doesn't sound like himself.

He walks on, and I do too. He stops, looking back down the road and then up at the crest of the hill. The Telford farm isn't far from here.

"I'm meeting someone," he says, "and you can't come."

"Who are you meeting?" I venture a guess. "Are you meeting a girl?"

"Amelia, you'd better get lost. Get the hell out of here and go back home." It's like he's threatening me. He's still smiling, though.

"All right, you win. I'm going home. I'll see you in the morning."

I turn and start walking back down the hill toward our house, but I'm panicking. This is way too much déjà vu for me. Should I go and wake up Joyce? We could come back with the car. I check my pockets for my cellphone. Damn, I left it at the house. I look around for other farms on this stretch of the road. There aren't any.

I hear Jack heading back up the hill, taking large strides now, moving quickly. When I can't hear him anymore, I stop and turn around. He's over the brow of the hill and no longer in sight. I don't have time for anything else. I turn around and head up behind him. It takes forever to get to the top of the hill, and now, in the distance, I can see the old farmhouse, dark and desolate. At first I don't see a barn. But as I get closer it appears behind the farmhouse, like a charcoal monster in the moonlight. It's one of those really tall ones, probably a hundred years old. The kind with boards that are dry and grey, some of them loose or missing. They always look like a stiff wind could bring them crashing down. I'm trying not to think about what happened here only five weeks ago. I'm focusing on Jack. That's the only way I can do this.

He must already be inside. I cut across the front of the farm property, toward the far side, and get to the barn door as quietly as I can. It's busted where there used to be some kind of bolt. I can just about poke my head inside. I move in slowly, carefully. I don't want to startle Jack, and I don't want to aggravate him.

The barn is gigantic. It looks even bigger from the inside. Moonlight is peeking through cracks between the boards, thin vertical lines of light reaching up into the rafters. There's a stale and musty smell. Lower down in the shadows I can dimly see stalls on one side and a kind of loft along the other, a platform running the length of the right wall, about five feet above the ground. As my eyes grow accustomed to the darkness, I see old junk stored underneath the platform and a few broken ladders leaning up against posts. In the centre the barn is empty from floor to roof; it feels like a medieval church. Jack is nowhere in sight.

I'm not sure I want to go any farther in. I listen. I hear a faint shuffling on the dirt and hay floor, coming from one of the stalls. I squeeze inside and whisper, "Jack?" The stall door swings open, making me jump. But I can't see him there.

I'm trying to control my fear. "Jack, grow up," I hiss. There's no response. I'm going to have to be patient. I'm going to have to wait him out. I listen again, and something like a cobweb brushes past my face. It's cold. My arms flail in an involuntary spasm. "Ugh, I'm getting out of here." But then I hear another noise, coming from a far corner. "Jack?"

Nothing.

Oh God, don't tell me there are animals in here. I'm staring hard into the shadows, looking for movement. But I'm not taking another step. I'm staying here by the door.

A gentle moan comes from somewhere high in the barn, and it draws me in. I'm looking up, turning slowly, straining in the darkness to see where the sound is coming from. I run my eyes along a major beam, a massive tree trunk that runs across the width of the barn at the top of the walls, some twenty feet up. It's Jack. He's crouching on the beam high above me, his head in his hands. He's crying.

"Jack? Jack, what's wrong?"

He doesn't answer.

"What are you doing up there? You should come down." I can't tell if he even hears me. There's something bunched up on the beam beside him.

It's a rope.

"Jack, please come down and talk to me."

He continues to moan and cry, and then his tone changes. He's still crying but he's also shouting, sputtering, angry. It sounds like "She said she'd come. She said she'd come." He sounds like a child having a tantrum.

What the hell? Now he's wailing—a tortured cry like nothing I've ever heard before. I'm stunned. This can't possibly be my brother. He seems completely mental. Or is he on drugs? I look around. Who is he talking about?

"Jack, you aren't thinking straight. You've got to come down. Right now!" I'm trying to sound tough, but he acts like he doesn't even hear me. "I'm going to call Joyce if you don't come down right now."

I'm standing directly below him, looking up. He's still crying and muttering, but now he begins to edge along the beam toward the rope. I watch, thunderstruck, as he ties the rope around the beam, leaving one long end dangling down. He tugs at the dangling end, pulling it up, and begins to loop it into some kind of slipknot.

"Jack, what the hell are you doing?" He drops the loop and it hangs from the beam. I try to sound calm, not to be hysterical. "Jack, listen to me! Can you just come down from there and talk to me for a minute? That's all I'm asking. Just come down for a minute."

How can I get up there? How fast can I climb?

He's straddling the beam, almost right over the loop. He's ignoring me. He's crying, saying, "She'll be sorry." That's all I can make out. He's going to hang himself! He reaches down for the rope. I scream his name.

Suddenly the knot in the rope comes loose. The rope drops from the beam, falling smack down on my shoulder as I duck my head, and then to the ground. I look up and see Jack staring down at the rope at my feet, staring right through me, a look of rage on his face. His eyes look psycho. He bares his teeth, glaring at the rope on the barn floor.

"Jack! Come down! Can you hear me? It's me, Amelia."

He rises to his full height on the beam and closes his eyes. His face looks frozen.

He starts to lean backwards.

Oh my God! "Jack!" I scream.

He falls backwards from the beam, landing with a sickening crunch only a few feet away from me. The straw sends up a cloud of dust in the moonlight. His eyes are closed, his body bent, lying still, as if he's dead. I collapse over him, screaming and crying his name, touching his face, frantically searching for a pulse in his wrist, his neck. It's faint but I can feel it.

Somewhere behind me, there's shuffling. Jack's eyes open wide, looking over my shoulder, and his mouth opens. Then his eyes close as if he's fallen asleep. I'm afraid to move him.

"I'll be right back, Jack. Stay here. Stay right here. I'll get help. You'll be okay."

As I run for the door I feel something cold and light brush over me. I beat the air but I don't slow down. I reach for the door. Just as I get through the narrow opening, I catch the letters *D-O-T* carved in the wooden frame.

Leaving Jack unconscious on the barn floor, I stumble along the dark country road, running for help.

11

*J*oyce is stony cold and focused. It's the way she's always been, in every crisis I can remember. Ethan and I are in the car with her, and she's got the engine in overdrive as we head up the hill on 12th Line. She's already called 911, and the ambulance and police are on their way. Ethan says I look like I've seen a ghost.

In two minutes we're turning into the Telford farm property, up the drive and over the rough field toward the old barn. Car doors fly open and slam shut, then we're out and running in the dark. Ethan carries a flashlight and its beam jerks violently in front of us as he runs. He's excited. Even the worst catastrophe has its entertaining side for him. I, on the other hand, am still crying. Joyce says nothing for now. The moonlight casts pale and wild shadows of us along the ground.

We get to the barn door, still open the six inches I had squeezed through, and together we push it open all the way. It creaks and moans and scrapes along the straw-covered dirt floor. In the moonlight that peeks down through the rafters, we can see Jack lying in a heap where I left him, and we run to him. His eyes are closed. He is warm—still breathing. We all talk to him at once.

"Jack. We're here!"

"Help is coming!"

"You'll be all right. You're going to be all right!"

We don't dare move him ourselves. Something might be broken.

"The ambulance is coming, Jack," I whisper, hearing the siren a long way away. "It's almost here. Hold on, Jack."

There is no response from him. I'm looking at him lying there almost dead. I'm holding his limp hand, my whole body shaking. It feels like a dream.

Joyce finally asks me what happened. I try to think.

"He had too much to drink, and I saw him leave the house after he got home from the party. I was worried about him, so I followed him." I'm struggling to get the words out. It's hard to breathe, there's so much pain in my chest. "I followed him here. He was horsing around up in the rafters when I found him. He was . . . horsing around." I hear myself lying. I'm not sure why, but I don't feel I can tell the truth right now. I remember the rope—that will give it all away—but when I look around, I realize that it isn't here anymore. It's disappeared. I didn't move it. Jack certainly didn't move it. I *know* I didn't dream it. I saw it fall—it hit me hard on the shoulder—but now it's gone.

"He just had too much to drink. I was telling him to get down when he slipped."

My heart pounds in my ears as I hear myself desperately trying to make what happened sound less scary. They wouldn't believe me if I told them the truth. The sirens get steadily louder until they're right on us. Then they cut out, car doors open and shut, and paramedics and two policemen appear at the entrance and run toward us. We scramble to our feet and back away to reveal Jack. Someone takes his pulse in his neck, shining light in his eyes and gently checking him over. Someone else runs back to the ambulance for a stretcher. One of the policemen has his notepad out and begins asking questions. Any witnesses? Who was here?

"Just me. I . . . I saw him fall."

"I'll need you to stick around for a statement, okay?"

I nod. I think I'm in shock.

Joyce is talking to the other officer. "Jack—Jackson Mackenzie. Seventeen years old. I'm his grandmother. His legal guardian. Joyce Stewart. These two are his brother and sister. We live a half mile down the road. Just moved in last week." The officer is listening, nodding.

We watch as the paramedics gently work on Jack, putting a brace around his neck, carefully straightening him out, rolling him onto a stretcher. I can't see any blood. Maybe he's okay. But when they move him, he doesn't wake up. *Open your eyes, Jack. Say something. Do something.*

Then they are gone, taking Jack with them, Joyce and Ethan following them out the barn door. The policeman asks me to stay behind. He says he'll drop me off at the hospital if I'd like. I'm left standing over the place where Jack fell while the policeman makes a phone call.

"Yeah, an accident in the Telford barn, on 12th. Jack Mackenzie. Looks like he fell. Yeah, they just left. The Mackenzie girl, the sister. Yeah, thought you might be interested."

The policeman finishes his call and says, mostly to himself, "This barn's seen a lot of action lately." Then he asks me to start from the beginning so he can take notes. I tell him how Jack arrived home from Halloween partying, then I realize I've got to mention that he and his friends were here earlier in the evening. He'll hear it sooner or later.

The officer looks around with his flashlight and catches something in one of the half-open stalls. Beer cans. A twelve-pack and empty beer cans, some in the box, some lying nearby. "Go on," he says.

I tell him what I told Joyce. The policeman looks up, flashlight in the rafters, the light moving slowly along the big timbers. I look around too as I speak, trying to control myself, trying to calm down. I feel so afraid. *Jack will be okay. He's okay.* The policeman scribbles something down, then looks up at me, waiting for me to continue.

"He was up there, kind of talking to himself—nothing I could make out. Gibberish, you know? Then he stood up and . . . and I was begging him to come down. I . . . I was terrified he was going to fall. I kept asking him to come down, but he ignored me." I start to cry again.

"Is that when he slipped?"

I nod and cover my face with my hands. He puts a hand on my shoulder.

"That's fine for now, that's enough. I'll take you home. Or to the hospital. Whichever you prefer."

"To the hospital, please."

I take a deep breath. I wipe the backs of my hands against my brows and hold them there for a moment, pressing my knuckles into the inside corners of my eyes.

"Are you going to be okay?"

I nod weakly and we turn to leave the barn.

That's when I see the rope, in a dark heap on the floor against the far wall. Standing beside it is Matthew, leaning against the wall, arms crossed, watching me.

12

I hear voices and open my eyes. I'm outside the emergency entrance of the hospital, being lifted onto a gurney. I see the officer talking to someone nearby as I'm wheeled through the glass doors of the entrance. I close my eyes again and feel the movement of the wheels rolling along a corridor, stopping, then starting again. And I hear my grandmother's voice.

"Fainted," someone replies.

Someone takes my pulse. A blood pressure band pumps on my arm.

"Amelia?"

"A little too much for her," a voice says.

"She's fine. She just needs to rest a bit."

"Amelia, can you sit up? There's a glass of orange juice for you here. Sit up and take a sip."

I don't want to. *Matthew?*

"Amelia?"

I finally open my eyes, reluctantly. My grandmother is standing over me, holding out a paper cup.

"Juice," she says. "You should drink."

She's got a vending machine coffee in the other hand.

I struggle to pull myself up on my elbow. Everything's spinning. I force myself to think. "Jack?"

"He's in good hands," she says. "He's safe." She hesitates. "He's still unconscious, but that's no surprise. There may be a break. He's in X-ray." Another pause. "There may be a break in his lower back."

Oh my God! I look at her face for the first time. She seems frightened. She holds out the juice again and this time I take it from her, still shaky. I take a sip, for her sake. I should have woken her up before I left the house. I wasted precious time following him alone. *Oh, Jack.*

I lie back on the stretcher and look around. We're in a corridor outside the emergency waiting room.

"I'll be okay soon," I say, trying to reassure her. "Where's Ethan?"

"He's checking out vending machines, looking for a snack."

There's silence, and suddenly I remember.

Oh my God, Matthew!

Morris Dyson answers the phone when I call in the early morning. He listens as I tell him that my brother had an accident in the barn last night.

"Your brother?" he asks. There's some mumbling and what sounds like a swear word. "Is he badly injured?"

"He's still unconscious. It's not good. There's a fracture in his lower back. They don't know yet whether it will heal properly. But right now, we just want him to wake up."

"Jesus! That's . . . a shock. He fell inside the barn? What was he doing there? Do you know?"

"I don't know, I don't know. He'd hung out in there earlier in the evening, drinking beer with his friends. Then later he went back alone." I take a deep breath, forcing myself to go on. "I followed him. I saw what happened."

"You were with him in the barn?"

I raise my free hand, cupping the mouthpiece as I whisper. "I lied to everyone. I said he slipped off a beam in the rafters because he was drunk. He wasn't *that* drunk. He let himself fall. He just did some kind of backward swan dive onto his head. On purpose." I can't believe I'm admitting this to someone I hardly know after lying to the cops and my family.

Morris mutters under his breath.

"And something else. He was crying, hysterical. Over a girl. I don't know what he was going on about, but he seemed really angry with her, really upset. He wasn't making any sense. He's never acted like that before. It was totally extreme."

"I see." That's all he says. I wish he'd say more.

"I mean, it reminded me of how Matthew talked about meeting a girl the night he died. At the time I was too jealous to think straight. But now I'm seriously wondering if she wasn't, you know, a ghost."

I've been talking fast while Morris barely responds. I hope he doesn't think I'm getting carried away with this.

"Okay. One more detail about my friend Paul," he finally says. "You know how the Sorensons discovered a word carved in Matthew's wooden desk at home? They said the word was *DOT*—in capital letters. Well, Paul's sister, Emily, told me that she ransacked his bedroom after he died, looking for clues that he'd been depressed. Under his pillow she found the word *dot* written in Paul's hand, on a piece of paper, about a dozen times."

"Oh my God, I just remembered—I think I saw *D-O-T* carved inside the barn, inside the door frame on the right side. I could be wrong. It just flashed at me as I was running to get help for Jack. I was so freaked at the time, I may have imagined it."

"Really?" he says. "That's very interesting. I think I want to check that out for myself."

"There's something else. Before Jack fell—or jumped, or let himself fall—he was kind of struggling with a rope on the beam. I was terrified because it looked like he was going to hang himself. But the rope actually fell from the beam before he could put it around his neck. As if it had untied itself. And then, even weirder, when I got back to the barn with my grandmother the rope was gone. It wasn't where it had fallen."

"Wow! Okay, listen. You've got to be with your family now, so how about we wait a bit before digging any deeper into this? I'll be in touch. I hope you don't mind if I use my son, Kip, as a bit of a go-between. He's been working at the Grey County Archives and doing some title research for me on the side. On the Telford farm. To find out if it has any secrets. He's a decent young man, once you get to know him."

"Sure," I say. "Why not?" We say goodbye and hang up.

I've told Morris all I'm going to tell him. Because maybe it was only my imagination—that last thing I saw.

13

As soon as school ends I go straight to the hospital, feeling hugely anxious. The entranceway is depressing, with its pale blue-green walls and antiseptic gel dispensers and parked wheelchairs, the gift shop with its get-well cards and knick-knacks and slippers, the harsh lights and white noise. I'm having flashbacks of my mother in her pink bathrobe and pale blue hospital gown.

I find Joyce in the intensive care waiting room on the third floor. She's reading a magazine but she looks like she'd rather be smoking it. She's been trying to cut back, not smoking in the house and that, so this must really be testing her willpower. She raises her bushy eyebrows in greeting, and I sit down in the empty chair beside her.

"Anything new?" I ask. It's hard to read her face. It's always pretty hard.

She shrugs. "The specialist is in there with him now. He said he'd come get me in a minute. Jack's awake."

"Oh wow! That's good, isn't it? That's great, isn't it?" You wouldn't know it from her voice.

"It *is* good. But . . . he doesn't have any feeling in his legs." She pauses and then adds flatly, "It looks right now like his legs are paralyzed."

For a second, I try to picture Jack not walking—not running or jumping or skating or skiing—but I just can't. Impossible. Instead, I imagine him starting physiotherapy in a few weeks, walking by Christmas, running in the spring track meets, good as new. If anyone can do it, Jack can.

Joyce and I sit in silence until she says she's going to run downstairs for a coffee and a smoke. She asks me to stick around in case the doctor comes.

I'm waiting for something to happen, for someone to come, feeling so tired my head bobs forward and it jerks me awake. I couldn't sleep last night. At about three a.m. I looked up the word *dot* in the online dictionary. "Full stop." That's more or less what it means. It's just a piece of punctuation. I lay on my back with my eyes open in the dark, Matthew flashing to life in my head. And when I wasn't seeing Matthew standing at the back of the barn, I was thinking of Jack.

Jack's room in intensive care is filled with machinery and bags of fluid hanging from hooks. His bed is at the far end, by the window. There's another bed as well, with a man in it who looks like he's sleeping, thank God. He kind of looks dead, actually, except he's snoring.

Jack is on his back, white sheet and thin blanket pulled high on his chest. He has some kind of cast or brace around his torso. Something stiff. He has a neck brace too. His face looks tired and pale. His hair is a mess, and he has a tube running from his hand. I catch sight of a bag of pale yellow pee peeking out along the side of the bed. His eyes are half-open, and he gives us a little smile when he sees us. I rush at him with a hug, careful not to hurt him anywhere.

We don't talk much. At some point I ask him if he remembers what happened, but he says everything's a blank after he went into the barn with his buddies. I let him know that I followed him into the barn the second time, when he fell. I was worried about admitting this, but he tells me he already knew. He says some detective guy dropped in to see him earlier. That surprises me. I wonder if it was Grierson.

Just then, the doctor walks in. He tells us that Jack is one very lucky guy, that the damage could have been a lot worse. He could have died. But he adds that Jack isn't out of the woods yet. He says he has an "incomplete" injury to the cable in the spinal cord that controls movement and sensation. That's better than a "complete" injury, obviously, and also it's low on his back, which is better than high. So the doctor thinks that with time and lots of therapy, Jack has a ninety-five percent chance of recovering. But for now his legs are paralyzed, and he's in for an "uphill climb." That's the doctor's phrase.

On the drive home, Joyce and I barely speak. The atmosphere is so tense that when she steers the car into the driveway and parks, we both just sit there. It's as if neither of us can move. She looks so stressed, I'm afraid she'll have a stroke. Finally I have to say something.

"I know he's going to get better. That's Jack. It's his nature. Don't you think he's going to treat this whole thing like a big training session? Like he's training for the Olympics or something?" She doesn't even answer, which is so not like Joyce. She just lowers her head. "I mean, if there's anyone in the whole world who can recover from this one hundred percent, it's Jack." I'm trying to sound positive but something pushes back. *Why Jack? Of everybody in the world, why did this have to happen to Jack?*

14

For the next few days I try to focus on school, try to think positively about Jack. Try not to obsess about that vision of Matthew. I remind myself I was probably hallucinating.

By Friday, Jack's out of intensive care and in a regular ward. To cut the boredom, we get him a new set of earphones and a little TV with a DVD player on a metal arm that can swing over his bed, and he gives us a list of movies to rent. They're all movies he's already seen, but I guess it helps to feel that some things stay the same.

On Saturday morning, Morris phones my cell and asks if we can meet at the Telford barn at two p.m. for a little survey. That's what he calls it. I say okay, but inside I'm dreading this. I haven't been able to get the sight of Matthew out of my mind. And I haven't said anything about it to Morris, because what if I only imagined it? What if it was only wishful thinking, like Dr. Krantz says? *Matthew, I've been talking to you all along, but in my mind you were still alive. Still living, breathing Matthew, your dark eyes squinting in disbelief at something I've just said, twisting in your chair to face me, raised eyebrows and a forgiving smile. I can still feel your heart beating against the palm of my hand. I never once imagined you as a ghost.*

It's a grey November day, early afternoon. Joyce is out back with Ponyboy and Marley, cleaning up after them and grooming them. It's like having a second job, but she seems to like it. Ethan is playing on his computer, as usual. I have the bathroom to myself for a while, so I stand in front of the full-length mirror in my underwear, feeling anxious. I look at my white body. Thank God summer is over and I can cover up with more clothes. My hair hangs down past my shoulders like black straw. I need hair conditioner. I think maybe I've lost some weight lately, though my hips still look kind of wide—to me, anyway. I wonder if I'm ever going to have the nerve to be naked in front of a guy. I mean, so far I've barely been seen in a bathing suit. It's not that I'm not interested in guys. I've just had zero experience. Except for a non-event with an Italian kid whose parents visited our neighbours the summer I was twelve, I've never even been kissed. And that kiss didn't actually land on my mouth. He meant it to, but he kind of missed.

Then, during the summer before grade eight, when my girlfriends were hanging out at the mall and comparing stories about getting groped by boys, my mom got sicker and sicker and I stopped going out much. There was no point in trying to explain. She died later that year, and I almost failed grade eight. After that, going to school made me feel sick to my stomach.

So much for my so-called love life. When other girls my age started whispering about their Saturday night dates, I pretended not to hear. But this year . . . who knows what might have happened? I probably would have lain naked across a railway track with Matthew if he'd wanted me to. In the dark, anyway.

I layer up as I dress. It takes a while to find a combination I can live with. A black sweater over a yellow tank top, and my blue jean jacket. I put on some clear lip gloss and tie my hair back with an elastic band. I try the ponytail high at the back of my head but it sticks out too much and looks stupid. I tie it low at the back of my neck—boring. This is nuts. *I'm acting like I've got a date with you, Matthew. A little late for that.*

I don't want Joyce or Ethan to see me leave, so I wait until they're both in the kitchen and then sneak out the front door. I walk south on 12th Line, and once I've reached the crest of the hill I can see Morris's car in the Telford farm's driveway. For the first time, I see the weathered grey barn in daylight. Now I'm really getting nervous. In fact I'm freaking out. When I think back to the night Jack fell, I remember bizarre sensations, mysterious noises. It felt as though that barn was crowded.

The difference today is that Morris is here in case I get spooked. I'm going to have to rely on him to get me through this. I hope he's up to it.

As I approach the property, he gets out of his car and leans against his bumper. He has a small camera on a cord around his neck, and he's carrying a bag. He's wearing a dark overcoat, the one I saw him in at the funeral. With his long grey hair and scruffy beard, his lined face and worn features, he looks like a biblical character, or maybe a European film director. I give a little wave as I approach, and smile as best I can.

"Hi, Amelia. Are you . . . okay?" He sounds about as nervous as I feel.

"I think so. I mean, I don't feel great about this." Don't feel great? There's an understatement. I feel like Frodo about to walk into the Land of Mordor. The only reason I can even contemplate stepping back into that shadowy place is that the love of my life might be in there. *Matthew, if you really are there, let me see you. Please don't hide from me.*

"Do you want to change your mind? We don't have to do this," Morris says. I get the feeling he's not sure about it himself.

"No. No, I haven't changed my mind. I *want* to do this. I really do."

"Well, the number-one thing you have to remember is that if, at any moment, you want to leave, you just say so. Okay?"

I nod.

"Number two, this is only research. I just want to get a sense of the place. No seance or anything. I'd like us to look around and take note of as much as we can. If there's enough light, I'll take a few pictures. Then let's get out and talk and compare notes about our impressions. Out here by the car. Then we'll see how we feel. Sound okay?"

"Okay."

Now all we have to do is go inside.

But standing outside the big front entrance, the door closed with a broken lock, I freeze. "Morris, maybe you should go first."

"Yes, of course," he says, and pushes on the wooden door.

It doesn't want to give, so he pushes harder, and finally it moves with a creak, scraping along the dirt floor, opening up into the cavernous space.

I look in and up. There's the smell of straw and dust. Right away, I have a flashback of Jack in the rafters, falling backwards. Lying on the ground. I grab the door frame to steady myself, hoping Morris didn't see me swaying. He reaches into his bag, pulls out a flashlight and turns it on, though the barn's much brighter than it was in the middle of the night. I step inside and the first thing I do is check out the frame where I thought I saw something carved. I can't make out anything, so I motion to Morris to bring his flashlight closer. He runs the beam along the frame, stopping it at about my eye level. The board is badly marked from a hundred years of use, and there are lots of gouges and cracks and lines. But the light illuminates one marking that's extra deep. It looks old and worn, like it was carved years ago. But it definitely looks like *D-O-T* to me. I wasn't imagining it after all.

Morris moves the light down a bit. It looks like there's a plus sign immediately below, but if there was ever more to it, it's since been crossed out with a whole bunch of what look like knife cuts.

"Maybe it was some kind of formula," I whisper. I don't know why I'm whispering.

Morris doesn't say anything; he just stares at it. He tries holding the flashlight at different angles, seeing if he can make the markings stand out more clearly. Finally he hits an angle he likes and takes a few pictures, with me holding the flashlight. Then, lowering the camera, he turns around to face the inside of the barn, and I do the same. I can hear myself breathing, feel my heart beating in my chest. But so far I don't see anything scary or strange.

We walk cautiously into the open space, looking up and around as we do. I can hear a crow or some other bird somewhere outside. A dog barks in the far distance. But there are no sounds in here except our own feet on the dirt floor. We stop in the middle of the barn and I point up to the rafters, to the beam that Jack fell from. Morris nods and stares at it for a bit, then takes more pictures.

Taking a deep breath, I turn to the wall where I thought I saw Matthew. There on the ground—just where I saw it that night—is the mysterious rope. I point it out to Morris, and he raises his eyebrows like he's impressed. We continue to walk toward the far wall, with Morris's flashlight dancing around corners, running along beams, scanning the loft along one side and the stalls along the other, before coming to rest on the tangled heap of rope. There's no one here.

Morris raises his camera to his eye again and takes a picture of the rope, then makes his way back toward the barn door, but this time he takes pictures along the way, going a step or two, focusing and snapping, then taking a few more steps. I stand with my back against the far wall and watch him, listening to the rhythm of electronic snaps and the silence in the background.

My fear has changed to disappointment. As Morris continues his picture-taking, I cast my eyes along the back wall again, seeking the rope. I shuffle closer and lean over it for a better look. It's old but thick and strong enough to have done the deed. I crouch down and touch it, untangling it a bit. The loop that I saw Jack make is still there. I run my hand along it. It's real, all right. I didn't imagine it. I know this rope was below the beam when I left the barn the first time, but when I came back twenty minutes later it was here. This could be the first true evidence I've ever had of something supernatural. *I* didn't move it. "So *who did*?" I whisper to myself.

"Who do you think?"

I lurch backwards so hard I lose my balance, landing flat on my backside in the dirt. Matthew is squatting in the shadows on the other side of the rope. A cold shock runs through me. Every muscle in my body wants to bolt, but I can't move. I feel my face contorting into a scream, but nothing comes out.

"Hi, Amelia."

Finally a tiny sound escapes me. Not a word exactly, and not a cry. More like a moan. I find my muscles and begin to move carefully, crablike, away from the rope, away from the love of my life, buried just last month in a casket in the ground. I move a few feet and then struggle to stand. I don't take my eyes off Matthew, who's still crouching by the rope, his dark eyes following me. I'm on my feet now, rubber-legged and shaking. I stare down at his face and try to speak.

"Did you . . . did you say something?" My voice is barely a whisper. He's looking up at me. Nothing. I'm hallucinating. I knew it.

And then: "About the rope? Yes, I moved it. I thought you'd want me to. He was going to hang himself."

Oh my God. Oh my God. Oh my God. "Matthew?"

Silence.

"Matthew?"

"Yes?"

"Are you okay?" My eyes fill with tears.

"I think I've been better."

I start crying, making a choking noise. "What happened?"

"I'm . . . I'm not sure."

"Amelia?"

A hand grabs my shoulder and I jerk. I'm so startled that my knees buckle, and Morris catches me as I go down.

"Amelia, what is it? What's happening?" Without waiting for an answer, he says, "Time to go." He puts an arm around my waist, hooks my arm around his shoulder and drags me away from Matthew, across the barn floor toward the door, and outside into the shocking daylight.

I hear myself screaming, a sound I've never made before. I can't form words. My legs are gone. Morris carries me over to the car and sits me down inside, leaving my feet dangling outside. Crouched in front of me, he waits with his hands on my shoulders, and after a few minutes I'm just bawling. When I'm only shaking, he jumps up and reaches into the back seat, pulling out a Thermos. He twists off the top and hands the bottle to me. His hands are shaking too. The Thermos stinks of cold coffee.

"I was afraid of this," he mutters.

I take a sip of the coffee. It's awful. I try to speak but he cuts me off.

"Amelia, forgive me. I shouldn't have brought you here."

"Morris . . ." Do I have the courage to say the words?

He's shaking his head. "Listen, I'm playing with fire and I know it. I'm using you to do my research and it's wrong. Your mother—"

"Morris, I think I saw a . . . a ghost."

"Okay." He takes a deep breath. "Okay." He pauses and looks down, like he's wrestling with something big, or maybe having a heart attack. "Who do you think it was?"

I drop my head into my hands and start to cry again. Does he think I'm crazy? I don't feel crazy. I feel pain. I feel grief. I want to go back inside.

"It was Matthew," I whisper.

"Did he speak to you?"

I nod, searching Morris's face. "Do you believe me?"

His eyes close for a second. "Yes," he says. "Yes, I do."

We wait in silence for a while, me sitting sideways on the passenger seat and Morris just outside, leaning against the open door. Finally I straighten up, take a big breath and look back at the barn. I pull myself to my feet and stand beside him against the car, waiting for the light-headed feeling to pass.

"I want to go back in for a few minutes. Just to see if he's still there. I want to ask him a few questions." I'm trying to sound as calm as I can.

Morris presses his fingers to his eyes, then drops his hands and looks at me. "I know how much he meant to you, Amelia, but I don't think this is worth the risk."

"I'd like to go back in," I say again. "I'm not doing this for you. *I* want to do it."

It takes a few minutes for either of us to make a move. At last we walk together toward the barn entrance. Morris says he won't stand too close to me, in case his presence interferes, but if anything intense happens he'll pull me out of the barn again and that'll be it.

We'd left the door open when Morris dragged me outside. Now

we stand at the entrance and peer back in. I brace myself. Matthew is still there, no longer crouching but standing where I left him, leaning against the far wall. He's watching us.

"He's still here," I whisper, and try to point in a subtle way.

Morris's eyes dart across the barn, settling on nothing. I can tell he can't see Matthew. We move to the middle of the barn and he asks me if I'm sure I'm okay with this. I nod and he tells me he'll wait there. He says that if I raise my hand, he'll be at my side in a second. I nod and begin to walk, keeping my eyes locked on Matthew, approaching carefully until I'm about ten feet from him. I stop and try to take him in. He's standing in shadow, but he looks real. He's wearing the same clothes he wore when I saw him last, in his father's pickup truck. He looks like he sees me just fine.

He suddenly speaks up. "Who's that?" He's looking at Morris.

"Oh, uh, just a writer who's doing some research. He has a column in *The Times*. Morris Dyson is his name."

"Is he going to take you away again?"

"I . . . I don't think so. But I don't know how long I can stay."

"Don't go."

We look at each other. I feel like I'm going to lose control again, but I fight it. I need to keep my head.

"Matthew, what are you doing here?" I recall what Morris said about those ley lines. "I mean, are you stuck here for some reason? Weren't you supposed to cross over or something?" It sounds stupid when I hear myself say it.

He seems to be thinking about that, and a rush of confusion comes over me, as if I'm picking up some feeling of intense disorientation from him. He says, "I don't know, but I think I must have done something wrong." His face looks clueless. That is *so* not like Matthew.

"Why do you say that?"

"Because it's like I've stopped living my life and I don't know how to start living it again."

I have a terrible tightness in my throat. How do I tell him?

"Don't you know what happened? Don't you remember?"

He shakes his head.

"I'm not sure how to say this"—I take a deep, shuddering breath—"but you died, Matthew. And everybody thinks you killed yourself."

He frowns. "No, I don't think so," he says, sounding unsure.

"There was a funeral. They . . . buried you."

He reacts to that with surprise, even amusement. Like maybe I'm joking. But then a wave of pain crosses his face.

I take another breath and go on. There's no point in holding anything back. "I think you're a ghost." I cringe when I say that.

Now he really is amused, and he breaks out in a grin. "You're kidding, right?"

"I have a confession to make. Remember how I always said I didn't believe in anything? Well, I was lying. I . . . I believe in ghosts. I've even seen a few. But I guess you could say I was in denial before."

His mouth is open, as if it's suddenly dawned on him that I'm not just teasing him.

"The point is, I've seen a few, so I know a ghost when I see one."

He looks at me hard now, and then gives a quick shake of his head. "Really? That's"—he searches for a word—"surprising."

"Yeah. I can imagine." He seems to be taking the news well, but maybe it isn't sinking in yet. Meanwhile, I want to get him to talk some more.

"Do you remember what happened to you in the barn? Anything at all?"

"Uh, just this horrible crying in my ears. At first I thought it was me, but then I lifted my head and saw this guy crying right in my face. When he finally calmed down, I looked back behind me and saw myself standing there. With a pitchfork through my stomach. It was pretty gross. I mean, talk about internal injuries."

His speech is slow and a little spacey, almost like he's stoned. It hurts to hear him speak so casually about something so horrible. "You're not the only one left with internal injuries, Matthew."

"I'm sorry," he says quietly.

He looks at me with this sad, confused gaze. I just stare back at him for a while, and then I ask, "And before that? What's the last thing you remember?"

"Mr. Telford showing me the barn, I guess. That was a Saturday morning."

"So you don't remember giving me a lift that evening?"

"No. Did I?"

"Yes. I mean, I thought it was you. Sure looked like you." I study his face, realizing that nothing feels sure. Nothing then, nothing now. "Matthew, how do I know you aren't just some figment of my imagination? Can you prove it's really you? Tell me something I wouldn't already know, something you never told me before. So I can check it out."

There's a long pause. Then he shrugs and says, "Okay. Well, I think I'm in love with you, Amelia."

I'm reeling. "I said something I *didn't* know." I'm trying to keep it light, but inside I feel like screaming.

"Oh." He pauses, like he's searching. Then he asks, "Can you really see ghosts? Because there's a red-haired guy with cool wire-rim glasses over there." He gestures toward the loft. "He could be one."

I whip around in the direction he's pointing. I can't see anything in the darkness.

"Like John Lennon glasses," he says.

"Who . . . who is it?" I'm trying not to freak.

"I don't know. His hair is kind of long. And red."

"Is he the guy you said was crying?"

"No, that's someone else. He's around here somewhere."

"Anyone else?"

"Oh, yeah."

"Matthew, I need to ask you something. That girl you told me you were meeting. Is she here?"

"What girl? I'm not sure what you mean, but I don't think there's a girl here."

I'm holding my hand over my mouth, trying not to cry. "But have you ever seen a girl in this barn, Matthew? Concentrate. I have to know."

"I don't think so . . . I don't know."

It's crazy, but I could sob with relief. At least there isn't another girl in the picture. "You told me you were meeting her."

He shrugs.

"Okay, how about *dot*? Does that word mean anything to you?"

"No. Should it?"

I tell him he carved it into his desk in his bedroom on the day he died.

"*Dot* as in dot-com?" he asks, but I shake my head. He says it means nothing to him and he doesn't remember carving it.

I need to find out one more thing. "Matthew, what happens if I touch you?"

Still leaning against the wall, he slowly sinks down until he's squatting, like he was when I saw him earlier. He reaches out to touch the rope. He moves it, just a little, in the dirt.

"I can touch some things, objects," he says, "but it's like I'm not all here. I don't know where the rest of me is." Still looking down at the rope, he asks in a quiet voice, "Am I really a ghost?"

He holds up his arm and looks at his hand. Then he holds it out toward me and rises to his feet.

I take a step closer to him, but it's as if the shadow he stands in is growing darker, or maybe my eyesight is growing dimmer, and now I can't see him as well. I lean forward, stretching my shaking hand toward his. But as I do, he fades even more, and where our fingers should have touched, I feel nothing but cool air.

I can't see him anymore.

He's gone.

15

sit beside Morris in his car in the Telford driveway, freaking out. It's like I'm having a nervous breakdown. I can't stop asking, "Why Matthew? Why me?" The fact that he's dead—that life can never go back to the way it used to be—is hitting me all over again. I look to Morris as if maybe he has the answers, but he just wears a pained expression, like he has a headache.

"It can't be easy for you," he finally says, shaking his head. He offers me his Thermos of cold coffee again, and I take a small sip before remembering how awful it tastes. As I pass it back, I notice a tremor in his hands. He apologizes and says he's going to have a quick smoke, and then he climbs out of the car. He walks a short distance away, dragging on the cigarette, pacing like crazy. When he comes back he apologizes again, says he's trying to quit. But I don't care about his smoking.

"I knew it," I say quietly. "I knew it all along. I knew my mother's ghost was real."

Then Morris tells me his story.

"Years ago, my wife and I lost a baby girl to crib death. It was just one of those nightmares you live through, waiting to wake up from it, except you never do. But then I started hearing my daughter crying down the hall in the empty nursery at night. At least, I thought I was hearing her cry. In the night, half-asleep, I'd run to her room. Of course, by the time I got there, the crying had stopped. It put me over the edge."

He's looking down, his chin practically on his chest, his voice tight and his eyes almost shut. We sit in silence like that for a minute.

"God. I'm sorry, Morris."

He shrugs heavily. "For a long while I thought it was just the feeling of guilt, but it wouldn't stop. What saved me was that I finally started thinking about the whole thing differently—just to keep from going crazy. I started asking myself whether I wasn't really hearing her ghost. And I started doing research. The more I studied, the better I could cope with it. My research took over my life, I guess. The sound of crying gradually stopped. But by then I'd lost my wife, and my son too. She got a teaching post at the University of Chicago, took Kip with her and found herself a new husband. So I've been digging myself out of a depression for years. This crazy ghost obsession is what keeps me sane. And sober." He mumbles the last part. "And I don't mind saying, your mom was a huge inspiration. Huge."

I ask him what he means by thinking differently, and he tells me that he stopped trying to convince himself that his daughter *wasn't* there and started asking himself what it meant if she *was*. He says his research shows that by far the most common connection to the spirit world is through sound. So the most "extrasensory" of the human senses is hearing. It's far more common to *hear* something supernatural than it is to *see* it. I'd never thought of that before.

"What else have you learned?" I ask him.

"Well, one of the reasons we can hear ghosts is that they can move stuff. Even though they aren't solid, they seem to be able to move things that are. Inanimate objects. So they can make a racket if they want to. It's only living things they have trouble with. The only way they can move living things is by possessing them."

Possession. *That* little trick. I've never thought of it like that before.

"I'm not a religious man," he goes on, "and I'm not sure I believe in an afterlife the way most religions talk about it. But after years of researching stories of apparitions, I'm convinced that a ghost is an emotional entity. The emotional fingerprint of a departed person."

"You mean like a soul?"

"Call it what you want." He shrugs. "The bloody mystery is how that energy survives the body and has an existence that some people can hear or even see." He looks over at me like he's looking for the answer in my eyes, but he realizes I don't have it, so he struggles to explain some more. "I'm just saying that ghosts aren't big thinkers. They feel. They feel the feelings they had when they were alive. So like everyone who can feel, they can suffer."

Listening to his gravelly, sad voice, I realize that for all the talk of ghosts I've heard throughout my life, I've never understood what they are. Morris sighs, like he's finding all this hard to say.

"Ghosts still long to connect emotionally with the living, only they're damaged in some way. They're traumatized. And it seems that some are outright emotionally disturbed." He pauses and then carefully goes on. "I think a ghost made Matthew kill himself. Maybe the same ghost that made Paul commit suicide. And that same ghost made Jack fall."

He starts up the car. "I'm sorry I put you through this, Amelia. It was selfish. I don't think you should ever come here again."

As we drive back up 12th Line, I'm thinking that I like Morris's theory a lot. I don't know how to tell him, and I don't know why, but

I realize I feel a bit better. Because I *did* feel emotion from Matthew. It felt real. And I always felt emotion coming from my mother's ghost too.

Morris lets me out on the road in front of my house and I creep in through the front door, managing to avoid Joyce, who is still out back in the paddock. I feel pretty rough and I don't want to be seen like this, so I slip into the bathroom.

Lying in a tub of warm water high with bath bubbles, the bathroom light turned off, I feel a kind of peace I haven't felt for a long time. It's almost sundown, the room is dark and warm and silent, and I'm finally calming down. But it's not only because of what Morris said about ghosts. It's because of the way he talked about ghosts *to me*. Like I was an adult. A sane adult. And for the first time, I feel like admitting that, yeah, I do see ghosts. I've seen ghosts all my life. So what? Get over it.

And then there's that other matter: the fact that Matthew— whoever, whatever part of Matthew I saw—finally told me he loves me. *Better late than never, Matthew.*

I've told Morris I'll do what I can to help him uncover the history of the barn. He's fascinated by Matthew's reference to the red-haired guy, and to the one who was crying. And he's intrigued that Matthew didn't remember our mystery girl. Morris thinks we can get at the truth without ever going back inside the barn. I don't agree, though I haven't said so. The question is, Do I have the guts to go back in alone?

Morris did make me realize one other thing: that something or someone in that barn may be causing people to kill themselves, or at least attempt it. That amounts to murder. So there really is a murderer on the loose in Grey County after all. But I can't think about that right now. I try to empty my head. I want to feel empty, in a good way.

I remember that when I was about eight years old, Mom rented a cottage on Lake Huron. The water was cold and the shore was rocky. There were big beautiful rocks you could play on, jumping from one to the other, trying to step only on the pink ones.

One evening after supper, my mom and I were playing cards in the screened-in porch at the back, facing the water. Jack was there too. And out on the lake, a long way from shore, there was this odd boat, bigger than a fishing boat, a faded green and blue. The sun was going down and there was a beautiful red sunset and the waves were rippling, red and shiny. My mom stood up and walked down the grassy slope toward the dock, and then she just stood there and looked at that boat. Jack and I jumped up and ran out after her.

I remember asking her, "What is that?" And she said it was a beautiful old boat. A really old boat. She said you never saw boats like that anymore. There were three people on the small deck. I could barely see them, but I could tell they were wearing strange clothes. I asked her why they were dressed so funny. I remember her looking down at me, and Jack in the background whining, "I don't see a boat." But after a few minutes the boat had moved a little, right into the path of the setting sun, and I couldn't see it anymore. Mom was shielding her eyes, still gazing out. Then she looked down at me again and touched the palm of her hand to my head.

A loud rap on the bathroom door startles me to death, causing a small tidal wave that splashes over the edge of the tub. I must have fallen asleep. The bathwater has cooled down and the bubbles are almost gone. Ethan is knocking and yelling, "Are you done in there yet? Someone called for you, you know. I didn't even know you were home, so I took a message. Some guy named Chip, or something weird like that."

"Out in a minute," I shout, grabbing a face cloth and soaking it in the water. I scrub my face till it hurts.

16

I step inside Toby's Tavern, still gasping from running four blocks, a pain in my side. I'm twenty minutes late. I really don't think I'm up to this. As I catch my breath, I look around. Toby's is one of those slightly shabby but cozy pub-style restaurants. It's Sunday, late afternoon, and there are just a few groups of guys here, drinking beer and eating nachos.

I check out all the tables and finally catch sight of a shaggy blond head, a hand lifting to his brow and saluting as I scan past. Kip has a small table in a corner near the window. A draft beer is half-empty in front of him, and he looks like he's been waiting for a while. Ugh.

This was Morris's idea. He's worried he's falling behind on a deadline, so he asked if Kip and I could do a bit of detective work without him. Maybe we should get to know each other a little first, he suggested, since we're going to be a research team. I'm dreading this.

I walk over to Kip's table, aware that I look like I just stepped out of a hurricane. I'm sure my face is red, and I'm sweating, too. Perspiring, I mean. From running and nerves. I try to smile and not seem too self-conscious. Wow! I suppose he's kind of hot. I say hi and sit down, tugging at my coat, trying to get it off, struggling to pull my arms out. Somehow I manage to turn the coat into a bloody straitjacket. I'm now wrestling with the sleeves, which are turned inside out and stuck, hanging from my elbows. Totally awkward. For just an instant I think his eyes flicker over my chest. I'm pretty sure. Maybe I should have worn my push-up bra. Then he looks me straight in the eyes, smiling. I finally get the damn coat off, but with way too much effort and flailing around. I apologize for being late, explaining that I had to wait until my grandmother was ready to visit my brother Jack at the hospital and could give me a lift into town. And that I ran from the hospital. Now I'm fighting to get the coat to stay on the back of my chair. Why is everything so difficult today? Kip smiles, his head slightly cocked like he finds this amusing, and waits for me to settle in.

"Want a beer?" he asks, looking over my head at a waitress a few tables away.

"You're kidding, right?"

"Why? How old are you?"

"Sixteen and three-quarters. How old are you?"

"Nineteen. By the time you get to my age, you don't break it into fractions anymore."

"I'm fine with a Coke." He's making fun of me. I'm not sure what's harder, looking at him or not looking at him. I'd better just keep talking.

"So your dad tells me you work at the Grey County Archives. Are you originally from Grey County?"

"No, I'm not from here. Born in Hamilton, raised in Chicago. I'm enrolled in university there but . . . taking a sabbatical."

"Sabbatical. Is that like sick leave?"

He laughs. "Not exactly. Kind of. I wanted a break. Also I'm sinking into debt. One year of college and I already have a student loan the size of some people's mortgages. So I'm taking a year off to make some money. My dad got me the job. He knows everyone there, since he's been mining the archives for his history column for years. And in exchange for room and board, I said I'd help him with his research. My moonlighting job."

"Must have been a shock, going from a big city like Chicago to a little town like Owen Sound. But nice to reconnect with your dad."

"You know, a little town is nice for a change. And who said my dad and I were disconnected?" He grins. "All right, a little. But I was also looking to get away. I needed to take some time out . . . to reassess the direction of my life. Happy?"

"Sorry to be so nosy. I really like your dad, that's all. But you seem young for reassessing your life already."

"Hey, you're never too young for a mid-life crisis. The sooner the better."

"Do you miss Chicago?"

"Yeah, I do. It's a great place—for Halloween costumes, especially."

"What? Oh my God. It's been bugging me, this feeling that we've talked before. Your eyes or something. When did you figure that out?" I'm totally floored. I can't believe I didn't make the connection.

"At the party."

"No! Are you serious? How did you know?"

"I don't know. I just did. Must have been your eyes or something." He's teasing again, smiling at me across the table. "And that other-worldly aura you have."

I smile back, thinking I should somehow have known that the mysterious Bob Marley twin was Kip. I admit he isn't as awful as I'd feared. "So why were you at that party, really? You didn't know anyone there, did you?"

"I didn't get the feeling you knew anyone either. Anyway, I told you: Brad's mom. She works with me, and she suggested I go. I really thought she might be there. She's hot. But turns out she's also heartless. Yeah, it was pretty bad. I left not long after you did. You were my last reason for staying."

"Sure." I laugh at that. "So when did you move up here?"

"In August. I lived on campus last year, and my lease was up. Before that, I lived at home with my mom and my stepdad, and I really didn't want to move back. They're both university profs." He grins again. "You know, you ask a lot of questions."

"Sorry! But wow, living with two profs—that must be interesting."

"Yeah, sometimes. Sometimes not. Anyway, my dad grew up in Grey County. He moved south and met my mom, then moved back here after the divorce. I was only ten and I went with Mom. So this was a chance to get to know my dad better. I mean, we've visited each other over the years, but that's not the same."

"And what's it like living with him now?"

"He's even crazier than I expected." He thinks about that a beat, then adds, "I like him."

"Well, it's nice that you have both parents in your life and they both . . . uh, love you. My mother is dead. My father's dead too, in a car accident when I was four." I suddenly realize that I sound self-pitying. I don't want to.

He looks at me for a moment before he responds.

"I'm sorry. That sucks." He takes a sip of his beer, probably trying to think of a way to change the subject. "I'm also an only child, so I'm kind of overvalued. Actually, I'm lying. There was another child, a baby girl who died."

"I know. Your dad told me."

"He did? I'm surprised he would mention that. Crib death. It wasn't great. My dad was wrestling with a few demons after that. My parents broke up a couple of years later."

"What do you mean by demons?"

"Nothing much." He's cringing a little now, like he said too much. "Yeah, well, he used to drink quite a bit. Sorry, Dad," he mutters.

I laugh. "Honestly, I won't tell on you."

"But he's been clean and sober, as they say, for six years. And he's fine."

"Are you going to go back to university next year?"

"That's the plan."

The waitress comes by to see if we'd like anything else. Kip asks if I'll share a plate of fries. I hesitate, fries being fattening and all, then say, "Sure."

"So enough about me," he says as the waitress leaves. "Tell me all about you."

"Nothing to tell." I'm starting to feel more relaxed. "Grey County, born and bred. Mom was from just south of here. Dad was from the city. I live with my grandmother Joyce, and my two brothers. My older brother, Jack, he's great. Crooked nose, good heart. My younger brother, Ethan, is a pain. That's about it, really. So what do you study at university?"

"Well . . ." He pauses, a look on his face I can't read, then continues. "I'm into classical Greek literature. But I'm not sure I'll stick with it."

"Really? Why not?"

"If I want to go any further with it I'll have to learn to read classical Greek, and as my mom likes to warn me, it's not exactly the fast-track to a paying job these days. She says it was okay for her generation but those days are gone."

"Ah. So what else are you interested in?" I take a risk. "Ghosts, like your dad?"

He laughs. "Not really, no. I'm what you'd call a skeptic."

"Oh. Does that mean you don't believe in anything?"

"You make it sound so negative. There are things I believe in."

"But not ghosts."

"Not really, no." He looks straight into my eyes when he says that, but I don't flinch or anything. It's because I'm not surprised. I could kind of tell he didn't buy into his dad's obsession.

"I think mythology's more real," he says.

"Mythology? I saw the movie *Troy* with Brad Pitt. You believe in that kind of thing?" I can't believe I just mentioned Brad Pitt.

"Well, in a way, I guess. Aeschylus, Sophocles, Euripides, Homer—those guys."

"They sound exotic."

"Yeah, they're pretty cool. And interesting. I'll give you an example. Have you ever heard of Prometheus?"

"Kind of. Maybe."

"Okay, well, Prometheus is famous for pissing off Zeus, the king of the Olympian gods, because he went behind Zeus's back and gave early humanity a few special gifts to help them survive, just when Zeus had decided he'd rather let them die out 'cause he thought they were such duds. Those gifts were what gave humans a leg up, so to speak. But Zeus was pretty pissed off, as I said, so for punishment he chained Prometheus to a rock on the edge of the world, with an eagle picking out his liver on a daily basis."

"That's nasty."

"Well, eventually Hercules came by and freed him."

"Phew!"

"I'm simplifying. But what's interesting are the gifts. The best-known is fire—Prometheus steals fire and brings it to humans. Which comes in very handy for heat, light, barbecues. But a lesser-known gift is hope. You know how Prometheus created hope? He took away people's ability to see into the future, including their knowledge of how and when they were going to die. According to Greek mythology, people's lives—and their deaths—are all predetermined. Knowing when they were destined to die filled people with resignation. But when Prometheus took away that foreknowledge, they were free to hope for the best. That's what 'Prometheus' means—'foreknowledge.' So instead of feeling discouraged by the knowledge of their deaths, humans started seeing life in a more promising way. Blind hope."

"You're right. That *is* interesting."

"Yeah, so basically they were better able to get on with living their lives because the future was unknown. Now, here's another neat thing: in Greek mythology the afterworld is called Hades, and there's a river there called Lethe. It's the river of forgetfulness. When people die, they take a dip in it so they can forget the life they just left behind."

I nod. It's a lot to think about.

He continues, "So taking away people's knowledge of the future lets them get on with living. And taking away their memory of the past lets them get on with being dead."

"So dead people have no memory." I think about that for a moment. "But ghosts seem to have a memory. At least some memory. Curious. Maybe it's memory that makes them a ghost."

"I wouldn't know. You're the ghost expert."

"You really don't believe in ghosts at all? Even when you're alone in an old, spooky mansion after midnight?"

"Uh, let's just say not yet. But either way, I prefer zombies."

I roll my eyes. "Right, I forgot. Jesus was a zombie."

"Well, only after Easter. More like a zombie than a ghost, anyway. I mean, if you had to choose. That's why he had that Doubting Thomas apostle stick a hand in his side wound after he was 'resurrected.' You know what I'm talking about, right? Gospel of John?

It was to prove he was still flesh and blood, not just a ghost. You may have noticed that the Bible isn't big on ghosts. Or even spirits or souls. Those ideas belong more to other religions. Pagan religions. And Shakespeare." He grins at that, like he finds it amusing.

"And don't forget Hollywood." I grin too. "So do you have a girlfriend?" I blurt. I can't believe I just asked that. It's like I had a moment of insanity or something. "I mean, not that it makes any difference," I add quickly. "I was just curious. I was thinking that if she lives in Chicago, you know, you must miss her. I mean, none of my business. You don't have to answer that."

"Wow, there's a non sequitur. But it's a relief that it doesn't make any difference and I don't have to answer."

"Non what? Is that Greek?"

"Latin. It's when something doesn't quite follow. Comes out of nowhere. And to answer the original question: not at this exact moment, no."

"You make it sound like you had one only an hour ago."

"Jeez, have you ever thought of a career in interrogation?"

He looks mildly uncomfortable, which makes him seem even cuter. I decide it's worth the effort trying to keep him that way. He must have to beat girls off with a stick.

"Okay, my turn," he says. "How about you tell me about Matthew?"

Now it's me who's caught off guard. I don't know what to say.

Kip's face goes a little red. "I'm sorry. That didn't come out right. I'm really sorry he died. And the way he died. I can't imagine. I'm . . . I'm sorry I brought it up."

"No, it's okay. Not much to say." A flood of feeling, as though I've had a little break from it and now it's high tide again. "He was . . . special."

"Were you two a couple?" he asks.

"You mean a 'couple' couple? I was working on that. Interrupted."
There's a long silence, broken only by the sound of a plate of french
fries being dropped onto the table. The plate just sits there. Awkwardly.

Finally he jumps in. "Well, whatever you had, it sounds special
all right."

The way he says that makes me wonder if Morris told him about
our barn visit. About Matthew's ghost.

"Seriously," I ask, "why don't you believe in ghosts?"

"They just don't make sense to me."

"Does the truth always make sense to you?"

He laughs. "Good point. Well"—he reaches across the table and
pats my hand—"let's just say, I believe you believe."

I pull my hand away, feeling irritated.

"Don't get me wrong," he says. "I'm thrilled that you and my dad
are teaming up. Almost as thrilled as he is. I think it's going to be fun."

That's disappointing, somehow. I'm pretty sure *fun* isn't the right
word for all this. "There's nothing fun about the Telford barn."

"No. No, you're right. I'm sorry."

Another minute of awkward silence.

"Well, we've covered quite a lot of personal ground," Kip says,
suddenly sounding all professional. "Shall we move on to business?
Research for Morris?" He pulls out a handwritten list on a piece
of paper.

"Okay, sure," I say, grateful for the shift in tone.

"Fry?"

"Sure." And we both take one.

"These are all the people who've owned the Telford farm." He
flattens out the list beside the plate of fries. He takes out a pen and
follows the names as he reads them out loud. "There have been only
four registered owners since the land was first sold to William McGrath,

a Scottish immigrant, and his family in 1888. McGrath—together with his wife, Margaret, and three children, William, Sebastian and Judith—built the farmhouse, which was registered in 1889. In 1912 the property changes hands, passing on to the younger son, Sebastian. Maybe the eldest son, William Junior, died young? Sebastian McGrath had a wife named Mary and four children—daughters named Frances, Dorothy and Cordelia, and one son, William. The next owner is registered in 1946, a Thomas McCleary. He married Linda and had three children, John, Mary and Daniel. And the most recent owner, Hank Telford, bought it from McCleary in 1966. He and his wife, Sarah, had two children: Paul—that was Dad's friend—and Emily."

While he's talking, with his eyes on the paper between us, I steal a glance at his face. Dirty blond, that's what my mother used to call that hair colour. A little wavy, a bit messy, and there's a shadow of beard on his chin and cheeks. He has nice cheekbones. His nose is maybe a little long. Well . . . perfect, really. There's a scar on his chin. You can see it through the stubble. And he does have a nice smile. Too bad about his attitude.

"That's all we know about the place so far. Dad wants us to track down anything suspicious in old newspapers or in records relating to either the property itself or the family members of the owners. I guess what we're looking for are things that connect somehow with what has happened recently. Mysterious deaths, that kind of thing?"

"Hmm, okay. So let's review what we know so far: Matthew Sorenson and Paul Telford died in that barn. Both suicides, both suspicious. And Matthew said there are at least two other ghosts there with him, a red-haired guy and someone he only described as crying."

"Got it."

So weird the way he doesn't believe in ghosts but then takes my word for something a ghost told me. What's with that?

"Oh, and just for the record: I asked my dad, and Paul didn't have red hair."

"Then maybe he's the one who was crying," I suggest. "So where do we start?"

"Well, how about I report back to Dad? Tell him how you and I have really hit it off. So well, in fact, we'll probably end up eloping to Vegas." He gives me a wink and I have trouble keeping a straight face. "I'll see if he's managed to set up a visit with Mr. Telford. He's hoping we can go along with him."

"That sounds fine. I think." He's a charmer, all right. Maybe he's a psychopath? Aren't they supposed to be charming? I take another french fry. "So what else have those ancient Greeks taught you?"

"That you can't fight fate." He grins at me.

Yikes. I can feel myself blushing.

About twenty minutes later, we step outside the pub onto the sidewalk. The November sun is already setting. I tell Kip I'm heading off to the hospital to join my grandmother. Just then, Morgan and Brittany come round the corner, and their faces totally brighten up when they see me with this strange hunky guy.

"Amelia! Hi! What's up? We've just been shopping. Who's your friend?"

They're both grinning very aggressively, all teeth, looking from me to Kip and back again, eyebrows raised high. I'm embarrassed at their unsubtle interest.

"Ah, Morgan, Brittany, meet Kip. Kip Dyson. He's a . . . family friend. Staying in town for a while."

"Hello, ladies." Flashing his baby blues. Shaking hands. The girls are all gaga. They might as well be wearing sandwich boards, they're so easy to read.

"Well, Amelia, make sure you bring Kip to my party next Saturday." Brittany turns to Kip, adding, "If you're still in town."

That winning smile. I fear she may be Kip's type. The cheerleader type. I'm moving away from them, nodding, waving goodbye, saying, "We'll see." Kip takes a few extra steps to catch up with me.

"What? I can't believe you weren't going to tell me about Brittany's party."

I give him a smirk. "This is the first I've heard of it. So congratulations, you're now on the grade eleven girls' hit list. Be very afraid."

At the corner of the street that leads to the hospital, I turn and hold out an unsure hand for a shake. He takes it and begins to raise it to his mouth for a kiss, but I pull it away. It's a reflex.

"Forget it," I say, and turn away from him, heading up the street alone. Only I can't resist one last look. He's still watching me, and now he's the one smirking.

"Okay, but we are *so* going to that party," he calls.

17

oyce is downstairs making dinner on Thursday evening, and I'm upstairs, staring out my bedroom window. There was a dusting of snow on the field early this morning, but by noon it had melted away. Our first snow of the season. The two horses are huddled together at one end of the fenced paddock as if they're whispering. I can see their breath in the air, like two friends complaining to each other. *You realize this means winter?*

Jack phoned me two days ago, sounding weird. He said he'd had a dream that he woke up in the barn. He was lying on the ground in the dark and his back felt like it was on fire. He said I was leaning over him and he could see me crying, but the sound he heard was coming from someone else. Some guy who was wailing hard and then started shouting angrily. Jack said it sounded like someone was standing right behind him, yelling, "You're dead! You're dead!"

A chill went through me. "You dreamt this?"

"You tell me."

I couldn't think of what to say. He said he wanted the truth and he sounded desperate. Very upset. I felt a rush of remorse. I admitted that there was more to what had happened than I'd told him or Joyce or the police, and that I just didn't think anyone would believe me. That's when it really sank in, what a big lie I'd told about him. I said I was so sorry. I promised I'd visit him the next day and tell him everything.

Yesterday I had a spare period before my lunch break, giving me an hour to slip away and head for the hospital. When I arrived, I checked out the old man in the bed next to Jack's to make sure he was asleep. His eyes were closed and his mouth was wide open, as if whatever he was seeing in his dream was giving him a fright. He looked about a hundred years old. Like he could die at any minute. I took a seat in the chair beside Jack's bed and pulled it close so I could keep my voice low.

I started with Jack and his friends arguing at around two a.m. after the party. I told him how I followed him when he snuck back to the barn. How he was so pissed off about that and told me to go home, saying he was meeting someone. He looked shocked to hear that, which I was afraid of. I was hoping that if he started remembering a bit of what had happened that night, he'd be able to answer some questions for me too.

"You seemed to be sneaking off to the barn to meet some girl," I told him. "That's the crucial detail. Because Matthew told me he was going to meet a girl the night *he* died. And Paul Telford—that's Hank Telford's son—killed himself in the same barn in 1980, after going on to his friends about some girl he'd just met. How I know that is a long story and I'll explain some other time, but you see what I'm getting at, right? I think what happened to you is the same thing that happened to them, and some mystery girl holds the key. Except in your case, you survived."

I explained that after he told me to get lost, I turned around and followed him again. By the time I got into the barn, though, he was already on the crossbeam, way up in the rafters and crying. Going on about some girl.

What I was saying really hit him then, and he started freaking out. "Holy cow! Are you kidding me? That's friggin' insane, man. That is definitely *not* me. Jesus, Ethan was right. *He was right.*"

Turns out Ethan had told Jack that he'd been possessed by an evil spirit, just like the guy in the movie *The Shining*. "Everybody knows that," Ethan said.

I told him that he couldn't breathe a word of this to Joyce or I'd kill him, but that maybe there was something to that evil spirit stuff. Then I said that I had to tell him the most important thing. "Jack, you didn't slip. At least, that's not what it looked like from where I was standing. You just let yourself fall backwards." I decided to leave it at that. He didn't need to know about the rope.

There was this stunned silence. "What? You mean on purpose?"

I nodded, but he continued to look dazed. I felt so sorry for him that I told him I was going to let him in on a secret he couldn't tell anyone. "*Anyone*—okay?"

He nodded, his head a little cocked to the side so that his nose looked straight.

"I've teamed up with this guy Morris Dyson. He's an expert in ghost sightings. And his son. We're going to dig into the history of that barn. We're going to try to figure out if it's haunted, and if so, who's haunting it." Jack just sat there, then turned to look at the sky through the window. "And I promise I will tell you anything I find out. But you have to keep this to yourself. Promise?"

"Okay. Promise," he mumbled.

———

I'm on my computer when Joyce calls Ethan and me to supper. *See you later, Matthew,* I say to my desktop photo, and I turn it off. Joyce has made spaghetti with meat sauce. It tastes pretty good, but she's given me too much and I can't finish it. Ethan, on the other hand, eats like a hog, blabbering about video games and blinking hard the way he does when he gets any kind of attention at all.

"You seem a little more energetic these days," she comments, looking at me suspiciously. Like I must be up to something. "You're . . . uh, feeling a little better lately?" She's looking down and playing with the pasta on her fork, waiting for my answer.

I guess it's true, I have been feeling better. Less miserable, I mean. I think it's because of this huge distraction I've had ever since I met Morris. And because of seeing Matthew again, of course.

"Yeah, I guess." I mean, there's not much more I can say.

Ethan says, "Yeah, you were in a really lousy mood, man. Like, for ages. Everybody said so." He looks at me with six inches of pasta hanging from his mouth, and he winces. *Yeah, well, your facial tic isn't getting any better,* I want to say. But I never would. He can't help it.

Then Joyce tells us that the renovation work will begin this weekend. The first job is to build a wheelchair ramp up to the door at the kitchen. The plan is to have Jack on a home visit over Christmas, so she's hoping to have the house accessible and his new bedroom on the main floor set up by then. She says we'll have to take things a month at a time after that, and see how he does in physiotherapy. You can tell she's taking this very hard. She's been a little different ever since his accident. But I honestly believe Jack is going to get better. I probably believe it more than I believe anything else in the world right now. I have to.

"Oh, before I forget, I've got a thing after school tomorrow. A study thing with a friend," I say, hoping that's as much information as Joyce needs.

"A study thing?" she says. "What's that about?"

"Oh, a history test next week. A few of us are going to get together to study. And watch TV," I add. I realize I was pushing my luck with the study line. Obvious crap. TV is easier for her to swallow.

"I'm getting a ride home. Should be back by eight."

Ethan and I are running out the door and down the driveway on Friday morning, backpacks full of books, homework and gym clothes. The bus will be by at any minute, and it doesn't wait for stragglers. All I can think about is my meeting with Morris and Kip after school in the Tim Hortons parking lot. Morris made an appointment for us to see Hank Telford, who's staying at his daughter's house in the first town south of here, at four-thirty. Morris told them he's researching some local history on farms in the county. They agreed to help, as a favour to an old family friend.

Sitting on the school bus as it barrels down the country roads, I can almost forget where I am. As usual, my mind drifts to Matthew. Ever since I talked to him in the barn that day, I feel less damaged, less mortally wounded, by his absence. I don't know if that's normal. *Matthew, I'm trying to work up the nerve to go into the barn again. This weekend. That's my goal. Just promise me you'll still be there.*

"Hey, what's up?"

What? Oh, it's just Peter. He's in my math class. He's also Jeremy's cousin, so he knows Jack. He drops down into the seat beside me like a cannonball. I'm so not used to being befriended. There was a time when I felt I had a better chance of being beheaded. But I guess it was my fault, mostly. I didn't want anyone to get to know me too well.

"How's Jack?" Peter asks. Everyone at school knows about Jack's fall, but Peter knows more about what happened than most, because of Jeremy being in the barn with Jack earlier that evening. I wonder if Jeremy thinks Jack was possessed too, thanks to Ethan's blabbing. I can't tell from Peter's expression.

"He's doing well. Really well, considering. I think he'll be good as new eventually."

"Great. That's great." There's an awkward pause, then he says, "Strange, eh? The accident and all? I mean, Jeremy says the barn is haunted."

"Yeah, well, I don't know about that. Sounds like something a little kid might say. Like my brother Ethan. But it's a good idea for everyone to stay clear of the place. Not because it's haunted or anything dumb like that. It's just pretty dangerous in there. Lots of rotten wood and junk lying around. Someone else could get hurt."

When you've got secrets, you have to learn how to lie. I don't like doing it but there's a lot at stake. It's not only because the barn is so dangerous. I don't want kids trashing it either. I have to protect Matthew.

All through my classes, I work at concentrating. I've decided that trying to keep my grades up is a good distraction. I'm both excited and nervous for the school day to end, though. I've spent a lot of years looking away from the weird things I've seen, and now, for the first time, I'm actually taking a closer look. It's hard to get used to.

And I hate to admit it but I'm also kind of looking forward to seeing Kip again. It's only because he's different from the other guys around here. That's all. I run into Brittany in the hallway on my way out of school and she immediately reminds me about the get-together at her place tomorrow evening. "You're going to bring your 'family friend,' right?" It's definitely Kip she wants to see, not me.

Soon I'm standing at the corner of the Tim Hortons, keeping an eye out for Morris's car. I catch sight of it pulling into the parking lot. Morris and Kip wave and I wave back, then I run through the parking lot to them. I open the back door and jump in, pulling my school bag in beside me.

Morris says, "Howdy," like an old cowpoke, with a quick glance at me in the rear-view mirror. Then his eyes are back on the road.

Kip turns around to face me from the front passenger seat. "Hey," he says with a big smile. "And how are you?"

"Good, thanks. And you?"

"Great. I'm great." He faces forward again. "We're on an adventure!"

I guess he's not getting out much.

Morris drives south out of town, past city hall, past the motels, past the cemetery and the golf course.

"By the way," he says, meeting my eyes in the rear-view mirror again, "just to keep things simpler, I'd like to introduce you as Kip's friend. Is that okay with you? It looks better if you're there because of Kip rather than me, if you know what I mean."

I'm not sure I do, but I say, "So I'm along because of Kip, not you?"

"Yeah, because you guys are friends."

"Fine with me." Kip winks at me like this is some kind of under-cover assignment. "*Close* friends, right?"

I can see Morris roll his eyes in the rear-view mirror. "Just friends is fine."

Kip looks back at me, his eyebrows moving up and down sugges-tively, which makes me stick out my tongue at him like a bratty ado-lescent. He laughs. Why did I do that? How juvenile! I focus on the view from the side window, fighting to wipe the smile off my face.

Within ten minutes we're pulling up in front of a white clapboard bungalow in an older residential block off the town crossroads. There are a few big trees out front, now bare, and dry brown leaves lie deep on the lawn. There's a large middle-aged woman standing in the front door, and she opens the screen as we get out of the car.

"Morris!" she shouts, a big smile on her face. He's up the porch steps in moments and getting a bear hug against her very large bosom. "It's been years," she says. "Oh my goodness! Is this little Kip? No way! The last time I saw Kip, he was a chubby twelve-year-old. Now look at you, looking down at your old man. How'd he get so handsome, Morris?"

"Recessive gene," says Morris.

Kip smiles at her a little painfully and holds out his hand. "Hi, Emily. Nice to see you again. This is my friend Amelia." He puts an arm around my shoulder, pulling me toward him. I feel myself stiffen a bit, but I nod and say a polite hello. His arm stays around my shoulder longer than it needs to, then he slowly lets me go. I feel his fingers brush my back as his hand falls to his side. Then he slips both hands into his pockets. Wow! Snap out of it, Amelia. I've got to keep Kip from messing with my head. I tell myself to take a deep breath and calm the hell down. I mean, does Emily actually buy it that I could be his girlfriend? She gives me a friendly smile and ushers us through her front door, then we all crowd onto the entrance mat, taking off our shoes and trying not to step on each other's feet. I'm super-aware of how close Kip stands. I can't help it.

"Let me take your coats," Emily says. "Dad's in the back room, watching TV. I told him you were coming over for a chat."

We follow Morris down the hall and stand at the entrance to the little room, a kind of den. It has a television in one corner and a sofa opposite, with Mr. Telford sitting at one end. On either side of the sofa is a chair, and there's a small coffee table in front. On the coffee table is a plate of cookies.

Mr. Telford looks scary frail. His thin frame is stooped forward. He raises the remote in a trembling hand and points it at the TV.

The screen goes black. Then he raises his hand to Morris. Morris walks over and clasps it in both of his, shaking it warmly. The old man has an artificial eye that stares into space, but otherwise he doesn't look as insane as I'd expected.

Morris takes a seat on the chair closest to him and quickly introduces Kip and me. Mr. Telford nods a polite hello and gestures for us to sit down. Morris and Emily start in with a lot of small talk about people they both know and family news and stuff. Mr. Telford seems distracted, or maybe it's just that he's hard of hearing. Emily has to repeat a lot for him. Then Morris asks about the 12th Line farm. He's playing dumb, asking if they know anything about its early past. Who built it, and that kind of thing. They don't know much. After a bit more chat, Morris asks if they have any plans to move back in. Mr. Telford shakes his head, pretty hard. Emily jumps in, explaining that when he's feeling better he'll meet up with a real estate agent to put it on the market. He's been planning to sell it for a long while.

"The barn was supposed to come down first," Telford says, moving around in his seat, all agitated. "It has to come down." Morris looks at him, nodding sympathetically. "I tried to keep it locked up." He gets a twisted expression on his face. "But it was no good."

"The barn's always been a source of pain," says Emily, "since Paul's death. He'd only stepped back into it after all these years to show the Sorenson boy the job. I'd heard about Matthew from a cousin down in Guelph. That he was real good at lowering barns. That he worked with a Mennonite crew and they thought of him as one of their own. Really level-headed and responsible. So I told Dad about him. It was just terrible, what happened."

It's so strange to hear her talking about Matthew in the past tense, having no idea what he means to me. Morris isn't letting on that he knows who Emily is talking about either. He listens, nodding, then says to Mr. Telford that it must have been a nightmare, hearing the day after meeting with him that Matthew had died in the barn.

Mr. Telford's looking down at the carpet. "I should never have brought him into it." He takes a shuddering breath. "The Devil's been holed up in that barn all these years, waitin' for his next victim. Now I know for sure." He looks up at Morris, his head kind of bobbing. "I suspected. I suspected it. But it's been thirty long years. I thought it would just come down."

Emily smiles and pats her father's knee. "Now, Dad, don't be saying things like that. You know it's all just bad luck. A terrible coincidence, is all. Paul and I used to sneak into that barn all the time when we were kids, through a loose board at the back. Never did us any harm. And even after Paul died, my kids used to play hide-and-seek in there sometimes. I had to go in to find them more than once."

Kip speaks up. "Interesting. So you never felt spooked by the barn?"

"Of course not," she says. "I mean, any old barn can seem spooky at night. That barn's nothing special. Now . . ." She seems to lighten up. "Tea or coffee, anyone?"

"Oh, tea sounds good, Emily," Morris says.

While she's gone, Morris tells Telford that there's something he's been meaning to ask him. Why did he keep the door padlocked? Even before Paul's tragedy, there used to be a padlock. What made him do that?

Telford says he had the steel shed on the property, all the storage space he needed, so he had no real use for the barn. "And even back when we bought the farm, there were already rumours about that barn, you know."

"Rumours?" Morris asks. Emily's come back with a teapot and cups on a tray. Everyone watches as she places it on the coffee table. "What kind of rumours?"

"Oh, talk. About something bad in the barn. The fella we bought the farm from, I only saw him once. McCleary was his name, I think. Thomas. It was what happened to his son. That's why they sold the place. His teenage son got into drugs. It was the sixties, right? My old neighbour on the north side, Munro, he said the kid got up to something awful. Found dead. Mutilated, eh? In the barn, he said. Suicide? Like hell."

Morris makes quick eye contact with Kip and me. "No kidding?" he says. "Jeez, Hank, that's an amazing story. I've never heard that before. You mean that when Paul died, you . . . you knew he wasn't the first? My God! What was going through your mind?"

Telford looks at him with his one good eye, like he's frustrated at having to keep repeating himself. "That barn. That barn is cursed."

Emily raises her eyebrows as if to say *Poor Dad*. She starts pouring tea, asking how we take it. She offers cookies and we each take one, but Telford passes on both. His body seems completely stiff now, and he's leaning forward awkwardly on the sofa.

Emily speaks up. "So, Morris, you can see why we need to pull the barn down before we put the farm on the market. Otherwise this guy"—she points a thumb at her father—"is going to be scaring all our potential buyers away. Dad, how are you going to get your money out of that place if you go on talking like that to whoever will listen?"

So that's what's bugging Emily—resale value. Now she changes the subject. She asks Kip what he's up to these days and he gives her the highlights—living with his mom and stepdad. A year at the University of Chicago. Taking time off to figure some things out. Hanging out with his dad. He grins at Morris, who smiles back, almost shyly.

"Say, Emily," says Morris, looking slowly around the room, "I'm just curious. Do you have any pictures of Paul back in the day? I don't have any old photos myself. Lost my school yearbooks, even, in a fire."

Emily jumps up and leaves the room. She's back in thirty seconds with a framed photo of a young man with brown hair and glasses. She hands it to Morris and he lingers over it for a bit. Finally he looks up, reaches out and hands it to me. I get the feeling he wants me to have a good look. I do, trying to memorize Paul's face.

While Morris and Emily chat some more, questions start plaguing me. What happens to Matthew if the barn is taken down? Is it possible he'll just disappear? Or cross over to some afterworld? It's something I don't really want to think about. It would feel like losing him all over again, and I can't go through that twice.

Fifteen minutes later, I suddenly realize that they are all getting to their feet, and Morris is thanking Emily and Mr. Telford for their hospitality and time.

"Now, you're not gonna write about this in a newspaper, are you, Morris?"

"No, no. Not at all. This is just some personal research, that's all. I do have one last question for your dad, though."

"What's that?" Telford says from the sofa.

"Mr. McCleary, the man you bought the farm from in the sixties. Do you remember anything else about him or his family?"

"Not much. Just his face. Big bald guy. Yeah. With a big red beard."

"Red beard?" asks Morris.

"That's right," says Telford. "Red."

18

I'm sitting in the living room on Saturday night, with Ethan playing a loud video game beside me on the sofa. I've got my eyes on the road outside. My bottom lip is starting to hurt from biting it all day. I have no idea what this is going to be like. It could be such a disaster. Finally I see car lights turn into our driveway, and I'm already standing at the front door when he knocks. I open it a little too quickly. Embarrassing, really. I don't want him to think I'm desperate, but I've been ready and waiting for a while. He's right on time.

"Hi . . . um, would you like to meet my grandmother, Joyce? She's just in the kitchen." He removes his shoes, and I whisper as he follows me in his socks, "Warning—she bites."

Joyce has been standing outside the back door of the kitchen. It's already dark, and she's got the porch light on—a bare bulb hanging from the roof. She's taking one last drag on a dying cigarette. She looks up at us through the door window, stubs the cigarette into a small ceramic ashtray on the railing and comes inside, her arms pulling a large grey sweater around her for warmth. It's mid-November and a chilly evening, even for cold-blooded Joyce.

"Joyce, this is my friend Kip Dyson. You know the local history columnist, Morris Dyson? That's Kip's dad." And I look back at Kip. "Kip, my grandmother, Joyce Stewart."

"How do you do, Mrs. Stewart?" He holds out a hand.

"Hello, Kip. Joyce will do." She reaches for her half glass of red wine on the kitchen counter, then holds out her other hand to shake Kip's. She peers at him through her bushy eyebrows, squinting slightly in the harsh kitchen light, and gives him a fast scan up and down.

"You aren't from around here, Kip, are you." It's her prosecutor voice.

"No, I'm from Chicago, but I was born in Hamilton. I'm just taking a break from school for a year, staying with my dad for a change of scenery. I'm working in the Grey County Archives office."

"School?"

"University of Chicago."

"Ah, that's nice." Her voice is a little chillier, probably because she's figured out that he's a few years older than me.

"So how did you two meet?" She keeps her eyes on him over the rim of her wineglass as she sips.

I'm scrambling for an answer to that one when Kip replies easily, "At the Halloween party a few weeks ago, at Brad's. If you can believe it, we were wearing identical Bob Marley masks. So you could say it was fate that brought us together."

Joyce looks genuinely amused at that. "Ah. Amelia hadn't mentioned you. Two Bob Marleys at one party in Owen Sound? That does sound like fate."

"Yes, and . . . that was also the night of Jack's accident. Hopefully he'll make a full recovery."

"Yes, well, time will tell." She is now leaning against the kitchen counter, peering at us. She's got this look on her face, like she's wondering about something.

"Well," I say, "I guess we should be getting on our way. We're just dropping in on a party at Brittany's. You remember Brittany, Joyce?"

"I do. Not one of your favourite people," she says.

"Oh, she's okay. I get on better with her these days." *Thanks for embarrassing me, Joyce.*

"Well, that's nice." Sarcastic, I'm sure. She looks at Kip rather sternly and gives him one last broad sweep with her radar. Finally she smiles. "You two have a good time. I'm assuming you'll get a ride home? From a sober driver, I mean."

"I think we can manage that," Kip says, placing his arm around my shoulder and leaving it there as we head for the door.

"That was a pleasant surprise," I whisper as we put on our shoes and head out.

"What do you mean?" he asks, opening the passenger door for me. Old-fashioned but nice.

"She really went easy on you, that's all. I thought she'd give you a hard time, considering that to her this must look like a date."

"Ah, a date." Kip gives a little shiver, like the very idea is creepy. He focuses on the rear-view mirror as he backs out of the driveway, but his eyes have narrowed, like he's trying to figure something out. "As opposed to what?"

"Pardon?"

"As opposed to a date?"

"I don't know. Our little charade. You know. Your dad's idea. To throw people off the ghost-tracking path."

"A charade. Right." After a minute or two, he turns on the radio and starts scanning through the half-dozen available FM stations.

"So . . ." he begins, then pauses. The silence feels a little awkward. He starts up again. "I passed up going to Toronto this weekend for this little charade."

"Really?" Why is he telling me this?

"Yeah, I have a few old friends who live there. Been bugging me to check out some new clubs in town with them."

"Oh." I try to sound casual but I feel crushed. I should have known this was a bad idea.

"I wasn't really up for it." He smiles as if to reassure me, but he looks disappointed.

"Must have been tempting, though," I say, trying to stay cool.

"Oh, I'm always tempted."

Something about the way he says that bugs me. I can't tell what's up with him.

"Seriously, you don't have a girlfriend?" Maybe it's none of my business, but I find that hard to believe. I need to know if he's just the two-timing flirt type of guy.

He laughs. "That depends on how you define *girlfriend*."

"Oh. I get it." At least, I think I do.

"Do you?" He looks over at me, and I can't read his expression.

Maybe Joyce is right. If she thinks he's too old for me, I mean. I give up trying to figure him out. I turn away and watch the farms fly by.

"I did a search in the archives today," he says finally, sounding more like himself. "I looked up the death notices for 1980 and found Paul Telford."

"Really?" I have to force myself to sound natural again. "Anything interesting?"

"Yeah, kind of. I found an article in the local paper with the headline 'Young Man Found Dead After Acceptance by McGill.' As if there was a connection. It said he was found in the barn on the family farm on

12th Line early the previous morning. Foul play wasn't suspected, and police were listing the death as an apparent suicide. And it goes on to quote a family friend who said Paul's acceptance to McGill University might have caused him to snap under the pressure or something."

"Really? Wow, I guess people are always looking for a reason." It reminds me of Matthew. We drive east along the highway in silence for a few minutes, and then Kip clears his throat.

"So just to get this straight," he begins, and I realize he's changing the subject again, "this isn't a date, right?" He looks over at me with this sly expression. "Which means you won't mind if I hit on Brittany tonight."

My jaw drops before I can stop it. I feel my face heating up. Why don't I just get out of the car right now?

"If you want to hit on Brittany, who am I to stop you? Free country. I mean . . ." How do I say this? "It *might* be slightly humiliating, seeing as how you've come to the party with me." I'm feeling humiliated already. I don't think I can even look at him.

"Because I'm your *date*, you mean?" He says that sounding all innocent.

I finally turn to look at him, exasperated. "I never said that. Brittany only invited me thinking I'd bring you along. So it's really you she invited, and you should feel free to do whatever you want. I'm sure Brittany will be *extremely* receptive."

I'm trying not to sound too upset, but I can't help it. What is it with this guy? One minute he's Prince Charming and the next, well, it's like I'm the ugly stepsister. Okay, I admit it: in my mind, this was kind of a date. My first-ever date, in fact. But whatever. Now I don't feel like showing my face.

We drive the rest of the way in silence. Finally, as we enter town, Kip asks me where exactly we're going, and I give him an address and directions. We arrive and park the car, then get out and walk toward Brittany's house. All I can think of is that it's too late to turn and run. We're standing awkwardly on her front porch, about to ring the bell, when I can't keep it in any longer.

"I think this is a mistake."

Kip just looks at me, then reaches out to push the doorbell. Waiting for someone to answer, he suddenly puts an arm around my shoulder, like he did back at my house. Only this time the grip is a little tighter. He leans into my ear. "You think too much," he whispers. Just in time for Brittany, all blonde hair and crimson lipstick, to appear at the door.

She opens up with a manic and wide-mouthed "Hey!" and welcomes us inside.

Kip turns to me with a wink. "After you, girlfriend," he says.

19

I'm strangely happy. I guess it's strange only because it doesn't feel familiar. Kip takes hold of my hand once he turns south onto 12th Line, and hangs on. I have to admit, I like it. Then he looks over at me.

"You know what? Before I take you home, I'd really like to drive by the barn. Just to see it. Do you mind? Would that bother you?"

I didn't see that coming. I gently pull my hand away from his. I have to think.

"Um, I'm not sure. I think your dad would freak if he knew." When I look over at his face in the faint glow of the dashboard lights, he looks innocent enough. I suppose looking can't hurt, can it?

He was just perfect at Brittany's party. Usually I dread hanging out like that, but Kip made it feel almost natural. He talked and joked with my friends, but he stayed at my side the whole time. And his arm was around me so much that I kind of got used to it. It felt amazing, actually. Everybody was acting friendly. We laughed quite a lot.

This stop at the barn may be a bad end to an otherwise great evening. But I guess it's too late for second thoughts now.

I point to the Telford property as we come over the crest of the hill. The night is overcast and there's no moon, so the barn looks like a huge black hole in the darkness. "There it is."

He drives slowly up the driveway, then veers off at an angle that aims the headlights at the barn. He turns off the engine but leaves the headlights on, and the circles of light fall on the grey barnboard about thirty feet away.

"Hmm," he says. "Maybe a *little* spooky."

We sit in the car for a few minutes, just taking it in. With the engine off, it's starting to get cold in here. Finally I speak up.

"What do you think? Had enough yet?"

"You know, I wouldn't mind sticking my head inside, just for a peek. Dad has a flashlight in the back seat. Want to come? I won't actually go all the way in or anything."

"Are you serious?" I'm shaking my head. "That's crazy, Kip. I promised your dad I wouldn't go back in there."

"You did?"

"Well, not exactly. But I know he'd be pissed."

He looks at me with a smirk, like he doesn't believe I'd let that stop me. Maybe he's right. I don't want him to go on his own.

"Just a peek, then," I warn him. "You have to promise me. And you have to stay right beside me the whole time." He laughs. "Kip, there's . . . there's something in there. Something evil. And it possesses people. Young men, anyway." But he's not changing his mind, I can tell. It's too late.

"Promise me you'll let me know if you feel the slightest bit strange," I say.

He laughs again. "As opposed to what?" He reaches into the back seat for Morris's mini-flashlight. "Listen, I promise. I hear you. Just a peek. Stop worrying."

We walk toward the front of the barn; the flashlight is hanging from a cord around his neck. The door is open a few inches, left like that by Morris and me last weekend. What if I see Matthew? I take a deep breath as Kip pushes the door open another foot and slips inside. Reluctantly I push in beside him, keeping my back to the open door, an arm's length away. It's really dark in here.

He puts his arm back around my shoulders. "It's okay," he whispers, giving me a friendly shake. "Don't worry. I'll protect you."

He grabs the flashlight in his other hand and begins to scan the barn walls, from left to right. I'm afraid to look but I force myself. I don't see anything. Or anybody. That's a relief. It's quiet and empty, or so it seems.

"Looks like a regular old barn to me," he says, not bothering to whisper this time.

We stand still, listening and peering for a few more minutes, our eyes getting used to the darkness.

"Had enough?" I finally ask. I'm eager to leave. And then I feel it. The cold, ticklish sensation I've felt before. It sends a shiver through me. What is it?

Kip turns toward me in the dim light and smiles. He pulls me closer and gives me a hug. His face is inches away from mine now. He's looking at me so intensely that it takes my breath away. He lets the flashlight dangle from the cord around his neck, lighting up the ground at our feet, leaving our faces in near darkness. He leans in closer, touching his forehead to mine. Suddenly his nose is burrowing into the nape of my neck, sending a different kind of shiver through me. His hand reaches around my waist. His mouth brushes along my neck, warm and moist. I feel his breath. Oh my God! What if Matthew can see us? I close my eyes. He kisses my cheek. My knees are going weak, and I hold on to his shoulders. His breathing is getting heavier. His lips move slowly across my face, hover over my mouth. I don't know what to do—

And then a horrible fear hits me. *What if this isn't really Kip? Oh my God! It's not Kip!*

In a split-second reflex, I push away and punch out as hard as I can. He yells, hands flying up to his mouth, and staggers backwards. Got to get him out! I barrel into his chest and shove him through the barn door. He's swearing behind his cupped hands, and I hear a muffled "What the hell?" as I grab his coat and pull with all my strength, dragging him farther away from the opening.

"Kip! Kip! Snap out of it!" I'm freaking out, shaking him by his shoulders as best I can. It's not easy. "Kip! Are you all right?" He's not answering. "Talk to me!" I scream as I keep shaking him.

He finally drops his hands and looks at me in disbelief. His lips are bloody, and he spits red.

"Am I all right? You punched me in the mouth!"

He touches his mouth gingerly, mumbling curses.

"Kip? Kip? Please just say something so I know for sure it's you!" I'm half crying now, trying to hold up his face, look into his eyes.

"Of course it's me!" He pulls away. "Who else? Bloody hell!" He's looking at me like I'm crazy. I feel the heat of embarrassment rise through me.

"I . . . I thought . . ."

"You thought *what?*"

"I thought you were possessed."

"Possessed? By what?" He sounds incredulous.

"It's full of ghosts in there! I mean, what were you thinking?" I'm starting to feel furious and I can hardly get the words out.

"I think it's safe to say I *wasn't* thinking," he mutters bitterly. "Clearly I wasn't *thinking* at all."

I'm shaking with anger and humiliation now, digging for some Kleenex in my pocket and shoving tissues into his hand. He holds them to his cut upper lip. Then he lowers the tissues, glances at the blood there and looks at me with his disbelieving blue eyes and flushed face.

I drop to the ground and start crying. He stands over me. I can see his shoes through my tears. It's a struggle to speak.

"Do you know what a scare you gave me?" I manage to ask. "Matthew died in there. And my brother could have died." I just can't believe this. I look up at his face. "I mean, was that your idea of a joke?"

He looks stricken. "Joke? God, no! I'm really, really sorry, Amelia. I really am. I wasn't thinking. Just . . . please, it was a mistake. A big mistake. I swear. I'm sorry. Let me take you home."

I suddenly feel like such a horrible idiot. "Your mouth . . ." I say, and he cuts me off.

"It's fine. I'll live." He's bending over me now, holding up my arms and pulling me to my feet. "Let's go."

He walks me to the car and we get in. Minutes later, we pull up to the front drive of my house in awkward silence.

"I'm sorry, Amelia, really," he says again.

I nod, barely whispering, "I'm sorry too."

I can't look at him. I can't believe I hit him. He thinks I'm crazy for sure now. And maybe he's right. I get out of the car and drag my feet to the front steps, listening to his car reverse down the driveway and head off up the road.

20

*I*n the dream I was caught in some kind of battle, all explosions and panic, ducking gunfire and grenades, overwhelmed by noise and cold terror. Now, in my dark bedroom, waiting for my wildly beating heart to settle down, I'm wondering what war has to do with anything. Except the dying part.

It was hard enough to fall asleep to begin with, and now it's four a.m. and I'm back to thinking about what happened last evening. I'm so embarrassed. But I can't believe Kip actually kissed me—in the barn. There's all the proof I needed that he really doesn't believe in ghosts. Which means he can't think much of me.

The problem is that I keep remembering what it felt like, being kissed like that. It was like nothing I've ever experienced before. I try to block it out. When I finally fall asleep again, about two hours later, I dream that I am back in the barn, his warm breath on my neck, his lips on my skin. But this time when I pull away, it's Matthew holding me in his arms, his eyes misty and half closed, his mouth slightly open, widening to a smile. My heart leaps. Then my eye catches someone standing behind him in the shadows. The moonlight shines golden on his hair. It's Kip, watching us, his blue eyes dark, his face sad. Like he's the one who's dead. This time when I wake up, I'm in tears. What's wrong with me?

Come Saturday morning, I'm still stuck on replay. The evening was so much fun, but then everything flipped and crashed. The next time I see Kip, it will feel awkward as hell. What should I say? Should I try to act like it never happened? And what if Morris finds out? I feel awful. But I shouldn't be the one to feel bad, should I?

I check my Facebook page. Morgan's posted some pictures from the party. There's one of me and Kip smiling at each other. I stare at his face for a long time. Then I practically smash the page closed and look at Matthew on my desktop. How could I have enjoyed being with Kip so much last night? What was I thinking? *You're the one I love, Matthew. There's nothing between Kip and me.*

I reach a decision: I'm going back into the barn today, by myself.

When I finally come downstairs, it's to the usual noise of Ethan playing a video game on the TV set in the front room. I stick my head in and ask him who's winning.

"Me," he says. "You wanna play a game?" His voice is hopeful.

"Maybe later," I say. "Maybe this afternoon." Poor Ethan, always looking for a little attention. I think he still really misses our mom. We all do, but since he's the baby of the family, it's harder for him.

In the kitchen I search the cupboard for breakfast. I can see Joyce from the window, out back with the horses. It's a windy day and the horses' manes are whipping around. So is Joyce's scarf, just like a tail. She's feeding them, talking to them as she works. You can tell she's talking, even from this distance. Her horses are the only things she loves. Well, and maybe Jack.

While I'm sitting at the kitchen table, munching on some cereal, my thoughts still lost in last evening, the kitchen door swings open with a bang that makes me jump, and Joyce steps inside. She works off her ankle boots and unzips her jacket, leaving it on one of the wooden pegs by the door.

"Good morning, young lady," she says, pulling off her gloves. "How was that party last night? I didn't hear you come in."

"Well, that's a good sign, isn't it? Means I wasn't singing too loudly when I staggered up the stairs." I'm hoping Joyce can take a joke this morning. "It was fine."

She's making a pot of coffee, spooning the coffee into the basket, and she does that thing where she darts her eyes at you over her glasses without moving her head.

"And how was your gentleman friend? Mr. Dyson? Did he behave himself?"

"Just about," I say casually. She'll prefer that to a simple yes, which she's less likely to believe.

"Hmph," she says, which roughly translates as "Men," and not in a good way. "Well, I don't mind you going out once in a while. In fact, I prefer it to you never going out at all. But he is a little . . . worldlier than you. That's my read. There's something a little too confident about him."

"I'm not sure what you mean." Maybe Joyce is right, but for some reason, even though he's upset me, I have a desire to defend Kip to her. "He seems to know a lot about a lot of stuff. About the Bible and Greek mythology. Interesting stuff. He's pretty smart, I think. His parents are big on education. His mother and stepdad are both professors."

"Ah, Greek mythology. That'll come in handy."

Joyce is good at sarcasm. It's irritating, really. I'm not bad myself but it must have skipped a generation, because I don't remember my mother ever being sarcastic. I have a flashback of her in the backyard garden, pulling a few small weeds out from around her flowers, running her fingers through the soil. Her head is down and a sun hat covers her brown shoulder-length hair; she's wearing her cotton gardening vest with the big pockets over a sweater and jeans. Her movements are careful and gentle. She slowly lifts her head, squinting in the sunlight, and smiles. "What a beautiful morning," she says to me. "Let's take the boys for a hike in Harrison Park after lunch."

"Joyce," I ask, out of nowhere, "how come the first time I told you I saw Mom in the garden, you seemed almost more upset than on the day she died?"

It's been a couple of years since I mentioned ghosts to Joyce. I don't know why this question slipped out today, but it's always angered me. She reacted as if I were telling a horrible lie. Or saying something too frightening to hear.

She's looking at the coffee dripping into the pot. Did she even hear me? Actually, I hope not. I don't have the courage to repeat it. Forget it. I'll finish my cereal and get out of here.

When she finally responds, it catches me by surprise.

"Any particular reason why you're asking me this now?"

"Uh, no . . . I don't know. Why?"

There's another pause, then she says, "Because I'm not blind, Amelia. Don't think I didn't notice something was up the night Jack fell in the barn."

Now I'm in trouble. "What do you mean?"

"I mean you were worried about Jack, yes, but there was something else too. I saw it in your eyes."

She doesn't mean to sound angry. I know that, but I have to keep reminding myself. That's what Dr. Krantz said; it's because she cares and she's worried about me. She's worried that if I think I'm seeing ghosts, it means I'm not well. That I'm suffering from a mental illness. Some people who are afraid for their kids have a way of sounding angry at them. She never meant to make me suffer on purpose. To practically ruin my life after Mom died.

"Amelia?"

"Yes?"

"Have you been seeing ghosts again?"

I think about Dr. Krantz, the months and months of visits to her office.

"No," I say. "No, I'm not seeing ghosts. I . . . I admit I was feeling very spooked that night. But I'm over it. It was just that the shock of losing Matthew sort of unhinged me." I can't believe what a good liar I've become.

"Well, that's a relief. You have to remember that you're probably in a similar emotional state now to the one you were in when your mother died. You've suffered another very difficult loss. That's what death is. It's losing something. And loss is the biggest challenge we face in life. Nothing lasts forever, including people. That's a fact."

Well, she's right about one thing: I hate the feeling of loss. Or is it the loss of feeling? I feel crushingly depressed listening to this, and I just want her to shut up. But I say nothing.

She walks over and puts a heavy hand on my shoulder.

"I'm okay," I manage to say in a calm voice. "Don't worry too much about me."

I wash my dishes, then climb the stairs back to my bedroom with what feels like a great hole in my chest. I sit on the bed for a while, then change into some warmer clothes: a turtleneck, a pullover, a thick pair of socks. Fifteen minutes later I'm bundled up and heading out the door.

"I'm going to take my bike for a ride," I shout to Joyce as I head for the kitchen door.

"Can I come?" I hear Ethan yell after me.

"Maybe next time," I say, slamming the door behind me. I head round the side of the house to the garage.

When I emerge, Joyce is walking in the opposite direction, heading back out to the paddock, a coffee mug in her gloved hands. She lifts one hand in a small wave. I swing a leg over my bike and settle onto the seat. This is the first time I've been on it since we moved. I didn't ride it much in town either, these last few years. But on these long country roads, a bike makes a lot of sense. Of course, that climb up 12th Line won't be a breeze. But I could use some exercise.

As it turns out, I have to struggle to get to the top of the hill. It's windier than it looks. But I stay on the bike until I can see the Telfords' farm in the distance. That's when I stop, get off and walk, pushing the bike along beside me. I need time to prepare anyway. Not that I know *how* to prepare for this, but I feel I should try. What's most important is that I keep my head. Don't panic. And if in doubt, get the hell out. If there are ghosts in that barn, good or bad, something tells me they won't come out after me, running down the road behind me.

The barn looks less frightening in the morning sun than it did last night, but I've learned from experience that that doesn't mean it's empty. There's a big black bird, a crow, up on the roof, staring down at me. Otherwise, nothing. Just the wind through a line of trees along the fence that divides the property from the neighbour's fields. The Telford house is unchanged. Curtains drawn and no sign of life. If there's any action on this property, it'll be in the barn.

The door is still open a foot or so. For a second the memory of last night comes flying back to me: Kip's warm breath, his lips. I try to beat that feeling away. How can I be such a pushover? It's Matthew I love. Kip's just a pretty face—and a flirt who assumes that every girl he meets wants to kiss him. That's been his experience, I guess. And obviously my feelings didn't come into it.

I lean my bike against the barn wall just outside the door and take a deep breath. Okay, so much for preparing. I feel nothing but dread. Why am I putting myself through this again? To see Matthew. *Focus on Matthew.*

I take a few steps toward the opening, lean inside, look up and around. So far, so good. I creep inside. *Matthew, are you there?*

Okay, the visibility isn't bad today. There are still dark corners and shadows, but at least the middle area of the barn is bright. On the other hand, the wind outside is louder than I've noticed before, and there's more creaking and howling high up in the rafters. I decide to walk around the inside walls, starting on the right side. For the first time, I'm trying to take in what I see, doing a kind of inventory.

There's a raised platform running the length of the wall on my right, at eye level. It's about ten feet deep, and underneath there are lots of rusted pieces of old farm equipment, still half painted in what used to be bright yellows and greens. I don't know much about what they are, or what they used to be. There are some things with blades that look like they'd be dragged behind a tractor. Very sharp in their day. Maybe still sharp. And there are some old wooden crates filled with cloudy bottles and rusty cans. I've never noticed them before. I guess this was used as a storage space for supplies, farm chemicals maybe. A few rusted metal containers look like they might hold gasoline or some other fuel. There are some hand tools too. Mostly they're in pieces, with cracked or missing handles. I guess this is where the pitchfork came from.

I approach the far wall and see the tangled bundle of rope on the ground, coiled like a snake right where it was the last time I was here. That's when I realize I feel something cold in the air.

"Matthew?" I listen. "Matthew?" I turn and there he is. Again there's that sharp shock at the sight of him. He's sitting back on the raised platform, leaning against the barn wall. His legs, slightly bent at the knees, are sprawled out in front of him on the layer of straw. His arms are loosely folded. He wasn't there a minute ago, or was he?

"Matthew!"

I catch my breath, then walk back toward him, slowly. I'm afraid he may disappear if I'm not careful. I can see his eyes following me as I get closer. He looks perplexed.

"Matthew?" He doesn't respond. Is there some trick to getting him to talk? And then he speaks.

"What was that about?"

"Uh, what was what about?"

"Last night."

Oh-oh. "You . . . you mean me, last night, here?"

"Yes, you and him, here, last night. What was that about?"

It's hard to read his tone. Not angry. Not curious, exactly. Searching?

"You know, I'm embarrassed to say it, but it wasn't about very much. The truth is, the guy I was with, that's Kip. He's the son of the other guy I was with last time, the history writer."

"Oh. And why did he kiss you?"

"To be honest, I don't know."

"Why did you hit him?"

"Because I . . . well, for a moment I thought he wasn't himself. That he was . . . possessed. I panicked. I thought I needed to snap him out of it."

"Possessed, eh?"

"Possession does happen, right? I mean, that's what happened to you, isn't it?"

"I don't know. Maybe, I guess." Now he smiles. "Something to think about."

"I've always wondered whether I could have done anything to snap you out of it. Like a slap across the face or a bucket of cold water."

"Ah." He shrugs. "Possession. If I can figure out how it's done, you'll be the first to know." He loses the smile. "Amelia, my mom and dad . . ." He stops there, like he doesn't remember what he wanted to say.

"Your parents. I saw them at the . . . at your funeral." I cringe saying that. I'm not sure how well he understands what's happened. He doesn't say anything, so I continue. "They're pretty devastated. They love you very much."

"Do they really think I killed myself?"

Maybe he does understand. "Well, I don't know for sure what they think, but that was what the coroner's report said. I think that's what they were told. If it makes you feel any better, they're convinced you're in heaven."

He looks around the barn. "I don't think this is heaven or anything, but they don't need to know that."

"Got it," I say. His family is so religious it seems unfair that he isn't in heaven. "Matthew, does this change anything about . . . your beliefs? Your religious beliefs?"

He holds his hand out in front of his face, fingers open, studying the palm, then turns it over and looks at the back of it.

"You know how people say they know something like the back

of their hand? My dad used to say that. Well, I do know the back of my hand. That's my hand, all right. But that's about it right now. I don't know much more than that."

That doesn't sound good, somehow. But I don't want to dwell on it. Too complicated.

"And what do you remember? What do you remember about your life?"

"Everything." And then he adds, "Kind of. I remember everything. I just don't understand what it meant."

"That sucks."

"Like, I don't understand how you meant so much to me and I didn't do anything about it until it was too late." He smiles, though his eyes look sad. "Now I can't even touch you."

That hits a nerve. I don't think I ever appreciated how important it is to be able to touch a living person. Involuntarily I think back to the light touch of Kip's mouth on my neck, then I smack the memory away. I hope Matthew can't read my mind.

"Tell me you won't leave me again. Okay?"

"Matthew, it's not like I can just move into this barn."

"But we belong together. That hasn't changed. Please say you'll stay with me?"

I blink back tears, swallow hard. I'm trying to think. "Can't you leave this place? If you want to?"

He says he's not sure. "It's hard to describe. Have you ever had one of those dreams where you know you're dreaming? Sometimes you can control the dream, but sometimes your dream controls you." He looks up into the rafters, as if searching for the right words. "I just feel stuck. Like everything around me is a little unreal and I can't do anything about it. If you stay here with me, everything will be okay." His eyes are still up in the rafters, as if raised to heaven. "If I really am a ghost, there must be a reason why you can see me and talk to me. It must be because we're meant to be together."

I shake my head. "Matthew—I've been seeing ghosts all my life. I was born this way. I don't think you were born to be a ghost. I'm afraid that being a ghost means something's wrong. Beyond being dead, I mean." I feel like he's not following me, and it's making me anxious. He's always been the smart one. Surely he doesn't think I can spend the rest of my life hanging out in this old barn? "Things have changed for us, Matthew. I'm still alive and you're . . . well, you're just not." It makes me feel wretched to say it, but I have to make him understand. "I know it's not your fault—but if I spend too much time in this barn, believe me, my grandmother will have me carted off to a mental ward."

"No. It's his fault."

He lowers his eyes to meet mine, then looks up again. I follow the direction of his gaze. High above me, directly over my head, are a pair of dangling shoes, men's work shoes. Above them I see legs and then a body, hanging by the neck from a rope lashed to a beam. A dead face. Eyes shut, jaw hanging open. Stifling a scream, I back away, staggering toward the barn door. My eyes stay on the body. It's a teenage boy in loose, old-fashioned farm clothes and suspenders.

"Matthew?" I manage to gasp, shaking. "Who . . . who is that?"

"I don't know his name. But he's trouble."

I'm nearly at the door now. "I've got to go, Matthew. I really hate leaving you alone in here."

"Oh, I'm not alone."

"I'm sorry."

"Then don't go, Amelia. Please stay."

"I'll come back. I promise."

I've got to get out of here. I turn to run the last few feet to the door and there, standing just to the side, is a face I recognize from the photo at the Telford house: Paul.

"Morris?" he whispers.

I freeze for a moment, too shocked to respond.

He whispers again. "What happened to Morris?"

I can't think. "W-what?"

"He looks like hell."

I grab hold of the door and lunge through. With feet planted firmly on the outside, I risk one last look back, searching for Matthew. He's just a shadow against the wall now. High above him, I can still see the body hanging from the rafters, neck broken. Just then, the head, lying unnaturally on the shoulder, snaps up and faces me. The body jerks and now the eyes are open wide, the mouth frothing and furious, cursing at me. It sounds like he's saying, "Get out!"

I dive for my bike, scramble to get my balance on the seat, then start pedalling furiously down the driveway, gravel flying. In no time I'm on 12th Line, gasping for air, my chest in spasms, adrenalin driving my legs as I pump up and over the hill.

Once I'm within sight of my house, I slow right down. I'm exhausted and hyperventilating. I have cramps in my legs and my side. My heart is about to burst out of my chest. I get off the bike and walk rubber-legged alongside it. I need to calm down. That was the most gruesome thing I've ever seen in my life.

The first thing I do when I get into the house is figure out where Joyce is. I'm completely freaked out, which I've seriously got to hide from her. Fortunately, she's still out back. I check that Ethan's still deep into his video game. Then I run to the kitchen phone, where I can keep an eye on Joyce through the back window.

I've got the Dysons' home number on a piece of paper in my wallet, and I pull it out and dial. The phone rings. Will Kip answer?

I haven't thought about that. But on the third ring, it's his father who says hello.

"Morris! It's Amelia." I'm still breathless. "I know you didn't want me to, but I went over to the barn this morning. By myself."

"I wish you hadn't, Amelia." His irritation takes me by surprise. "I'm serious. What happened? Can you talk?"

"Not for long. Joyce is out back." I take a deep breath. "I had a long talk with Matthew, and . . . well, I saw Paul. I recognized him right away."

"My God!"

"Uh, yeah. It was strange. He asked me what happened to you."

"What happened to *me*?"

"Yes. He . . . he said you looked like hell."

"Tell him thirty bloody years is what happened to me. Jeez! Anything else?"

"Uh, that's all from him, though I only saw him at the last second, on my way out." The vision of the boy hanging from the rafters flashes before my eyes. "Let's just say I was in a hurry."

"Why do I get the feeling you're leaving something out?"

"I don't really want to talk about it on the phone. Could the three of us get together soon?"

"Well, Kip's not here. He's in Toronto. He took the bus down early this morning. He's taking a few days off work, he said. Some downtime. But you and I could meet up. I can fill him in later."

"Okay, sure," I say. I'm disappointed but I try not to sound it. "I could meet you after school on Monday." I guess I'm not surprised that Kip went down to the city after all. I mean, why wouldn't he? Especially after what happened when we were last together.

"Monday's good. I'll be working in the library. Upstairs in the reference section. Why don't we meet there? And in the meantime,

Amelia—stay out of the barn. *Please?* I'm prepared to arrange to get it taken down for the Telfords if I have to, just to keep you out of it. It's not safe."

"Believe me, I've had enough!" I say, and we hang up.

I feel better having talked to Morris. He's the only one I really can talk to. But now what am I going to do?

Matthew, you're trapped like a prisoner in that horrible place. How am I supposed to save you from that?

I waste nearly an hour getting caught up with Morgan on Facebook. Someone's posted some funny pictures of Jack and his friends in his hospital room. Morgan and I discuss which essay question we're going to pick for our English assignment. We have to analyze one of three soliloquies from Shakespeare's *Hamlet*—the "To be or not to be" speech, or one by Hamlet's father's ghost, or one by Polonius. I haven't decided yet. Then Morgan asks me about Kip. I was afraid of that.

"OMG! SOOO QT!" she writes. Then she tells me Brittany is SOOO jealous and I'd better keep an eye on him. I have to tell her that it's not serious between us, we're just friends.

With benefits, I hope.

No, I write back. *Not likely*, I add.

Maybe the best way to get over losing Matthew. Take advantage of Kip. Not in a bad way. Just have some fun. Just saying.

I answer that I don't think I could do something like that.

Sucks to be you, then. And she adds a smiley face.

When it's time for bed I turn out the light, but I sit back up in the pitch-dark and decide that tonight I'll leave my desk lamp on. I lie down and consider what Morgan said. I think about the look on Kip's face just before he kissed me. His smile was so gentle. Could he have feelings for me? But no. He's just doing what he does best.

21

I'm on my way to the public library, deep in thought. I've been doing some thinking lately about why I see ghosts when most other people don't. I've done Internet searches on ghosts in my spare time, and on people who see them. Mediums, that is. Or clairvoyants. I've tried to uncover as much as I can, and you know what I've been able to find? Almost nothing. Why don't scientists research this stuff more? I don't get it. It's crazy how ghosts are such a big part of our lives—if you really think about it, people mention them all the time—but no one seems to care whether they're real or not. Unless they happen to see one for themselves.

I find Morris at a corner table on the second floor, in the reference section. He has his laptop computer and a file of newspaper clippings spread out in front of him. As I approach the table, he looks up and starts shoving papers and clippings back into the folder and clearing up part of the table, offering me a seat beside him. He takes a quick look around to make sure there are no eavesdroppers, then gestures with his thumb to the file he's been working on.

He says it's for a column about another historic building facing demolition. A grand old three-storey Empire Loyalist mansion. It's been run as a restaurant, changing owners about three times in the past ten years, and no one has been able to make it work. But back in the late 1850s it was a last stop in the Underground Railroad—the secret route to freedom for slaves escaping from the cotton plantations in the Deep South. Apparently it was also a tavern and brothel for sailors, back when the town was a thriving port for ships on the Great Lakes.

Morris sighs and says, "This beautiful old house is haunted. She's just a child. Sometimes she's in the garden, sometimes one of the upstairs rooms. There are so many recorded sightings that the last few times it's been on the market, the real estate listings have had to include a clause acknowledging reported paranormal activity. Some owner back in the 1980s won a lawsuit against a vendor for non-disclosure. No one wants to live in a house with ghosts, no matter how much they don't believe in them."

We talk about the whole idea of living people being possessed by ghosts, the way Matthew must have been when he was driving the truck. Morris says it seems as if the ghost possesses the body, memory and emotions, but not the whole identity. Which is why both Matthew and Jack still recognized me even though they were possessed. It seems they still remembered something about their real lives. I ask whether I could have snapped them out of it if I'd tried to, if I'd tried harder. Morris says he doesn't know. I think about how I punched Kip, and feel foolish all over again.

"Depends on the intensity of the ghost's obsession, I suppose. It seems that a ghost is a person who hangs around after his death rather than moving on to another dimension, because he's obsessed with a memory he's carried over. He re-experiences the emotion of it, whether it's a place or an event or a person. It's like a powerful flashback. Like post-traumatic stress disorder. In some ways, I think that's what ghosts suffer from."

"Well, for starters, death is pretty traumatic," I point out.

"But dying itself doesn't seem to do it. Because not everyone who dies becomes a ghost. Something goes wrong, beyond just the dying part. Or at least that's the theory."

I tell Morris about my trip to the barn on Sunday. About how I saw Matthew and we talked for quite a while. I've already told him about seeing Paul Telford, but I struggle with how to describe the rest.

"I saw someone else too," I finally admit. It's the real reason I had to see him today.

"Really? The red-haired guy? The McCleary boy?"

"No. No one red-haired."

"Oh? Who did you see?"

"It was more like a 'what.'" I take a deep breath to steady myself before carrying on. "A dead body. Hanging from the rafters."

Morris's eyes narrow and his jaw tightens. "I was afraid of that," he says in a low voice. "Now you understand why I didn't want you to go back in there." He swears to himself, elbows on the table, head in his hands.

"I admit it was scary, but as soon as I saw him, I backed the hell out of the barn. I didn't feel like I was in any danger." I'm kind of lying. That's not how it felt at the time.

"Jesus."

"Okay . . . there was one more thing: the last thing I saw as I left the barn. I took one look back behind me, and as I did, the body—which looked totally dead, by the way—kind of jerked to life and the guy moved his head to face me, broken neck and all. He opened his eyes and looked right at me. He seemed seriously angry, and he said something—I think it was to get out."

We sit in silence for a few moments. Finally Morris shakes his head and mutters, "Jesus Christ." Then he looks me in the eye, pointing a finger at me, and says sternly, "No. More. Barn. Visits."

"You won't believe this! He's been eavesdropping when we thought he was sleeping!" That's how Jack greets me when I drop in on him after school. He's talking about the old guy in the next bed.

"He asked me this afternoon which place I meant when I talked about the Telfords' farm. He asked if I meant the farm on 12th Line! Said he knew the family that lived there when he was a teenager. I told him you were interested in the history of the property, so he said for me to wake him next time you came over. He said the place has a *curse*."

I raise my eyebrows and look over my shoulder at the old guy. He's sleeping.

"What's wrong with him?" I whisper.

"He's got a broken hip. But I think he's got pneumonia or something too." Jack asks if this is a good time to wake him up. I nod eagerly.

"Mr. Clinton? Excuse me, Mr. Clinton."

The old man stirs and opens his eyes. He coughs a little and clears his throat, then smiles at us and nods. We smile back at him.

Jack says, "Mr. Clinton, this is my sister, Amelia. I told her that you overheard us talking about the Telfords' farm on 12th Line, and that you know a bit about its history."

Mr. Clinton smiles and nods again, for rather a long time, until I prompt him, asking how he knows that particular farm. It's obvious that talking is an effort for him. He takes his time, pausing every few words.

"My grandparents . . . lived across the road. The war years." He stops to catch his breath. "They were friendly . . . with the McGraths. Mr. McGrath, it was his . . . his parents built the farm."

"What a coincidence!" I say. I look at his bleary eyes and quivering lips, wondering how much longer he's got. And whether I'd see his ghost leaving his body if he died right now. A morbid thought, I know.

"I overheard you young kids . . . a few times, talking about the . . . accident in the barn. About strange things going on." He goes on to tell us how he heard rumours about that farm when he was a young man. About a terrible tragedy that people talked about for years. "A sad, sad story."

He sputters, breathing with great effort, his mouth open as if his tongue is too large. I have a flashback of my mother's head on the pillow, her bony face, her eyes closed, her breath barely there. I hate that memory more than anything. Then Mr. Clinton clears his throat and starts up again.

"His folks, they moved away . . . not long after that. Couldn't stay."

His folks? Whose folks? The old man clears his throat and starts coughing again. Jack and I exchange worried glances. I'm not sure if we should politely wait it out or offer him some kind of help. Maybe he's not coughing at all. Maybe he's choking. I'd better do something.

"Can I get you some water, Mr. Clinton?"

He can't seem to answer. I go to the door and lean out into the hall, looking left and right for a nurse. He's still coughing. I dash down the hall to the nursing station.

Moments later, Jack and I watch in alarm as a nurse fusses over Mr. Clinton, putting a pill under his tongue and giving him oxygen. "You've been talking too much again," she teases him. Behind the oxygen mask, his eyes are closing. He's falling asleep. Damn!

But Jack and I visit for a while longer, and just as I'm leaving, Mr. Clinton, his eyes still closed, raises his arm from the elbow, and his hand opens as if to touch something. I come closer.

"I hope you're feeling better soon," I say. Not likely, I'm thinking. I see his lips move, his fingers beckoning me to come closer, and when I do, he speaks in a raspy whisper.

"They said it was an accident." He shakes his head. "No one believed them."

22

*T*he carpenters arrive early Saturday morning, waking me up with their electric saws and drills and hammers, one working on the back-door wheelchair ramp and another in the dining room, now Jack's new main-floor bedroom. He's coming home in a couple of weeks, hopefully in time for Christmas. He's making such good progress, his doctor says. By then, we want to have the bedroom all set up, the walls painted and the furniture in place.

Over the last few days, I've managed twice to slip into the archives office to go through old county records and newspaper clippings. I've been looking for something, anything, about the McGrath family on 12th Line in the 1940s. And I finally found it. But I've been holding off calling Morris until the weekend, hoping Kip is back in town. The more time goes by, the more I find myself wanting to hear his voice. I just want to get back on friendly terms.

Last night I saw a movie in town with Morgan and a few others. Brittany asked me where Kip was, acting all curious. I think she's already figured out we aren't really hooked up and she's pleased about that. But I've been thinking about it a lot, and I've decided that the only reason I find Kip so distracting is that his take on things is kind of different. He's not predictable, that's for sure. And I admit he's seriously handsome. But that's it. I'm not saying he's not a nice person or anything. I just can't figure out what's going on in his head. And how can you trust someone like that?

I take the phone up to my bedroom to get some distance from the sound of construction work, not to mention Ethan's ears. I take a deep breath to calm myself, in case Kip answers, then dial Morris's number. But it's Morris who picks up. I tell him about the old guy in my brother's hospital room, then I tell him that I've been checking the county records and going through some old newspaper files.

"I found a death notice of a soldier named William McGrath III, September 22, 1945. Then I found out more about the death in the newspaper archives. He was a decorated war hero who'd spent time in a German concentration camp as a prisoner of war. He died the night of his homecoming party . . . on 12th Line. Get this: the article says he shot himself with his own revolver in 'a misadventure.'"

"Wow, that's terrible. Sounds like maybe there's more to it."

"Exactly, 'cause the old man in Jack's room said they called it an accident but no one believed them. That's exactly what he said."

"So the question is whether we can find anyone else in the county who knows the story, who's still alive. Family descendants, maybe."

"That's what I'm thinking. That's what I'm going to try to find out."

"Maybe Kip will give you a hand. He got back last night."

That sets off a little wave of panic, but I try to sound perfectly casual. "Oh, well, that would be great." It would be a disaster if Morris suspected anything awkward between us. "I've been thinking of checking out where this McGrath guy is supposed to be buried.

Just want to see the gravestone. It's the little old cemetery on 18th Sideroad. Not that far from 12th Line."

I like the idea of having something to occupy myself. As soon as I hang up from Morris, I change my clothes quickly and freshen up. I tell Joyce, who's in the kitchen watching the back porch construction, that I'm going for another bike ride. I want to hurry off before Ethan can beg me to let him come too. I don't want him hanging around, asking questions.

The sideroad intersects 12th Line a few roads north of us, up toward the highway. When I reach it, I turn east. The land around here is a bit hilly, which means it's a lot of work on a bike, but every once in a while there's a beautiful distant view of either the valley in the southeast or the bay to the northeast. All through the county there are crossroads with signs that identify where villages used to be, a hundred or more years ago. They usually had their own little churches, with cemeteries attached. These days, a lot of those churches have been converted into second homes for city folks. Others are gone and all that's left are the cemeteries with their rusty wrought-iron gates. Sometimes even the graveyard is gone, and nothing is left but a sad collection of the most ancient markers, all bunched close together, like a gravestone garden.

At the crest of a hill I can see down the road a long way. I spot the little cemetery I'm looking for. The church that once stood there is only a stone foundation now. I coast down the hill and leave my bike at the gate, then do a quick scan of the graveyard. There's no one around, which is a relief. Taking a notepad and a pen from my coat pocket, I set out into the rows of gravestones to find the name McGrath.

For a while, I'm so focused on what I'm doing that I don't pay attention to the sound of the odd car driving by. So when I hear a car door slam shut, I jump. It's like being jerked awake out of a hypnotic trance. Kip, dressed all in black, his dark golden hair striking as usual, is coming through the gate, walking toward me through the cemetery.

At first I'm frozen. He looks so handsome and the setting is so romantic, it's like watching a scene in an old movie. I feel mesmerized. But then he breaks out in a laugh and I snap out of it and smile.

"What?" I ask, a little defensively. He's wearing a black wool coat that reminds me of the sixties. Cool.

"So this is what you small-town girls do for fun. Have you found what you were looking for?" he asks, holding out his arms and wrapping them around my shoulders in a split-second hug.

Being that close, even for a moment, makes me veer awkwardly and almost lose my balance. He did it so casually, like nothing was wrong. I feel a surge of happiness. Thank goodness. Maybe we can put what happened last weekend behind us.

"Take a look at this," I say, eager to show off my findings. I lead him over to one of the largest monuments. *McGrath* is chiselled in large lettering along the top on each side. Below that is a series of names and dates.

"Here's the original family," I say, pointing to the first name. "*William McGrath 1852–1912.* He's the patriarch. Then there's the matriarch, *Margaret McGrath 1855–1924*, and finally"—I crouch down and run my gloved fingers along another name—"a baby, *William McGrath 1890–1891.*"

Kip lingers over the names, then stands up and walks around the monument. He stops and bends down behind it.

"And this must be a daughter, Judith," he says. "She died in 1918, at the age of twenty-six." He walks over to a smaller gravestone with two names chiselled into it, one above the other. "*Sebastian McGrath 1895–1948*," he reads out loud.

"He's the son who inherited the farm," I say. "He married Mary Simons, who was born in 1896 and died two years after him, in 1950. They're the ones who lived at the farm through the Second World War, and it's their son, William, named after Sebastian's dead brother, who died in 1945. His grave is over here."

Kip looks impressed, and that gives me a ridiculous amount of pleasure.

We walk over to a third gravestone, taller and more elaborately decorated, which reads *Sgt. William McGrath III 1922–1945*.

"That's our war hero," I say.

We stand silently before the gravestone. It's beautiful. The inscription reads,

> *Forever our hero.*
> *Forever in our hearts.*
> *Rest in peace,*
> *'Til we meet again.*

"I don't know if your dad told you what I found out, about how this guy survived being a prisoner of war, only to die when he was back home barely a week. On the night of his homecoming party. The records say he shot himself in the head, by accident, but this old guy in the bed next to my brother in the hospital knew the family. He told me no one believed it was really an accident."

"Yeah. Dad told me." Kip nods thoughtfully, still looking at the stone.

I flip back through my notebook. "So one last thing to mention is over there—" I point and we walk over to a small square stone, set flat in the ground. "It's a grave marker for another baby, *Frances McGrath, 1918*. So according to the birth records for the family, that leaves two other daughters, Anne and Dorothy, and I haven't been able to find them here. But if they got married they would have changed their names, and they might be buried with their husbands somewhere else."

"They could still be alive, though, right? How old would they be?"

I check my notes. "Let's see. Anne would be ninety-one and Dorothy would be eighty-eight. So yeah, it's possible. Who knows?"

We stroll out of the cemetery, and Kip stops in front of my bike and glances over at the car.

"Want a lift home? I think I can get this into the trunk if you'd like. I hate to drive off and leave you to struggle up that hill."

"Well, if you think it can fit, I wouldn't refuse."

He opens the hatch at the back and then takes hold of the bike. I hurry to grab on, claiming the back half. We carry the bike to the car and slide it in but can't quite get the hatch to close.

"It's okay," he says. "We're not going far. I'll blast the heater."

We get into the car and he starts the engine. At first the cold air makes me shiver. He looks across at me, and then smiles and looks away. Now I notice the dark circles under his eyes.

"How was your week in Sin City?"

"I did all right. What doesn't kill you . . . you know."

We drive in silence for a few minutes, until he turns onto 12th Line. Then he glances sideways at me.

"Look, Amelia, I want to apologize again. What happened last weekend . . . well, that's the dumbest thing I think I've ever done. And believe me, there's lots of competition."

My heart races but I'm trying to stay cool. "It's okay, really. Let's just forget it. I admit I was pretty upset at the time, but only because I was afraid. For you, I mean. And just . . . caught by surprise. I think we should forget it happened." He doesn't say anything to that, so I go on. "You know, I went back into the barn by myself on Sunday and talked to Matthew again. The first thing he did was ask about the little scene the night before. He actually saw it. Saw *us*."

Kip looks over at me and his brows come together like he's perplexed, or even worried. He doesn't say anything.

"You don't believe me, do you?" I say. He just looks up the road. "I was thinking about it after that night, and the look on your face now made it all come back. Because you would never have kissed me in the barn like that if you thought there were ghosts in there." It suddenly seems so obvious to me. "So to you, I'm either crazy or a liar."

He gets this pained look on his face but doesn't say anything; he just continues to focus on driving.

Finally, as we're approaching my house, he says, "Amelia. I . . . I'm sorry. I don't believe in ghosts, so how can I believe *you* see them? But I don't think you're crazy. I really don't. And I don't think you're a liar either." He shakes his head. "I don't have any explanation for any of this. I'm not trying to find one, either. I'm interested in helping to solve the mystery of the barn, though, which kind of surprises me. Maybe I'm a chip off the old block after all."

Once we're in the driveway, we sit in the car in silence for a minute. I feel so torn. I'm upset with him, and yet that was probably the nicest apology anyone's ever made to me. Then he puts a hand on my shoulder and his grip fills me with vague hope. But he just gives me a friendly shake and lets go.

"But hey, why worry about what I think?" he says. "It's not important. Maybe I'll be a convert before this whole thing gets solved. Either way, I promise not to piss off your dead boyfriend ever again."

I'm in my bedroom on Friday night, wasting time on the Internet, when the phone rings and Ethan bangs on my door saying it's for me. Poor Ethan. Looking kind of depressed, he hands me the phone.

Joyce says he's got this big project due on Monday and he's barely started it. She says his marks are going downhill. I should really try helping him with his homework next semester.

"Your new boyfriend," he says with a smirk, and immediately I feel less sorry for him.

I wait until I'm sure Ethan's out of earshot before saying hello. Kip asks me how I am. I say I'm fine, and I ask him how he is. He says he's fine. He says he's done some research on Anne and Dorothy McGrath, and he's found records of both their marriages. Anne married a guy named William Stinton, and Dorothy married a guy named Philip Ross. He's also found death notices for their two husbands and for the older sister, Anne, but he hasn't found anything for a Dorothy Ross.

"So it looks like she might still be alive, unless she left the county," he says. "But there's no Dorothy Ross in the phone directory. I'll keep looking."

"Ross? I know an old lady named Mrs. Ross. I can't remember her first name, but I'm sure it wasn't Dorothy. I'd remember that 'cause of *The Wizard of Oz*. I read *Great Expectations* to her when I was in grade nine. It was a volunteer program, reading to seniors with bad eyesight. Maybe she's a relative of Dorothy's? That would be amazing. She's in her late eighties too, I think. If she's still alive."

"Where did she live?"

"In a seniors' residence south of town on Highway 6. Near Williamsford."

Kip says he'll mention it to his dad, see if he knows her. I tell him I'll try the name on my grandmother, who knows a lot of seniors herself. Then we say goodbye and hang up.

For a long time I sit on my bed with the phone in my hand. His tone was friendly enough, I guess, but a little businesslike. I have to admit that I feel nostalgic when I think back on that get-together at Brittany's. I miss how he was that night. How he made me feel.

I type his name into the search engine on my computer. The first thing that comes up is some girl's Facebook pictures. One of those parties where everyone is pretty drunk and the girls all look like they're competing for spots on some "bachelor" reality show. And in one of those pictures I recognize Kip sitting on a couch, a beer in his hand, smiling for the camera. Pressed up against him is a girl with long red hair and a tight yellow tank top with her lime green bra straps showing. Her eyes are also on the camera, her mouth open in a wide grin, her tongue lightly on her bottom lip, as if she's threatening to nibble his ear. Or lick it. It must be from the summer, because she's not dressed for the cold. Her name is Serena somebody. I wish I hadn't looked. I'm such an idiot. I've got enough awful images crowding my head already.

I force myself to shift focus. Could it be that old Mrs. Ross is William McGrath's sister? As I'm wondering about that, something comes back to me: that nightmare I had about being trapped in crossfire in a battlefield. The feeling of fear was overwhelming. That was the night after Kip and I went into the barn together. A chill passed through me just before Kip kissed me. Was that the ghost of a terrified young soldier, now trapped in the barn with Matthew and the others?

23

I wake up Saturday morning to the screaming of a smoke alarm going off in the kitchen. Heart pounding, I pull on my bathrobe and run down to find the room filled with the smoky stench of burnt toast.

"Ethan!" I yell, and yank the toaster plug out of the socket. Then I throw open the kitchen door and grab the toaster with oven mitts, putting it outside on the back deck, where all of our cooking disasters end up. "Ethan!" I grab the cutting board and start fanning the smoke detector on the ceiling. I fan as hard as I can, and eventually the smoke alarm cuts out. "ETHAN—!"

"I'm right here." He's standing behind me in his pyjamas, blinking wildly, sounding defensive. "My toast!" he says, as if burning his toast was something *I* did.

"Your toast was on FIRE!" I yell at him, winded from fanning the smoky air. "There were actual flames. The curtains could have caught fire. The whole kitchen! You're lucky Joyce isn't here. That's the third time you've set off the smoke alarm this month. What's with you?"

As if I have to ask. Obviously he was playing some video game. He gets so caught up in whatever he's doing that the house could burn down and he wouldn't notice. "Don't be such a stoner, Ethan. For chrissake, it's not the nicest way for me to wake up in the morning."

"Well, how did I know it was gonna get stuck? I just wanted some lousy toast. Jeez. There's nothing to eat around here." He says that like it's the biggest injustice.

I'm about to yell some more, because I really don't think he gets it, but instead I take a hard look at him and notice how miserable he seems.

"Okay, fine. I'll make you a grilled cheese sandwich." His face lights up. "Happy?" I ask, still slightly irritated.

"Happy!" he says. He starts to dance around in his bare feet, jabbing his hands in the air.

"Although there's no reason you can't make your own."

"Yours are better," he says, still dancing.

Joyce is working down at her friend Rita's riding stable all day today, so I figure I should offer to help him with his big assignment. "Joyce says you've got a project due on Monday and you've barely started it. If you want, I could help you a little with the research. What's it on?"

"I forget. Something."

"Great, Ethan. Really great. Well, I'll start your grilled cheese if you get the assignment sheet."

He runs off upstairs to his room and I search the cupboards for the frying pan.

Actually, it's already been a heavy week of research for me. Every evening I've spent about an hour searching the Internet for ways to prove the existence of ghosts. The fact that Kip doesn't believe me bothers me a lot, and I'd love to be able to say, *See? I told you.* So I've been researching methods for capturing ghostly images and sounds on video or audio recorders. The problem is that none of this stuff is super-convincing to skeptics. Even I have a hard time believing that most of the pictures on the Internet are really of ghosts. They don't look like any ghosts I've seen.

Still, there are special cameras that pick up things you can't see with the naked eye, and others that you just set up and leave on. I'd love to get hold of something like that and take it into the barn. At the very least, maybe it could pick up moving objects or sounds. Something I could shove in Kip's face. What I wouldn't give to hear him say, *Wow, you weren't kidding.*

I'm putting the finishing touches on Ethan's grilled cheese when he walks in with a badly crumpled piece of paper—his geography assignment. "That took a while," I say. He says he had trouble finding it. The assignment is about aboriginal peoples living around the Great Lakes. He has to choose a particular location and write about their connection to the land there. There are five options, but Manitoulin Island is the one he wants to do.

"Remember when we visited?" he asks.

I do. That was the summer of Mom's first operation. We took the big car ferry from Tobermory and stayed in two motel rooms—me with Mom, and Joyce with Jack and Ethan. We went for a hike because Mom wanted to see Dreamer's Rock. That's an ancient aboriginal site where for thousands of years teenage boys would go on vision quests. Off by themselves for days at a time without food, they'd go into a kind of trance and start dreaming, and in their dreams they'd see themselves as grown men and learn their destiny. Must be nice to get that kind of direction in life. But Dreamer's Rock was hard to find, even with a map from the local band office. Mom was still recovering and was so tired that we kept having to stop and rest.

"You were only seven," I say. "What do you remember?"

"Ice creams. From the store near the beach. And Mom bought me a thing to dig in the sand. A bulldozer thing. And I got a sunburn on my shoulders."

"Yeah. I remember that too." I watch him eat his grilled cheese sandwich. His eyes aren't focused on anything in the kitchen. I can tell he's back on Manitoulin Island.

"That place was full of ghosts," he says, out of the blue.

It practically makes me jump. I have a flashback of a young man sitting under a tree by the water, looking like he'd been there for a thousand years.

"How do you know that?"

"Jack told me. He read it in a book or something. It used to be an Indian burial ground. That's why Mom liked it there."

I ask him what he means by that, and he says, "Nothing." He says Mom just liked interesting things.

"Well, anyway, I'll help you find some information on Manitoulin Island. You can use my computer."

We're just getting set up in my room when Morgan calls me for a chat. I leave Ethan at my desk and tell him to get started without me. "Just type 'Manitoulin' into the search engine and bookmark any sites that have good information." Then I take the phone downstairs for privacy.

Morgan tells me everything that's happened lately in the lives of everybody she knows. Like how Brittany went on a date with her brother's friend who's at Georgian College. Then she asks about Jack—she usually gets around to Jack. When is he coming home from the hospital? And does the doctor think he'll make a complete recovery? Just before we finally hang up, she asks about Kip.

"What's he up to these days?"

"Oh, not much. We hung out for a while yesterday."

"Really? What did you do?" Somehow, visiting the cemetery on 18th Sideroad doesn't sound right, so I tell her we went for a drive and a walk. Morgan seems so excited by that, you'd think it happened to her. "Really, girlfriend. You'd be an idiot to let that guy slip away."

I hang up and just sit there, thinking about Kip and Matthew. They're just so different from each other. Is it so evil to wish I could have them both? Then I remind myself that I can't have either. Not in the real world, anyway. Finally I remember Ethan up in my room.

"So how's it going?" I ask as I reach the bedroom door. Ethan jumps and I know I've caught him at something bad. "What are you looking at?" I demand. The pale image of a ghostly figure disappears as he hits keys in a guilty panic and closes the page he was looking at.

"Ethan, who said you could stick your nose in my stuff?" I'm angry, but mostly because I'm embarrassed. I'm the one who's been caught red-handed with a folder full of bookmarked pages on ghosts. A folder I just labelled "Stuff." Great. If he tells Joyce, I'm dead. "What the hell are you doing? You're supposed to be researching your geography assignment, not spying on me. Is that your idea of doing homework?"

"Well, excuse me," he says, blinking and twitching excitedly. "But it's not my fault I accidentally opened your stupid files. And guess what? You're in trouble if Joyce finds out what you've been looking at. Because she doesn't like it when you talk about ghosts. Everybody knows that."

"Everybody knows that?" Ethan's favourite line. "Well, everybody doesn't know much, then. And that was just some research for a friend. And it's none of your business. I was about to delete those pages anyway."

"Oh yeah? Well, what about special cameras for shooting ghosts? What was that for?"

"I don't know. I didn't ask. I was just doing someone a favour."
I gesture that I want him out of my chair. I want him out of the
room, in fact. "So do you mind?"

He stomps past me, all agitated and indignant.

I shut the door behind him and head over to the computer.
I wonder how much he actually saw. I know I was gone a long time.
Damn it! For the rest of the afternoon I stay in my room, reading
and reviewing everything in my "Stuff" file folder, and deleting the
bookmarks one by one. I know I can find them again easily enough
if I want to, but for now it's best not to have them around.

I wonder if Ethan will tell Joyce on me. I really don't feel in the
mood to help him with his project anymore. But while I'm deleting
everything, I decide to give Morris a quick call. I want to tell him
about a few of the sites I've visited on the Internet, and about the
special cameras.

"I think we should check out a few of those things, to see if we
can get some proof of the ghosts in the barn."

"I'll look into it, Amelia, but I don't want you going back into
the barn, remember?"

"Not even with you?"

He doesn't answer.

When Joyce gets back from work, I catch sight of her through the
front-door glass, struggling with a bunch of grocery bags and trying
to open the door with one free finger. Ethan is preoccupied with yet
another video game, so I run down the hall and pull the door open
to give her a hand. I suppose Joyce has her hands full most of the time,
in more ways than one. Most women in their sixties aren't working
almost full-time, supporting three teenagers and basically running the
whole household. This probably isn't what she wanted to do with her

life right now. I bet she'd rather be taking motorcycle trips through South America. Or at least relaxing and riding her horses.

As I'm helping her put the groceries away, I decide to bounce a question off her. Since she knows a lot of seniors in the county—she's done some volunteer work in her day, and gives seniors special discounts on riding lessons every summer—I ask if she's ever come across an elderly woman named Dorothy Ross. She'd be the last living descendant of the McGrath family, I explain, and it happens that they built the Telford farm. She looks at me twice when I say that but I just keep talking. Morris Dyson is doing some research on nineteenth-century farming families, I tell her, and Kip is helping out. I said I'd ask her for him, as a favour. But Joyce tells me the name doesn't ring a bell.

Later, from up in my room, I can hear her talking to Ethan downstairs and I try to listen in. She asks him about his project, and he says he worked on it a little but he's taking a break. That's a lie. I'm pretty sure he's been watching TV or playing video games all afternoon. But I don't hear him tell her anything more than that. He's going to flunk grade nine if he doesn't smarten up.

Later I notice him from my window, walking across the backyard and out behind the paddock, sneaky-like, by himself. Joyce is in the kitchen, working at dinner, so I decide to see what he's up to. I head downstairs, shove on my boots and throw on my jacket. The sky is full of dark clouds and it makes everything seem too dark for this time of day, even if we are getting close to the shortest day of the year. When I walk around the back of the paddock, I find him hunched over, his back to me.

"What are you doing?" He jumps, caught for the second time today. He's in the middle of lighting a cigarette. Must be one of Joyce's. He's using an orange plastic lighter, also one of hers.

"What the hell?" I'm genuinely surprised. "I can't believe you're smoking. Are you stupid? Joyce is going to kill you." I guess we are always talking like we could get killed by Joyce on any given day.

"So? None of your business." He's pretty upset that I caught him. He barely knows how to use the lighter, so I don't think he's been smoking for very long.

"Really? And where did you get that cigarette?"

He shoots me this sharp look, and for the first time ever I feel like he hates me. He doesn't answer.

"Cigarettes aren't good for your health," I say, softening slightly. He rolls his eyes, like I'm some kind of idiot. "Everybody knows that."

"So do you want to get cancer? Like Mom?" I immediately feel guilty for putting it that way.

"So what if I do? What do you care?"

It really bothers me, the way he says that. It hurts. "God, what is your problem?" I don't wait around for an answer. I turn and start walking away from him, but as I leave I toss some advice over my shoulder. "You'd better have breath mints on you, that's all I can say."

I realize that I'm not going to tell on him. And he's probably not going to tell on me.

When I get back up to my bedroom, there's an e-mail from Morris that makes me forget about my irritating little brother.

I've found Dorothy Ross, nee McGrath. She goes by the name Dee Ross. Phoned around to a few seniors' homes and tracked her down at Williamsford Manor. Turns out Dee's her nickname. Says she hasn't been called Dorothy in sixty years! Small county, eh?

24

ip, in dark sunglasses, is at the wheel. I can't help feeling happy just to be with him, and excited because we're driving south on Highway 6 to visit Mrs. Ross, the lady I used to read to. Except now we know that she's also Dorothy McGrath, the oldest living person with a connection to what is now the Telford farm. She's the granddaughter of the original Scottish homesteaders. Unreal. I'll be so happy to see her again. And it's great to be seeing her with Kip.

His hair seems a little longer than when I saw him last, even though it's only been a week. It's curling at his collar. He's wearing a black turtleneck sweater under his black wool coat. I'm trying not to be too obvious about staring at him. So far, he hasn't had much to say.

Morris said that Mrs. Ross sounded fine on the phone. Sprightly, he said. He told her he's writing about some of the first families in Grey County with the help of two young researchers—that's us— and we'd like to interview her and ask her what she remembers about her grandparents. On the phone she laughed and replied, "Not a lot," but she said she'd be happy to chat. Morris told her she might recognize one of us. "Well, it'll have to be by the voice," she said. "My eyes don't recognize much anymore."

Morris gave us a crash course on interviewing. He said we should try not to sound like we're digging too much. It's better to come off as only curious and interested. Don't react too much to what she says, he advised. And don't worry about the silences. Hold off and wait for her to fill them. And then he gave us a mini-digital recorder. I told Morris and Kip I'd prefer it if Kip did most of the interviewing. Morris shrugged and said okay, but he told me that it's a skill I should eventually pick up.

"Just to review," Morris told us, "the public record is that Dorothy's brother Willy died by accident after coming back from the war. He'd been a POW in Germany, and when he was liberated at the end of the war, he came home to a hero's welcome. A week or so later the family threw him a homecoming party to celebrate, and at some point that night he 'accidentally' shot himself with his own revolver. In the head. That's all we know. So your job is to find out more about her brother's death, without sounding suspicious. We don't want to upset her."

Sitting in the passenger seat now, I steal another little glance at Kip. He's keeping his eyes on the road, deep in thought. Finally he speaks up.

"I almost forgot. Dad was doing some research on the Internet and found something pretty cool—a native heritage site on the south side of Blue Mountain called the Scenic Caves. You know how interested he is in ley lines and that kind of thing? Well, he was looking into some local native legends about ghost roads, which I guess are routes the spirits of the dead travel on their way to some afterworld. He's found a place that's supposed to be a kind of gateway to a ghost road, and it cuts through Grey County from somewhere around

Craigleith, heading west, to just south of Owen Sound and out toward Lake Huron."

"The same line his ghost sightings are on?"

"That's it."

"Holy jeez!"

"You should look it up. It's pretty awesome."

We pull into the lodge parking lot and leave the car under a row of naked silver birches, then head up the entrance steps and into a warm reception room. Mrs. Ross is waiting for us near the front desk. It's wonderful to see her. She hasn't changed a bit. She's still my idea of a perfect elderly ninja warrior. She's short but she holds her chin up and stands straight, with those round blue eyes that don't see much and a little smile. She's wearing a deep purple knit sweater and black slacks. She walks toward us carefully, using her white cane, and holds out a thin, veiny and graceful hand. She must have been so pretty when she was young. And I bet there's more than one resident in this place who thinks she's still pretty.

"Mrs. Ross, it's me, Amelia Mackenzie. I read *Great Expectations* to you two years ago."

"Amelia!" Her face lights up. Honestly. She really looks happy. "Amelia! Of course it's you. Of course, my dear. How are you?" Her voice is warm and only slightly shaky. She's reaching out her right hand, searching impatiently for mine. She finds it and gives it a squeeze.

"I'm good. I'm fine, thank you. And this is my . . . uh, research partner, Kip Dyson." It's a little awkward calling him a research partner, but I figure I'll play it safe. "Kip is Morris Dyson's son. You know Morris, don't you?"

"Of course I do. By reputation! How are you, young man? Pip, is it?" She grins and holds out her hand to him for a gentle shake.

I laugh. That's the name of the hero of *Great Expectations*. "Kip," I say, a little louder. "Kip Dyson." I think she was just teasing me.

She invites us to follow her to a lounge around the corner beyond the reception desk. It's like a super-large living room with four different upholstered couches, all pale pinks and greens. Each one is set up like a separate little space, with a coffee table and a couple of high-back chairs. The place has the feel of somebody's home, with nice broadloom and pastel-coloured walls, framed pictures and several fireplaces. There are flowers in vases around the room, and floral patterns on the draperies and throw cushions. The only institutional touch is a small table in one corner with stainless steel urns of coffee and tea, a stack of white cups and saucers, and small packets of sugar and milk in a basket. Mrs. Ross looks right at home here, like she decorated the place herself.

There are only two other people in the room, an elderly white-haired couple sitting close together on one of the couches at the far end, talking and holding hands. Kip and I notice them at the same time, and he leans into me, nudging me with his elbow and whispering, "Isn't he too old for her?"

It catches me off guard and a little laugh escapes me. I hope Mrs. Ross doesn't think I'm laughing at these old lovebirds. But did he mean something by that? Was he saying something about us? I look at him, but now he's smiling at Mrs. Ross as she points out the coffee and tea across the room.

She invites us to help ourselves, so Kip and I walk over together and pour three cups of tea, opening packets of sugar and milk. For a moment it feels like we're playing house.

While I'm stirring, he leans in close and whispers, "How's that deadbeat boyfriend of yours?"

Is that supposed to be funny? "I'm going to ignore that," I say. "But it's nice to see you," I add, as casually as possible. I'm looking down at the teacups, feeling embarrassed at how much I mean that, even though he knows just how to put me off balance. I can't figure out whether he's flirting with me. I change the subject. "Isn't Mrs. Ross lovely? She's my idea of the perfect grandmother."

He smiles. "Sure. But I kind of like your grandmother. She's cool."

"Hmm. I'd rather be like Mrs. Ross when I'm old." I think about that, then add, "That's how I picture my mom would have been . . . if she'd lived."

He gives me a curious look. "I'm too busy wondering what kind of twenty-year-old I want to be to worry about stuff like that."

I balance two teacups on saucers and he takes the third, and we head back across the room together, him hinting that he's prepared to race me if I'm game. It's tempting, but I resist.

Back at the couch, as we settle in with our tea, Kip chats up Mrs. Ross about Williamsford Manor, and talks about the kind of research he does for his dad's articles on heritage properties and social history around Grey County. Then he puts on his interviewer's cap. He's a natural. I guess he gets it from his dad. He takes out the small voice recorder and asks if she minds if he records the conversation. She hesitates, laughing, and says there will be so many blank spots where she forgets what she was going to say. "I suppose you've got a fast-forward button for those bits?"

"It's voice-activated," he says. "It stops recording during silences. So no worries at all. Take your time."

She reluctantly agrees to the recording, and he thanks her and turns it on.

For the next twenty minutes or so, Kip asks Mrs. Ross about her grandparents. Where in Scotland did they come from? What does she know about their life before Canada? What does she know about their early years, building and working the farm?

She was born after both grandparents had passed away, so mostly she talks about things her mother told her. Their lives were very hard, her mother said. There were many years when they struggled just to feed themselves through the winter. They grew root vegetables and bartered for flour. Eventually they bought several cows. Babies were born at home, and when people died, that was at home too. They'd head into town once a month, to either Owen Sound or Meaford, and over to the small church on the next line every Sunday. The closest schoolhouse was on the same road, a forty-five-minute walk in spring; in the winter snow it could be twice that.

The conversation moves naturally to Mrs. Ross's own childhood and family memories. Most of the time she talks, she looks somewhere between us, and far away.

"What do you remember most about your father?" Kip asks.

Her eyes glisten and she smiles. "How hard he worked," she answers. "People today wouldn't believe how little leisure time those folks had. Dusk till dawn. The way people today can kill time, it's dreadful. Back then, there was barely a half-hour to spare for a radio show, not the hours every day that people spend in front of the TV now. Even children worked hard. I remember my brother, Willy, chopping wood for hours on end, day after day, and stacking it in rows as high as he could reach. It was wood that kept us alive in winter. Warmed the house, cooked the food. I know it sounds like an exaggeration, but we had to work day and night through the spring and summer and fall to make it through the winter. Just like the squirrels. Those were the Depression years. We had so little. But all I feel when I remember that time is joy." She chuckles. "I don't know if that's because life was so much simpler, or because my memory is so poor."

I break in. "I think your memory is amazing. I can barely remember what happened last week." But what I really want to do is get her to talk about Willy. I screw up some courage and catch Kip's eye for support, then take the plunge.

"Mrs. Ross, was Willy the war hero in the family? I know one of the McGraths came back from the war with military honours."

She smiles and nods. "Yes," she says. That's all.

"Actually"—now it's Kip's turn, and he's speaking carefully, looking down—"when we did some research, we found that there had been a tragedy written up in the local paper." He pauses and looks up at her. "Was that Willy who . . . who died so soon after the war was over? A terrible accident, the newspaper said."

Her smile fades. Her eyes look through Kip. "My brother died, yes. It was . . . a tragic loss for the family."

"And that kind of death—an accident, I mean—well, there was no shortage of accidental deaths on family farms in those days. Still, this one must have been so hard on your parents, with him being fresh back from the war."

"That's true," she says.

At first I feel bad that we're pushing this, but you can see that she's casting back in her mind, and she seems willing to talk. We let her pick up the story when she's ready.

"It was particularly difficult because we'd missed him so much when he was away at the front. He was the family favourite, you see. Willy. And then my parents were notified that his plane had been shot down, and there was no word about whether he'd survived. But we were told that some airmen who'd crashed toward the end of the war were captured and shipped off to camps. So we never gave up hope. The whole family prayed nightly for his safe return. When we got word that he was alive, that he'd been found during the liberation of German camps at the end of the war, we felt our prayers had been answered." She smiles a little now, but weakly.

We are both looking at her intently, nodding in sympathy. It's hard, knowing where this is going. We wait for her to continue.

"We planned a homecoming party for him. Not right away, but about a week after his return. We wanted to make sure he was rested. We didn't know what to expect. What kind of shape he'd be in, physically or mentally."

"And what shape was he in? Do you remember?" I'm feeling a little more comfortable asking questions.

"The day he returned? He was thin, pale. But he was grinning from ear to ear. He had tears in his eyes as he put his arms around each of us, one by one. Holding us so tight. I still remember how it felt, my arms around his neck that day. I did love my brother." Her eyes drop again, looking into her half-empty teacup. "He had always looked out for me. He was so protective. Too protective, maybe. But that is one of the happiest memories of my life, the day he finally came home."

We all sit in silence. It seems like minutes go by before Kip says, "I can't imagine what it must have been like—having him survive the war only to die in an accident. A shooting accident, wasn't it?"

"Yes. Yes, it was. On the night of the homecoming party. He accidentally shot himself with his own revolver. We never knew what happened exactly. All we knew was that he had shot himself. In the head."

"My God! I hope you don't mind me asking this, but how did you know it was an accident? Were there witnesses?"

"It was my father who found him. He said it was an accident. He said he could tell." Her voice drops off a bit with those last words.

"It's just that"—Kip is choosing his words very carefully now—"these young men, coming back from that horrific experience, I suppose a lot of them must have suffered from what they call post-traumatic stress disorder today. I think they used to call it shell shock back then."

Mrs. Ross's red eyes look out across the room, focused on nothing. "Yes, that's true. I . . . I do believe it's possible my brother suffered some of that. I believe my parents were aware that it could have played a part. But I suppose the truth is that it was easier somehow to think of his death as an accident. I mean, it was desperately difficult, but still easier than the alternative. So many people were at the farm that evening, and there was so much happiness, so much celebrating. Music and dancing. Willy seemed happy. We were all so relieved."

"Why relieved?"

"Well, you see, he'd had a sweetheart before he left for the war, and while he was gone she married someone else. We tried to keep it from him at first. But he kept asking after her, and we finally had to break the news to him. And he took it quite badly. But the night of the party, he seemed completely over it. He was happy. That's why no one could believe that he could change so drastically. So quickly. If it wasn't an accident . . . well, the Lord wouldn't answer our prayers and bring him back home safe and sound only to abandon him to such despair, would He? That was what Father said. The Lord wouldn't do that to him. To us."

At this point, I'm sitting on the edge of my seat. Everything she says is starting to sound familiar.

"And since it was an accident," I say, "he was able to have a proper Christian burial, which he clearly deserved."

Mrs. Ross looks my way. "Yes."

"How did the family cope after that, Mrs. Ross?" asks Kip. "It must have been so hard losing Willy. He was the only son, right?"

"Yes. My parents didn't cope well, I guess. I don't think they ever recovered. They sold the farm that year. My father died shortly after, and my mother a couple of years after him. No, they never recovered from Willy's death."

"Why did they sell the farm, though? Didn't that make things harder?"

"They couldn't go on living at the farm without Willy. No one could after that. So it was over. My father never walked into the barn again."

I realize with a jolt that before that moment, I didn't know for sure where Willy had died.

"The barn?" Kip asks, clearly thinking the same thing.

"Yes. Willy died in the barn."

The urge to make eye contact with Kip is enormous, but I fight it. Instead, I focus on the little voice recorder on the coffee table.

"Besides, I moved away, married Philip Ross the next year. That was the boy I'd been going with since high school. He'd been in the army too, and we'd been engaged the whole time. I'd been waiting for him for five years. So I was looking forward to my life with Philip." Her face brightens a bit.

We smile, allowing the break. We sip our tea. We all seem to relax just a bit. Then Kip's expression changes again, his brow creasing. His voice is gentle.

"But those poor boys who came back from the war, they didn't get any counselling the way they would now. For the emotional trauma of what they'd been through, I mean."

Mrs. Ross nods, and I can see the strain in her face. She's fighting back tears. Finally one breaks over her pale bottom lashes and onto her cheek. Seeing it makes me feel awful. She speaks in a shaky voice.

"No. No one talked openly about things back then. Willy . . . Willy wasn't entirely himself that day. I mean, he was happy enough. But . . . well, I was the last person to talk to him that night, before he died."

"You were the last to talk to him?" said Kip. "That must have been very hard for you, afterwards."

She lets out a sigh. "Yes, it was hard. I'll be honest with you—

I really don't want to remember that. It's too . . . upsetting." It takes a long time for her to continue. "He was acting strangely the very last time we talked. Just outside the barn." Now her eyes are brimming with tears. She looks up, shaking her head. "You know, I've never admitted that to anyone before." She reaches in her pocket for a tissue with a trembling hand, dabs her eyes and blows her nose. We wait as she composes herself, and she finally says, "People today are much more aware of the emotional needs of our army vets, aren't they? At least I hope so."

For a long while on the drive back to my place, neither of us says much. When we left her, Mrs. Ross was still gracious and polite but she looked shaken. And what did we gain? Well, one more suicide victim for our list, that's true, but no mystery solved. And still I'm left with one nagging thought. Finally I decide to test it.

"Kip, remember how Mrs. Ross said that Willy found out the girl he was in love with had married someone else? He must have been heartbroken, wouldn't you think?" Kip looks over at me and nods. "Well, your dad said something about ghosts—that they are almost like the emotional energy left behind by dead people."

"Yeah, so?"

"Well, Willy's romantic setback kind of reminded me of Paul's just before he died. And how his sister, Emily, said he was all excited about hooking up with some mystery girl, remember? He'd had a fight with his girlfriend. And then I was thinking about my brother. At the Halloween party, when I talked to him, he was really depressed about Morgan. He's been in love with her for years, and she kind of leads him on, then pushes him away. That night he told me he'd had enough, and he was going to give up on her."

"What's your point?"

"The point is, he did seem broken-hearted. But when he was heading back to the barn, he told me he was meeting someone. It was obvious it was a girl. That was the big giveaway that something wasn't right. And when I think about his weird ramblings before he fell, he kept repeating, 'She said she'd come,' or something like that. I guess I'm wondering if there's a connection between romantic trouble and getting possessed by some ghost in this barn. I mean, I see a bit of a pattern. Don't you?"

Kip is frowning. As he turns into our drive he says, "There's just one thing." He stops the car, engine still running, and turns to me. "What about Matthew? How does he fit in?"

This is hard to admit. "It was pretty complicated. But Jack told me that Matthew was worried his parents wouldn't approve of him and me as a couple. So it's possible that he was feeling a little heartsick as well. Over me."

I've never thought of it like this before, but hearing myself say it, I can see the connections. Am I dreaming? Or am I on to something?

"I don't get it. Why wouldn't his parents have approved of you?"

"They're just really serious churchgoers. So I'd be a lost soul to them."

"Ah. A pagan."

"Maybe I'm imagining this, but it's possible this barn ghost connects with guys who have girl problems. Maybe because he had girl problems of his own."

"You mean there are guys *without* girl problems?"

That annoys me. "I mean serious ones."

"Oh, serious. Of course," he says, nodding, slightly sarcastic. "So who is this mystery girl? The one Jack and Matthew both said they were going off to meet?"

"I think she must be the original heartbreaker. The one who started all this trouble." Then it hits me. "She must hold the key to the word *dot*."

He suddenly leans over, brushing my hair back from my cheek. I hold my breath. "One last question," he says. He looks away, out the car window.

I wait for him to go on, and it feels like it takes forever.

Then, finally, "Are you still in love with him?"

At first I'm kind of stunned. Am I still in love with Matthew? I don't know if I can answer that honestly, but something in Kip's face makes me want to try.

"I still love him, yes. I think I'll always love him. But . . ." It's so hard for me to admit this. "It's not quite the same now that he's dead." As soon as the words have left my mouth, I feel horrible. But a ghost isn't a great substitute for flesh and blood.

Kip looks away again. When he turns back to me, he's smiling. "Well, I can't tell you how happy I am to hear that."

He leans in and gives me a peck on the cheek. It's over fast. Nothing like the kiss in the barn.

He says, "See you later, ghost girl."

25

I've been experimenting with my desktop picture. I've cut myself out of the photo and zoomed in on Matthew's face, his dark straight hair falling down over his dark narrow eyes, his grinning mouth, a bit of those square shoulders. He's closer now, but less in focus. I zoom in even more, until he's just a blur. I stare at the blur for a long time.

I've been thinking about Matthew when he was alive. I guess you could say he was a bit of a smartass, but not in a bad way. Everything seemed kind of straightforward to him. He never seemed to doubt himself, or the world around him either. The fact that he worried about how his parents would react if he dated me was an eye-opener, though. Maybe not everything was black and white for him. Love can make a lot of things grey, that's what I think. But now that Matthew's getting used to being dead, he's seeing things as uncomplicated again. If I love him and he loves me, we should be together. Simple. Except that it's not simple at all. I wish I could feel as confident as he does about everything. Or anything.

I think back to the day Morgan took this picture. The fire alarm had gone off at school and we'd all had to leave the building. It was a false alarm, but we stood on the sidewalk waiting for the fire trucks to arrive. Morgan snapped the picture just after we'd gotten the green light to get back into class. We were feeling a little pumped and excited by the disruption. In the instant she snapped the shot, my eyes were on her and Matthew was looking at me. I wonder what life would have been like if I'd paid more attention back then. If I'd known that he loved me. Everything could have been so different. I might have found out what it was like to kiss him, to feel his arms around me. I zoom back out until we're both in the photo again. He's sharper now, and farther away. I wonder if kissing him would have felt as good as it did with Kip.

Morris e-mailed me last night and told me to do an Internet search on the word *Ekarenniondi*. Turns out it's the name of an ancient aboriginal village. Over on the south side of Blue Mountain at the Scenic Caves mentioned by Kip, there's a popular hiking trail leading to a lookout and a huge rock that marks the spot of a Petun village. The Petun people were a small native tribe that lived around here for thousands of years before being wiped out by the Iroquois about four hundred years ago. Ekarenniondi means something like "where the rock sticks out." What's interesting about the rock is the legend that goes with it. It was supposed to be a sacred gateway marking the start of the journey the newly dead had to take to get to the "Village of the Souls." The really cool thing is that stationed at this rock was a mythological creature known as Oscotarach, meaning "the head-piercer." He would pierce the brains of the dead, one by one, as they set off on their journey. According to the legend, Oscotarach was removing their memories of their past lives so they wouldn't feel so bad about missing the people they'd left behind.

Makes you wonder if he sometimes screwed up and left a piece of memory behind.

I also did some research about those ley lines, or ghost lines, that Morris mentioned. I found out that they were named by Alfred Watkins, a British archeologist, in 1921. Watkins found all kinds of examples of four or more ancient sacred sites in a row in the landscape. The old English word *ley* means a kind of trench or valley. *Geophysical anomalies that point to an invisible earth-energy network.* I wrote that line down, word for word.

I'm still contemplating Matthew's face when Morris phones. I'm excited to hear that he's got hold of two special cameras he's going to try out at the barn.

"I want to come with you," I say.

"Absolutely not. It's safer if I do this myself."

"But isn't the whole point to see if the camera can pick up the same things I see? You need me there to tell you where to aim it."

He hasn't thought that through. I can hear him agonizing across the phone line.

"It'll be fine," I tell him. "I'll be much better than last time. I've had a chance to deal with everything, emotionally."

He says he needs to think about it. Then he tells me his latest news. "You'll love this," he says. "I heard about your heartache theory—about the boys in the barn all having girl problems when they got possessed. Do you remember George McCleary's son? The one Hank Telford told us was found dead in the barn? I found his sister. She has a law practice in Orangeville, and I managed to get her on the phone last night. She said her brother—his name was Danny—was an easygoing guy who loved folk music and played the guitar and wore his hair long. Red hair, she said, like his dad's. He wore hippie beads and tie-dyed T-shirts and, like many people in the sixties, was into experimenting with drugs. She said he had a girl-friend he was crazy about named Loretta, but she had broken up with him two days before he died. She'd left him for another guy, apparently. So Danny's sister was surprised when she heard later that he'd told one of his friends—the last person to see him alive—that he already had a new girlfriend. He seemed all excited about her, but wouldn't say who she was.

"They found him in the barn the next morning. He'd cut the arteries in his arms and bled to death. Practically cut his arms off, she said, with some blade from an old farm machine. Both arms. The conclusion was that he'd gone psychotic from a bad acid trip—that and heartbreak over Loretta. She said the new girl was a lie he made up to try to make Loretta jealous. She said everyone believed Danny's death was drug-related. End of story."

"Morris, I've never said this out loud before, but we've got to stop this guy. This evil ghost? We've got to figure out how to make him stop."

26

*I*t's snowing lightly again. Looking out my bedroom window at the paddocks, I watch the snow settling on the backs of the horses. Morris wants me to meet him on the Telford property—he might run into my grandmother if he picked me up here—but I'm not looking forward to riding my bike up that hill in this weather.

Jack is coming home from the hospital tomorrow, and the house is just about ready. Having him around again will be good for all of us, especially Ethan. Joyce says he failed his geography assignment last week. If he'd stay off the video games once in a while he'd do better, but it's like he has no motivation at all. I wonder if he's still working on his new smoking habit.

I keep myself busy with a bit of homework and cleaning up my room until after lunch, then get ready to go out. The idea of returning to the barn seems about as exciting as anything I've ever done, and as scary—both at the same time. I'll be relieved if I can see Matthew again and nothing much has changed with him. It's weirdly comforting to know he doesn't seem to be aware of time passing. It makes me feel less guilty about not having the nerve to visit him more often.

I tell Joyce I'm off to meet up with some friends, and head out of the house. As I pass the living room, I see Ethan; he's sitting on the floor in front of the TV, and his eyes follow me along the hallway. I ignore him and pull open the front door. The snow covers the road in a thin white sheet, so I decide to leave my bike behind and walk. Once I hit the crest, the Telford barn looms ahead, giving me the usual feeling of dread.

How do you deal with an evil spirit, anyway? That's something no one ever talks about. I've been in that barn six times now, if I count both times I was there the night of Jack's fall and both times I went in with Morris. And though I didn't know it, that psycho ghost was in there each time too, watching, listening, maybe standing right behind me. God knows what's up with him. But he takes the fun out of this experience, that's for sure.

Morris's car is parked in the Telford driveway. As I get closer I see that there are two people in the front seat, and I get butterflies in my stomach realizing that Kip came too. I wish he didn't make me feel this way. I flash back to the night we came here together, and wonder again what it meant and where it might have led if I hadn't freaked out. And whether he'd ever try it again. I'm sure he's decided I'm just too weird to bother with.

As I walk up the driveway, I notice a For Sale sign on the front yard by the road. That complicates things, for sure. Kip gets out of the car to greet me.

"Hey!"

I take a deep breath and smile. "Hi there. I didn't know you'd be here. What did you say to Morris to get him to let you come?"

"Oh, I had to agree to be the lookout while you guys are inside, watching for any trouble. Or real estate agents," he says, gesturing to the sign. "He says I can come inside for emergencies only." He grins, looking back at the barn.

I wish he'd take this a little more seriously, like his dad does.

"And what's Morris up to?" I ask, seeing him bent over in the front seat and looking busy.

"Just prepping his equipment." He leans toward my ear. "Should be interesting."

Morris looks up from whatever he's doing and waves at me. Then he gets out of the car, a small camera in hand. He opens up the back door and pulls out a large duffle bag. He looks excited, like a little kid.

"Amelia, how are you? Ready for this? Here's what I'm thinking: we'll go in and do a survey, find out who you can see and where they are exactly. Then I'll start snapping and we'll see if anything registers. Okay?"

"Sounds good."

"If possible, I'd like you to try to talk to whoever you see, but at the same time you'll need to direct me to where they are, so I know where to point the cameras. I've got an infrared lens to take pictures in the dark, and I've got a motion-sensitive camera that might be able to pick up a blur of movement, even if it doesn't actually pick up the image of what's moving."

He takes one last look at the contents of his duffle bag. "One more thing: I was thinking I'd bring along the recording of your interview with Mrs. Ross, to see if her brother, Willy, is in there. Play a bit of it in the barn. See if it draws him out. Just an idea." He shrugs and turns to Kip. "So you'll stay within earshot and keep your eyes open for property hunters or whatever?" Kip salutes and Morris turns back to me. "All set?"

"Uh, sure," I say, trying to sound sure. Glancing at Kip, I ask myself if I'm ready for this. He opens his eyes wide and shudders, pretending he's frightened. It's impossible not to laugh, but maybe that's because I'm pretty nervous.

"I still think you should have brought your Ghostbusters vacuum, Morris," he says as we head toward the big barn door. "He actually has one of those," he shouts after me.

I'm feeling a little weak-kneed as Morris pushes on the door. He shoves it all the way open, to let in as much daylight as possible. Then we both stand in the entrance, letting our eyes get accustomed to the dim interior. It's quiet and empty. I brace myself and step inside.

Morris moves over to one side of the door with his bag, sets it down rather noisily and begins to take things out: a flashlight, two cameras, a large lens attachment and the small video recorder. While he fusses with his cameras in the corner, I step lightly along the dusty floor. As usual, the cracks and holes in the boards of the walls and roof cast dramatic light in some places, while others are darkly shadowed.

There's a shadow catching my eye on the loft platform along the wall. As I get closer, it takes the shape of Matthew. He's sitting down, leaning back against the wall, legs bent in front of him, one elbow resting on a knee. He's looking at his hand, just like he was the last time I saw him. That's a little strange. I approach quietly, then stop and turn to Morris. I whisper, but loud enough so he'll hear me.

"Matthew's here. Sitting there against the wall. Right there under that cracked board. Should I talk to him?"

Morris has jumped to his feet with one of his cameras in hand, and he gives me a thumbs-up sign. He starts to circle behind me in the open middle space of the barn, all the while adjusting his camera settings.

"Ignore me," he whispers. "Just let me know if he moves or anything."

I nod and turn back to Matthew. He's still there, only now he's looking at me and smiling. I smile back at him and wave hello. I walk closer.

"Matthew! It's so great to see you again. It always feels like some kind of miracle. Hard to get used to."

He's watching me but doesn't respond.

"How are you?" Behind me, I hear Morris swearing under his breath. I ignore him and focus on Matthew. "You look exactly like you did when I was last in here. Do you remember that? You were sitting there—looking at your hand, even—like you are now. Do you remember what happened? That . . . creepy guy? Hanging from the rafters up there?"

Matthew glances up, cocking his head to the side, then looks back down at me. "That guy? Yeah, he's mad."

"What do you mean? Mad crazy? Or mad angry?"

"Both. He's angry at someone. His girlfriend, I guess. I wish you could get her in here to talk to him. Calm him down. She must have really done a number on him. And you should see the temper on this guy."

"I think I've seen it."

"Amelia, can I ask you a question?"

"Anything, Matthew. Anything." I hear Morris cursing and fiddling with his camera behind me.

"Is everyone dead, or is it just me?" He looks depressed. "It's just me, isn't it?"

I wish I could say something to cheer him up. "Well, I think everyone who's hanging out in this barn with you is dead. And it's only a matter of time, right? Until the rest of us are dead, I mean. Until I'm dead too. And time doesn't seem to matter to you much these days, so maybe I'll be joining you before you know it." I'm saying this but it's not like I'm eager to join him in his weird ghost world. I feel a twinge of guilt about that. I wonder if he can guess. I'm also aware that Morris can hear what I'm saying, even if he can't hear Matthew's end of the conversation.

"I'd put it off if I were you. I miss my life." He's looking down at his hands again. "You know what they say: you don't know what you've got till it's gone."

I don't want this to get too sad. "Hey," I say, "you remember the 'paved paradise' song?"

"I guess so."

"Do you remember that time Nick threw his plate of spaghetti at the cafeteria wall?"

He smiles. "I remember the look on your face, yeah. I remember the look on Mrs. Gibson's face too."

"Do you remember your locker combination?" He looks at me like I'm nuts. "Never mind," I quickly say. "I was just curious."

Now his face has gone completely blank, like he forgot what he wanted to say. I can hear Morris's camera off to my left. I hear a snap and then something that sounds like "Ouch."

"Matthew, suppose I ask you to take a walk with me through the barn?"

"You want to go for a walk?"

"Yes, I do."

And suddenly he gets to his feet. It takes my breath away to see him standing on the platform, towering before me. He walks to the edge and I can definitely hear his footsteps. I don't know what that means. Is he still kind of solid somehow? Or am I only hearing what I think I should be hearing? He sits down on the edge of the loft and drops to the floor about six feet away from me. I hear him land. I take a step toward him, but the closer I get, the less clear he is to me in the dim light. It's like I'm far-sighted, like one of those old people who can't read close up. Or like zooming in on his photo until he's gone. I decide to stay a couple of arm's lengths from him.

"Are you going to stay with me this time?" he asks.

His question catches me off guard.

"Because I love you. And you love me. We were meant to be together, and we should stay together always. Here."

I feel like I'd better change the subject.

"Matthew, you know there's a ghost in this barn that's responsible for your death, right? And the deaths of a few other people too." I'm looking around, but I don't see anyone else.

"Yeah?"

"Well, I'm not crazy about spending too much time around him."

"He can't hurt you. I won't let him."

"You can stop him?"

"Yes."

"How do you know?"

"I already have."

"What do you mean?" He doesn't answer but just looks at me, tilting his head a little. "Well, I'm grateful for whatever it is, but still . . ."

"You're safe with me. Please stay with me? Don't go."

I have a flashback to that moment in the library shortly before he died. *Don't go*. His fingers tight around my wrist, keeping me at his side, the clenched muscle in his fist, his forearm, his neck. I could have leaned over him, kissed him on the head, relaxing his tense jaw and bringing his lips to mine. Instead I panicked and ran. It seems so long ago. Now we stand face to face, looking at each other, but he might as well be a hologram. A sigh escapes me. How can I tell him it's hopeless?

I hear a creak above me, somewhere in the rafters. I look back at Morris. He's heard it too and he's looking up. There it is again.

We stand perfectly still. I scan the roof's sloping boards, many of them loose or broken, until something catches my eye. It's one particularly long board, gently moving back and forth, hanging high above us by a few nails. It's creaking. It could come completely loose, I'm thinking. Fall on us. Now it stops moving. I look back at Matthew, who's also looking up. I glance at Morris. He appears concerned. Then he raises his camera to his eye and points the lens toward the board. He swears softly and lowers the camera.

"This thing's not working in here," he says. "I don't know what's wrong."

There's another creaking sound, this time from a different part of the roof. Another board moves back and forth, like it's being loosened by an invisible hand. Footsteps behind us make us both jump.

"Me. Just me," whispers Kip. "Why am I whispering?"

"He should get out." It's Matthew. He says it flatly. He means Kip.

"Kip, you shouldn't be in here," I say. His sunny smile seems so out of place right now.

"Kip," says Morris, "I thought I asked you to stay outside."

"I just wanted to warn you that someone drove by and slowed right down, taking a good look at me and your car. Don't be surprised if a concerned neighbour is phoning the cops right about now."

The sound of another creaking board cuts him off. It's louder than the others, and in another part of the roof. We all look up at it swaying loosely. Suddenly there's a loud crack of breaking wood and the board comes flying down. We jump aside as it lands with a heavy thud, raising a cloud of dust at Kip's feet.

"Jeez! That was close," says Kip, surprised as hell.

We look up again, eyes darting, ears straining to hear. Another board moves, only slightly at first. Gently. Then the movement gets harder and louder. We huddle closer together, our backs to the door, inching away from the noise. Then it stops. We stand still, holding our breath, looking up into the rafters, saying nothing.

Minutes go by.

I look around for Matthew, but now I can't see him. The barn is silent.

"I think we should go," Morris says.

"Yeah. Flying boards are bad," Kip says, sounding, for the first time, a little nervous.

"I don't know," I say. "Could we stay just a little longer? Maybe play a bit of the voice recorder and see what happens?"

Morris walks back to his bag, muttering again about how the cameras aren't working properly. He pulls out the recorder and brings it over. As he does, I notice Matthew back in the shadows.

"Matthew?" I refuse to worry about what Kip might think. "What just happened there? Is it dangerous for us to be in here?"

Matthew gives Kip an unfriendly glance. Then he looks at me. "I told you I can protect you. I promise."

"Well, is there a young man in here who looks like he might be a soldier from the Second World War? A guy named Willy? Or William?"

Matthew seems to be checking out Kip again, but he glances sideways across the barn to the wall where the stables are. He nods in that direction, and when I turn to look I see a dark form emerging from a stall. Coming out from the shadows is a young, thin man wearing a loose-fitting service uniform and a cap. I feel a strong sense of fear, of danger and chaos, like I had in my dream.

"G-good day, ma'am," the soldier says timidly.

"Willy?" I'm looking around for Morris. "Can I call you Willy?" I move a step closer and look again for Morris, who's holding the recorder. "I was hoping to run into you."

Willy has curly, sandy brown hair. His cheekbones are high and sharp and his eyes are sunken. I guess you'd say they look haunted. That's because of his time in the POW camp, probably. His uniform looks well worn, but it's clean and pressed. He's looking at me with an exhausted expression.

"Your sister told us all about you," I say.

"My sister?" That perks him up.

"Yes, your sister Dorothy. Dee."

"Dorothy?" He looks around anxiously. "Where is she?"

"Dorothy lives not far from here. We met with her earlier this week, and she talked about you a lot. She loves you so much. But she hasn't seen you in sixty-five years."

"Is she safe?" he asks. He sounds worried.

Out of the corner of my eye, I catch Kip taking the recorder from his dad's hand as Morris fiddles with settings on the second camera. I focus on Willy.

"Yes, she's great, I'd say. But she feels bad about losing you so soon after you returned from the war. Do you remember that?" I hear Kip come up behind me. "What happened, Willy?"

Willy shakes his head. "Something terrible," he says. "I . . . I think my gun went off."

"Do you remember how it happened? Was it an accident? Or were you upset? Did you do it on purpose?"

He looks shocked at this suggestion. "On purpose? No! I didn't want to die. I wanted to live. That's why I survived in the camp. I wanted to live." He sounds lost, like he's losing his train of thought. He's sinking somehow, fading back into the shadows.

"Willy?" I try to pull him back. "Willy, who else is in here with you? Is there . . . is there a girl in here?"

"No," he says, shaking his head.

"Do you know who else is in here?"

"Jimmy. Jimmy's here." Fear crosses his face and he starts to fade again.

"Wait, don't go. Stay with me a little longer. Please? Who's Jimmy?"

But Willy's not listening. He's turning away. I look around for Kip and Morris, and I spot someone over by the corner where Morris left his bag. It's Paul, just standing there, watching us. He's wearing a tan-coloured corduroy blazer and a light blue cotton shirt with white buttons. He's wearing glasses with thin brown frames. It's impossible to imagine him drinking some vile solvent on purpose. He doesn't look the reckless type.

Just as I'm wondering about Danny, the red-haired boy who died here in the sixties, there's another sound, like the shuffle of feet high overhead. I dread looking up into the rafters, but I force myself.

No one and nothing there, or not that I can see.

Morris is standing to the side, behind Kip. I whisper, "Paul," and motion with my head toward the corner. Morris turns rapidly to look in Paul's direction, eager at the thought of seeing his old friend, but I can tell from his face that he's not seeing anything. Kip looks at me questioningly, the voice recorder in his hand. He lifts it slightly toward me, offering it. Then he tilts his head up and his eyes narrow. He's heard something too. He looks back at me. Our eyes meet, and for the first time he seems to be admitting that something strange is going on.

I reach out and take the recorder from him, pressing the play button. I turn up the volume as loud as it will go; it isn't very loud, but in the barn, with everything suddenly still, the sound fills the space.

I can still see Willy standing in the shadows. "Willy, do you recognize your sister's voice?" I ask him.

I don't know how he is going to take this. He stares wide-eyed at the recorder in my hand, his face brightening with recognition. He's frozen like a statue. He seems to smile and then he starts to fade.

"Willy, don't go." I can barely see him now.

I search for Paul, but I can't see him anymore either. Finally I look around for Matthew. He's standing behind me, eyes focused on the rafters, a worried expression on his face.

"Matthew? What's happening?"

His head shakes slowly from side to side. He looks back down at the recorder, then up into the rafters. He's fading too. And then he's gone.

On the recorder, Mrs. Ross has been talking about how hard her father worked on the farm, the long days. Now she's talking about Willy chopping and stacking wood for the winter. I hear rustling coming from one of the stalls. Then I hear something behind me. I shiver and look at Kip. He seems to shiver too. I try to see Willy, but I can't.

"Everyone's disappearing," I whisper as panic settles in. What's happening?

Mrs. Ross's voice starts to sound kind of distorted and I hear creaking overhead, high in the rafters. The sound of shuffling along the huge crossbeam. I can tell that Kip hears it too. He's straining his eyes, staring into the shadows above us.

There's a sharp crack, almost like thunder, and another piece of barnboard breaks loose from the roof and comes hurtling down, this time rocketing toward Morris. I scream his name. He tries to leap aside, but it smacks him on his left shoulder before slamming to the ground. It has grazed the side of his face, scraping his cheek, and he's holding his shoulder in pain, staring in disbelief at the board at his feet. The recorder has slipped from my hand but it's still playing Mrs. Ross's voice as she struggles with her emotions over Willy's death. The sound is louder now.

"My God, are you okay?" Kip has rushed to Morris's side.

"Let's get out of here," Morris says tersely.

"Amelia!" Kip says.

We've barely taken a step when the rope, a knotted loop at its end, slowly lowers from somewhere high in the rafters. Where did that come from? We freeze where we are, mesmerized. Then it stops, hovering just a few feet above our heads. A wave of cold runs through my body and I feel my eyes pulled to the ground. At our feet, in the dirt, a line is being drawn, slowly, as if by an invisible finger. No one moves. A second line cuts through the first, forming a cross. *Oh God.* We keep watching as a circle gradually forms in the dirt beside the cross. *What does it mean?* I look up at Morris. There's a drip of blood running into the grey stubble on his cheek. Kip points at the ground. Beside the circle another has started forming, running clockwise from the top. At the bottom it stops, then jerks up in a straight sharp line that makes me jump. It's like a backwards D. And then it hits me. Not a cross, not a circle—it's *Dot* spelled backwards. And then the rope drops.

It happens so fast that I barely see it landing like a lasso over Kip's head. His hands fly to his throat, grabbing hold of the rope as it tightens and chokes him, then jerks him up by his neck so that he's barely touching the ground, legs flailing. I scream and jump up, grabbing hold of the rope above his head, trying with all my strength to pull it down. Morris does the same, yelling Kip's name, hauling on the rope above my hands. It doesn't budge. I search the shadowy rafters. There's no one holding the rope. There's a choking sound. Kip is being strangled.

"Kip . . . Kip . . . hold on!" I drag down on the rope, my outstretched arms above his head, the two of us hanging face to face. His blue eyes are wide with shock and his face is turning red. His feet kick, struggling to touch the floor. I'm screaming and crying, "Morris, Morris, do something!" Mrs. Ross's shaking voice still fills the barn.

"Hold on, Kip!" Morris yells. "Hold on!" Kip's fingers grip the rope against his throat. "Is there anything sharp in here?" Morris shouts at me. "To cut the rope!" His eyes dart to a spot under the loft as his hands tighten their grip above Kip's head. "Over there!" I twist to see, scanning through the broken pieces of farm equipment under the loft.

Kip's lips are turning blue. His eyes are closing. Mrs. Ross's voice is so loud now that I can barely hear Morris. "Oh my God!" I'm screaming. I don't know what to do.

I see an old wooden crate of bottles and let go of the rope, running over to dump out the crate and racing back with it to Kip. I plant the crate below his feet and grab his ankles, trying to help him step up on it. He struggles to find his balance, but the extra height makes the rope go slack. Morris and I claw at the tight slipknot, loosening it as fast as we can. Above us the rope begins to pull taut again, before we can get the noose over Kip's head. In a rage, Morris grabs hold of the rope and yanks on it as hard as he can. For a second nothing happens. Then the rope is suddenly released, dropping so hard and fast that it sends Kip and Morris crashing to the ground.

In the dirt of the barn floor, Morris and I fight to get Kip out of the noose, desperately dragging the rope over his head. Somewhere nearby, Dorothy's voice stutters and she begins to cry. Kip is on his hands and knees, face close to the ground, gasping and heaving. I can barely breathe myself but my arms are around him. I want to pull him toward me, hold him tight. But we've got to get up.

Morris jumps to his feet first, looking up into the rafters. "Get out now!" he yells.

We struggle to our feet and start backing out of the barn, Kip staggering and leaning heavily on me, but Morris runs over to one of the stalls and begins to climb up, like he's insane with anger. I look up and see the farm boy staring down from a beam high above us. Half of his head and face are blown off, all blood and ragged red tissue. I scream, "Morris! Morris, don't!"

He stops, looks at Kip and me near the barn entrance, and then jumps back down with a thud that raises more dust and straw. He runs to us.

"Take him under the arm," he says to me, positioning Kip between us, his arms over each of our shoulders as we lurch toward the door.

Bursting into the daylight, we nearly knock over someone who has appeared from nowhere, blocking our way. It's Ethan.

"Whoa, what the heck?" he yells as we push past him. "Amelia, what happened?" He's blinking and twitching excitedly.

We stagger, the three of us, ten or fifteen feet away from the barn, then sink to the snowy ground, with Morris and me trying to control Kip's landing. We're all heaving and gasping for air like we've been holding our breath for five minutes. At first we can barely speak. Morris examines Kip's neck. There's a bright red welt, like a choker, right around it. I feel like I'm going to pass out, just from seeing it.

"Are you all right, Kip? Are you all right?" I'm crying. I can't believe what just happened. My arms are around his shoulders. I would squeeze harder but I'm afraid he's hurt. "Kip?"

"I'm okay . . . I'm okay." He's nodding, shaking, still coughing and struggling for air.

"What the hell is going on here?"

This time we all look up in surprise. My arms drop from Kip's shoulders. It's Detective Grierson. His police cruiser sits parked behind Morris's car in the driveway. At first we're all too stunned to respond. Then Kip speaks up.

"It was just a freak accident," he says between gasps. "I . . . tripped and fell . . . got caught up in a rope hanging from somewhere . . . almost hanged myself." His voice drifts off and he swears under his breath, a look of complete shock on his face.

I grab his hand. I can't help it. I whisper in his ear, "Oh my God, Kip, I've never been so scared. Are you all right? Really?"

He nods. "You?"

I nod. *No, not really. Not at all.* I quickly wipe at my watery eyes and my runny nose. I look at Morris, pale and shaken, blood on his cheek. He nods, breathing heavily, eyes on Kip.

Grierson, his hands on his hips, feet apart, is looking down at the three of us kneeling in the snow.

"Dave," Morris says finally, "this must look pretty strange. But it was just an accident, like Kip said. Gave us a fright."

"Morris, this looks strange even for you."

You can tell that Grierson and Morris have crossed paths before. Grierson glances at the barn door and we all look over. Ethan's standing inside, near the doorway, facing out. I'd forgotten all about him. He's got the voice recorder in his hand. It's gone silent and he's just staring at it.

"Ethan, come out of there," I say. He doesn't seem to hear me. "Ethan?"

Grierson walks over to the barn and heads inside, passing Ethan. A minute later, he comes back out with Morris's bag in his hand. He dumps it on the ground by our feet.

"I don't want to know what you guys were up to. But you are on private property, and unless Hank Telford has given you permission, you've got no business being here. If I find you here again, you'll be charged with trespassing. I mean it this time, Morris. Enough is enough." The three of us, still down on the ground, are silent. "Now what are we going to do about that mystery rope-burn?" he adds.

I speak up, trying to keep my voice from shaking. "We'll go to my place and put something on it. We'll take care of it."

Kip gets to his feet, staggering slightly, and Morris and I stand up too. Morris turns to Grierson.

"Thanks for the warning, Dave. I can tell you, we won't be back."

"Ethan!" I yell. "We've got to go." He looks up at me from just inside the barn. "Come on!" I yell again. "What are you, deaf?"

He drags his feet out of the barn and we head over to Morris's car. Grierson stands by and watches us as we get in—Kip in the passenger seat, Ethan beside me in the back—then gives us a last look before getting into his own cruiser. He backs out onto 12th Line and waits for Morris to back out too. He follows us until we turn into my driveway, then pulls to the edge of the road in front of our house and stops. We see him talking on his cellphone. Then he takes off up the road.

With Ethan here, none of us can talk about what just happened. We sit in the driveway and wait in a tense silence, trying to recover before going inside.

Joyce appears at the living-room window, looking out at us, a phone to her ear. She slowly puts down the receiver.

27

We get out of the car and stand together in the middle of the driveway, psyching ourselves up to deal with Joyce's wrath. Ethan stays off to the side, looking a little smug. He knows I'm the one who's in trouble. I take a deep breath to try to calm down, then approach the front door, with Kip and Morris following close behind. Just as I reach for the doorknob, it turns and the door opens. Joyce is standing there.

"Well, well," she says. "Sounds like you fellows have been up to no good in the Telford barn. Mr. Dyson, nice to finally meet you. Kip, nice to see you again." She holds her hand out for both to shake and invites them inside. She seems strangely civil, but cool.

"Nice to finally meet you too, Mrs. Stewart. Please call me Morris."

"And you can call me Joyce."

She stands against the open door and we have to file past her into the hallway. She leans in toward Ethan as he passes and quietly and firmly tells him to go to his room. As he heads down the hall, she turns and takes a hard look at me and then Kip. We probably look wrecked. Like we've been playing roller derby or something. Kip's jacket is ripped under the arm. And I'm beginning to realize I've got a bit of a limp. Must have twisted my ankle.

"Kip . . . um, has had a little accident," I say, trying to sound normal. "Just want to find him a cold cloth for his neck."

"Ahh." In the hallway light, Joyce is looking steely-eyed at Kip. "Nothing serious, I hope?"

He tries to protest but she insists on taking a peek under his collar. "That must hurt," she says.

She gestures for us to join her in the kitchen, and Morris and Kip take seats at the table. She leans against the counter, arms folded across her chest. I'm pretty sure she's furious but she seems really controlled. I reach into a drawer for a freshly laundered dishcloth and soak it under cold water. I wring it out and hand it to Kip, who smiles a thanks at me and very gently wraps it around his neck.

"So"—Joyce looks at Kip—"how did that happen?" From the tone of her voice, I'm not sure she's expecting the truth.

"Well, a dumb accident really," Kip says. "There was this rope hanging in the barn. I was up on a beam, trying to take photographs for Dad's farm collection—old barns, outbuildings, that kind of thing—and I . . . uh, tripped. Tripped and fell, got tangled up in the rope. Just the way I fell, I actually got my head caught in a loop and . . . uh, damn near hanged myself. Just stupid bad luck."

"No kidding," Joyce says, a little flatly. "I guess you can't be too careful in old, abandoned places like that. There's no shortage of bad karma in that barn."

Morris raises his eyebrows.

"Mr. Dyson?"

"Call me Morris."

"Okay, Morris. You were going to say something?"

"Yes. I could use a smoke. Would you join me out on the back porch?"

"Well, why not?" she says, taking a jacket from a hook on the wall.

Morris rises from the table, gingerly, and grabs his coat from the back of the chair. He takes a quick glance at Kip and me, then follows Joyce out the door. "Trying to quit," I hear him say as the door slams behind them.

Through the kitchen window, we watch them walk to the far side of the porch. Joyce pulls two cigarettes out of her pack and hands one to Morris. She takes out a plastic lighter and lights hers, then hands the lighter over. They turn toward the paddock and lean on the wooden porch rail, their backs to the window.

Kip and I look at each other across the table. His face is pale now, his hair super-messy and his mouth slack like he's in shock. For a second he reminds me of a little kid. Then he gives me a weak, quivering smile.

"Holy crap. I feel like I just went through some initiation ritual. For a satanic cult."

"Well, I think you passed with flying colours," I try to joke, but then the fear washes over me again and takes my breath away. I have to hide my face for a minute. It's too awful to imagine how that could have ended.

When I look up, Kip is focusing on his hands, which he's placed palms down on the table before him, like he's trying to steady them. Then he says in a low voice, "I'm sorry I didn't believe you. About ghosts, I mean. But that was . . ." He searches for the right word. "Very convincing." He glances up at me, his blue eyes bloodshot. Then he quickly looks away, shaking his head and swearing under his breath.

We sit in silence for a few seconds. I'm thinking about how badly I wanted to prove to him that ghosts exist. But not like this. I look at his hands and I'm embarrassed to realize that I have such a strong desire to touch him right now. To put my arms around him. Finally I reach out, but only to brush my fingers lightly along his knuckles. Then I draw back and put my hands in my lap.

"If we hadn't got you out of there in time, I would never, ever have forgiven myself." I look up at his pale face. "Never."

His hand slides, palm up, along the table toward me. I don't hesitate to place my hand in his, and we sit quietly and wait. Feeling his warm touch is such a relief, I try not to think about anything else. When we see Morris and Joyce turn and walk back toward the house, our hands release. They bring with them a gust of chill wind that smells of cigarette smoke.

Morris slumps into the chair beside Kip and me. He looks awful.

"Morris and I had a chat about the barn," Joyce says. She turns to Kip. "Beer?"

"Sure," he says, surprised. "Thanks."

She walks over to the fridge and gets him a beer, flipping the cap off with an opener, then grabs one for herself and a couple of cans of cola for Morris and me. I watch Kip take a gulp from the bottle. Morris reaches out for his can of pop, his hand still shaking slightly. Then he looks at Kip and me.

"I've told Joyce everything we know about the history of the barn. About the four suicides leading up to Jack's fall. And our suspicions about Jack's fall."

My jaw drops. I can't believe it. He looks at me and raises a hand, gesturing that it's okay.

"She already knew something was going on, so there was no point in trying to cover things up. We didn't get into this looking for trouble, but now it's serious. We're trying to solve a mystery before someone else dies, and there's no ordinary way to deal with it. We can't just file a complaint with the police, or dial 911 for help."

He turns to me. "Joyce believed me when I told her we didn't bring Ethan into this and have no idea how he tracked us there. But her bigger concern is you, Amelia. Your grandmother doesn't want you having anything more to do with the barn, and I agree with her."

My jaw clenches. There's a silent tension in the kitchen, and finally Joyce speaks.

"I told Morris I don't believe in ghosts. If he does, that's fine, but he's got no business involving a sixteen-year-old girl in his ghost hunting. Especially you, Amelia, given your history of . . . apparitions. I'm not going to stand by while you get sucked back into an obsession with dead people. That's not the way to get on with your life."

I knew it. I knew it would come to this. I'm looking down at my hands, balled up in fists on the table before me.

"Joyce"—I'm struggling to control myself—"it's not like that. It's not Morris's fault. And it's not my fault. It's not something I can just stop. It's . . . it's not going to stop." I feel like exploding at her. "This is the way I am." It's all I can do to get the last words out.

Kip reaches across the table and takes one of my fisted hands, holds it in his like he's trying to warm it. I keep my eyes on his hands as they go blurry.

"Amelia," Joyce says calmly, "just because I can't believe in ghosts doesn't mean they don't exist. I realize that. But I don't want you taking chances in dangerous situations. And seeing ghosts, whether they're really there or not, is not good. It's not good. Even if you're sane now, it'll drive you mad eventually. I do not want you going back into that barn. Is that understood?"

As she says that, Ethan walks into the room and everyone at the table seems to straighten up. Morris clears his croaky throat. I yank my hand from Kip's and quickly wipe my eyes. When did he come downstairs? How much has he heard?

"I'm thirsty," he says, as though nothing unusual is happening. He doesn't even look at us. He walks over to the fridge and takes out a carton of milk, all eyes on him. He takes a glass from inside the nearby cupboard, and we all sit in awkward silence as he drinks, slowly, like he's just killing time.

Finally Morris asks, "What grade are you in, Ethan?"

"Nine."

"Ah. Then you might know the daughter of a friend of mine. Jessica Nielsen? Is she in your class?"

"Yeah. I think so." He finishes his milk, then hoists himself up on the counter by the sink, legs dangling, making himself comfortable, like he's not going anywhere. He's gazing around the kitchen as if it's terribly interesting. Joyce raises her eyebrows and turns to Morris.

"Well, I guess you'll have to be getting back into town. It's been nice meeting you face to face." She turns to Kip. "I do hope you take care of that neck."

Kip catches my eye as he reaches for his coat on the back of his chair, and he leans in, saying in a low voice, "I'll call you." I wish he didn't have to go.

Joyce and Morris have stood up but I stay where I am, feeling too weak to move.

"Amelia asked me about an old gal you were trying to track down," Joyce says, like she's making small talk. "She thought she might be in one of the local nursing homes. Did you ever find her?"

"Oh yes, we did. Dorothy Ross. We found her in Williamsford. It turns out she's someone Amelia met before, from that reading program for seniors. Yes, she was very helpful. Lively gal for eighty-eight. She goes by the name Dee."

"Dee? Funny she'd call herself that. In the old days, the nickname for Dorothy was Dot." Joyce shakes her head. "Now that's a name you never hear anymore."

Our jaws drop in unison. Ethan looks over at us with a smirk and says, "Everybody knows that."

28

 ack's come home. What a relief! It is just so nice having him back in the house. When Joyce and Ethan went to the hospital to pick him up, I stayed behind doing some last-minute cleaning. To celebrate his arrival, I made a big brunch for everyone. Joyce had done a major grocery shop, so we had bacon and sausage and scrambled eggs and toast and pancakes. Brunch is a tradition in our family, something my mom used to do on special occasions. It was a success, more or less. Only one egg broke on the kitchen floor, and one pancake fell behind the stove. The sausages got a little burnt and had to be put out on the back porch till they stopped setting off the smoke alarm. They had a kind of charcoal crust but they were still declared to be "perfectly edible." The scrambled eggs turned out great. The bacon too. Everyone likes it crunchy anyway.

It was a wonderful family meal, a true celebration. Joyce seemed quite emotional, toasting Jack's return with orange juice. I wasn't that hungry but it helped take my mind off what happened yesterday, at least for a short while. I loved seeing Jack smiling at the table again.

And Ethan ate enough for all of us. You'd think he hadn't eaten in years.

Ethan seems quieter than usual, despite Jack coming home. I guess he's sensing that something serious happened yesterday, though I can't see how he picked up very much. Thank goodness he only showed up after the worst of the drama.

Me, I've been so grateful to have Jack to focus on. I woke up this morning with a shock of adrenalin, my hands flying up over my chest like I was falling, my heart pounding. I couldn't remember the dream, only yesterday's nightmare. How the ghost in the barn almost killed Kip.

At the back of my head, I haven't been able to stop thinking about what happened to him. What almost happened. It made me realize something: from what I've seen of the ghost world, it's a poor substitute for this one. If you really care about someone, death is still the worst possible thing. And sometimes, when you imagine someone's death, you find out just how much they mean to you.

I hated it when Kip had to leave yesterday. I didn't want to let him out of my sight. I'm hoping to get over to their house this afternoon for a few hours. We have a lot to talk about. When he and his dad left, it was in a kind of stunned silence. I watched them through the living-room window, Morris with his arm around Kip in the driveway.

Kip called later to say he was worried about me. How crazy is that, when he was the one who almost got killed? But he said he was feeling better. I wanted to tell him how relieved I was to hear that, how much it meant to me, but it was hard to find the right words. "Kip," I began, and there was this awkward silence, but he cut in gently, saying, "Amelia, I know." Then he said he and Morris have been asking themselves just what happened to send the ghost into orbit. It was almost as if playing Mrs. Ross's tape set it off. And that's the biggest question on their minds: Did Mrs. Ross leave out the most important part of her story? *Her* part?

A few hours later Joyce mentions that she's got some more shopping to do in town, and as much as I dread being alone with her in the car, I ask if I can bum a lift. As it turns out, we drive into town mostly in silence. It's pretty awkward but it's better than talking. She lets me out in the mall parking lot and I walk downtown, turning east at the hardware store, toward the Dyson house.

It's Kip who opens the door, surprising me with a big bear hug. It feels wonderful having his arms around me, my face against his neck, my chin on his collarbone. He's only wearing a T-shirt but he feels warm. He smells good, too. I let out an involuntary sigh, which I hope he doesn't hear, and feel myself go kind of limp. I don't want him to let me go. When he does, I sway slightly before straightening up, a little embarrassed, and say hello. I have to force myself to snap out of this trance. It was just a friendly hug, after all. But wow!

"Dad's downstairs in his cave. I'm pretty sure he's been awake most of the night."

"I know I was. How's the neck?"

"Better. I'll live."

"Good. You'd better."

We head through the kitchen, past the counter and sink full of dishes, and downstairs through the basement door. "Watch your step," says Kip.

"Watch your head," says Morris from down below. "How are you, Amelia? I felt bad about just leaving you yesterday. Are you holding up?"

He's sitting on the couch. A bunch of handwritten papers are on the table in front of him, along with an empty coffee cup. The cameras are nearby, at his feet. I don't think he ever did get a shot of anything. He looks even more haggard than usual, his dark grey hair pointing every which way and big bags under his eyes. Both he and Kip look rough and unshaven, except in Kip's case that looks pretty hot. Morris just looks unhinged. He invites me to sit down and Kip remains standing, leaning against the door frame. I take a seat on the couch.

"I'm okay. But I'm sorry I was such a baby yesterday. Joyce just pushes these buttons with me, and I don't know, I want to bawl. I'm sorry about melting down. Kip's the one who almost got lynched." We both look up at Kip, standing and shuffling his feet. He looks agitated. But why wouldn't he?

"I hear you didn't sleep much last night either," I say to Morris.

He smiles and shrugs. "I'll admit it was pretty . . . well, frightening at the time." He's still looking at Kip. "But I think some good came of it. Straightened out my back." He touches an ear to a shoulder and winces a bit. "Better than a chiropractor, pulling on that damn rope." His deep, gravelly voice still manages to sound as laid-back as a cowboy watching over a herd of cattle.

"I'm thinking about putting in a call to Emily Telford. It's time we talked about that barn coming down. Also, I'm thinking we should call Dorothy Ross again. Now that there are a few new questions to ask." He riffles through some of the papers in front of him, looking for her phone number. "I thought I'd call her while you guys are here. But first, Amelia, did anything else happen yesterday that you didn't have a chance to tell us about? And what was that about Ethan showing up, by the way? Jesus, what timing! Anything we should know?"

"About Ethan? Not much. He's just a natural-born snoop who's always trying to figure out what everyone else is up to. But I did want to tell you about something I saw after the rope fell and we'd got it off Kip's neck. You know when you started climbing up the side of the stall? I saw him. The same one I saw before, hanging from the rafters. This time he was up there looking down at us, and one side of his head and face was covered with blood. It was like there was a hole blown in his head. It was like . . . well, it was like the injury I imagine Willy had, when he shot himself. That's what it looked like to me, anyway. That was when I screamed at you, Morris, and you stopped and jumped back down, thank God."

"Your scream scared the hell out of me. But I guess that explains it."

"Yeah. And when I spoke with Willy, he seemed to know the killer ghost personally—back when he was alive, I mean. He seemed really freaked by him. He called him Jimmy."

"Jimmy? So now he has a name."

"Oh, and by the way, Willy said there's no girl ghost in the barn."

"Well, I think that's because our mystery girl isn't a ghost. It's Mrs. Ross." Morris closes his eyes for a moment, then turns to me. "I'm afraid your grandmother is right: the barn is completely off limits. The Telfords need to take it down, and the sooner the better. I'll tell them whatever I have to, to get them to move on it."

I've been trying not to think about this, but I knew it might come up eventually. My heart sinks. What happens to Matthew if the barn is destroyed? I'm not ready to face that.

My worry must show on my face, because Morris adds, "I'm sorry, Amelia." Kip is looking at me with a strange expression, but he doesn't say anything.

Morris continues, "I don't think we can stand by while some unsuspecting family buys that property, knowing what we know. I'd like to see the barn torn down immediately."

"With a wrecking ball," Kip mutters.

I turn to Kip. "I don't blame you for feeling that way, but let's just think about this. Is the problem really the barn, or is it the location? Morris, I thought your research pointed to lines in the landscape where ghosts tend to appear. Ley lines."

"Right," Morris says, sounding cautious, like he doesn't trust where I'm going with this.

"So maybe getting rid of the barn wouldn't make any difference. Maybe the ghosts would just hang out in the field."

"Or maybe they'd get back on course, crossing over to some afterworld." Kip must be paying more attention to his dad's theories than he lets on. "Maybe this barn is what's holding them up."

Morris cuts in. "Well, we don't know for sure if getting rid of the barn would solve anything, true. But there's a long tradition of destroying haunted houses, and maybe that's because it works. Maybe a building becomes transformed by the presence of ghosts, becomes like hallowed ground."

"What do you mean? Isn't that something religious?"

"Well, the expression 'hallowed ground' used to mean the ground was holy or blessed. Like at a sacred site. But maybe the true meaning of 'hallowed' is closer to Halloween, as in 'spirit-ridden.' It could be that a haunted place loses its innocence—becomes hallowed in a bad way, in other words—and the damage can't be undone. The place can't be saved. And it becomes part of the problem."

"But what if there was a way to get rid of Jimmy and leave the barn as it is? I mean, if the other ghosts aren't hurting anybody, can't we leave them in peace? Shouldn't we be thinking about how to do that?"

"Okay, so there are only friendly ghosts holed up in the barn. Then what?" says Kip. He's starting to sound irritated.

"Well, what if—I'm just saying—what if a ghost could actually, maybe, get used to his situation, and start to feel comfortable, even? Being a ghost among living people. Couldn't that happen?" Both

Morris and Kip are looking at me strangely now, like they don't know what to think. "I'm just wondering." They must know I'm talking about Matthew. They're not stupid.

"Then there's that other mystery," says Kip, his eyes steady on me. "Why does Amelia care more about the dead than the living?"

I'm speechless. Morris shoots a concerned look at Kip, like something's just occurred to him. Then he turns to me.

"Let's forget about the barn for a bit and focus on Mrs. Ross." He gets off the couch and moves to his desk to make the phone call. He says he's going to have to be a little more honest with her this time about what we're really up to.

While he's dialing the number, Kip takes a seat beside me on the couch and his arm goes up along the back, behind my head. He leans over to me and in a low voice, so he won't interrupt the phone call, he asks where my "boyfriend" was during that "magic rope trick" yesterday. "I'm curious," he says. "Was he rooting for me, do you think? Or maybe just enjoying the show?" His face is very close to mine, making me nervous.

I try to stay cool. "Once everything went crazy, I was pretty focused on you and the rope," I say. "I didn't see anyone after that, except Jimmy with half his head blown off. But you know, maybe Matthew did help. Because he says he was the one who let loose the rope when Jack was going to hang himself with it. He probably saved Jack's life, so it's possible he saved yours too."

"So still your superhero, then?" Why is Kip acting so hostile?

"Well, I can't just abandon him to a wrecking ball."

"Why not? Because he might get hurt? He's dead, Amelia."

Looking into his angry blue eyes, I'm lost for words. I turn away to watch Morris on the phone, talking in a low, intense voice. Kip taps lightly on my chin to get my attention again.

"Has it ever occurred to you that maybe ghosthood can change a person's character? Bring out his dark side?"

"Matthew doesn't have a dark side."

"Ah, I see. Well, the rest of us mortals tend to." I resist responding. It's not his fault if he doesn't know the real Matthew. "Amelia, you are going to stay out of the barn from now on, right? Will you promise me? You know yourself, I could have died in there yesterday."

"I know, Kip. Believe me, it's all I've been thinking about. But I don't know if I can promise."

"Well, sometimes you've got to make a decision even when you don't know for sure. I'm serious. I'll burn the barn down myself tomorrow if you can't stay out of it." He pulls his arm away and straightens up. I didn't think he could be this aggressive.

I get up and walk over to one of Morris's bookshelves and start checking out the titles. I don't want to feel angry at him, but I do. I glance back at him on the couch. He's looking away and seems upset.

"Well, that's not good." Morris puts down the phone. "She just hung up on me."

"What? Are you sure she hung up?" I ask. "Maybe it was an accident."

"Preceded by the words 'Please don't ever call me again'? No, she was seriously pissed off."

"What was it that upset her?"

"Well, I told her that more than a few young men have died in that barn, not just her brother. She didn't seem to want to hear that. But when I asked if she'd ever been called Dot, that's when I really hit a nerve. She got angry and cut me off. Said she had to go and told me never to call her back. I doubt we'll get anything more from her."

"That's awful! I can't believe Mrs. Ross would act like that."

Kip finally speaks up. "Maybe we don't need Mrs. Ross. I mean, we found out a lot about the other deaths through our own research. Maybe there's a 'Jimmy' buried in the death records too."

Morris nods slowly. "This trouble started before Willy's death, that's for sure. And Mrs. Ross is caught up in it somehow. She's afraid of something."

"Afraid?" says Kip. "Or feeling guilty?"

A short while later Kip takes me home, but he barely says a word during the drive. He's angry with me, and I know it's because he doesn't want me going back into the barn. But if the barn is coming down soon, I've got to go in one more time, by myself. If only to say goodbye.

He pulls into my driveway and stops the car.

"Kip?" I reach over to touch his arm but he stiffens, so I pull back. "Kip, why are you so angry? I'm sorry if—"

"Don't be," he says, cutting me off. "This whole ghost world of yours . . . I guess I just don't get it. I mean, you're a psychic sixteen-year-old with a dead superhero boyfriend, and I don't know what the hell I'm doing with you. I can't handle it." He seems to relax a bit, then looks at me with a sad smile. "It's just that I can't compete with a ghost. That's all."

"I don't know what you mean. You don't have to compete with Matthew." I'm feeling panicky. "Besides, he's not my boyfriend."

"Really? Does he know that?"

"There's no competition, Kip. Matthew's different . . . so different from you."

He rolls his eyes and I hear him take a deep breath. "You should go now," he says softly.

I get out of the car and walk into the house like a zombie. Joyce is yelling from the kitchen, asking if anyone's seen her new cigarette lighter. That's the second one to disappear lately, she complains.

"Maybe you should check under Ethan's pillow," I mutter as I head upstairs.

She shoots me this look, like it's going to be my fault if Ethan's acting any weirder than usual. I'd like to remind her that he's always weird, all by himself, but I take one look at her face and decide to keep my mouth shut. I head for my bedroom and shut the door behind me.

I don't know what to do about Kip. But I can't worry about that right now. I've got to see Matthew. I've got to warn him that the barn may be destroyed, and I don't know what effect that will have on him. I can't just stand by, not caring what happens to him. He still means too much to me.

29

hen I woke up this morning, tired after lying awake for hours last night, I found a short e-mail from Kip in my inbox, sent after midnight. He'd spent some time in the archives yesterday, he wrote, and found a death notice, dated September 1941, for James Wallace, a seventeen-year-old farmhand from Saskatchewan. Wallace was found in a barn on 12th Line in Grey County. Cause of death was listed as suicide. Hanging.

He added that he was thinking of going on a last-minute vacation to Mexico with some Chicago friends, flying out Boxing Day. Then he said he was sorry about being in such a bad mood yesterday, and told me to forget what he'd said. What did he mean? Which part? Was that supposed to make me feel better? It didn't.

I can't believe I actually have to go to school this week. Only a few more days before the Christmas break, thank God, but what a waste of time. My head feels a million miles away from the classroom. When I'm not thinking about Kip or Matthew, I'm thinking about James Wallace. What was up with him? Did some ghost make him kill himself, just like the others? Or was he the very first, the one who started it all?

After school I decide to run down to the archives office before it closes. I know I may find Kip, but that isn't the only reason I want to go. I have some new research to do.

A quick scan from the entrance and I immediately catch sight of Kip's thick, dark blond hair bent over a file, hanging down long enough to hide his face. He looks up briefly as I walk toward him, my heart picking up speed, but he doesn't say hi. His supervisor is nearby, and he treats me like I'm just another person dropping in to look something up.

He seems tired, and he acts cool and distant. "Can I help you?" he asks politely. I can't tell what he's feeling. I try to smile but I'm embarrassed, feeling my face go warm. I decide to go along with his professional tone.

"I'm just wondering if I could do a search, a newspaper search, on a young man who died about seventy years ago near here. Just wondering if any reporter from a Grey County paper wrote an article about him. The name was James Wallace."

"Ah." He lifts his eyebrows. "Well, let's see." I follow him to another part of the office and he shows me a chair in front of an old microfilm machine.

"No search engine I can just plug his name into?" I ask innocently.

"Afraid not. But you have a date to work with, right?" Strange, I think, pretending we don't know each other. I can't help it—I search his face for some kind of sign, and our eyes meet. The corners of his mouth twitch, almost into a smile, then he looks away. "You know how this works, right?" he asks, pointing to the machine.

"I don't know how anything works," I tell him.

He smirks. "You'll figure it out. Call me if it gives you trouble." He walks back to the front desk. I watch him cross the floor until he's out of sight.

My hunch pays off. There's a whole article written by a Mrs. Ruth Berger about the short, tragic life of Jimmy Wallace. He was taken into foster care by a family in Meaford at the age of twelve, transferred by the Children's Aid Society from somewhere in Manitoba. "What many never knew about," the article reads, "was the notorious case that had stunned a rural community and filled the town papers out west." Turns out he was the victim of brutal abuse as a child. His stepfather used to tie him up and beat him in the back shed, leaving him locked up in there, sometimes for days on end, without food. The stepfather also beat a dog to death, and that was the last straw for the neighbours. They called in the police, who discovered the full extent of his crimes against the boy, and the stepfather was thrown in jail. "The tragedy," wrote Mrs. Berger, "was that all the good Christian kindness of the Meaford family who took that child into their home couldn't undo the damage of years of abject cruelty. In the end, in spite of five years of loving support, the boy took his own life, as if to finish the work of the devil he'd called his father."

I make two photocopies of the article, folding one in half and writing Kip's name on it. I hand it to the archive supervisor, asking if she would mind passing it to Kip Dyson. He's only twenty feet away, standing behind a bookcase, hidden from view. I can see the top of his head as it turns my way, but he stays where he is.

I pick up the phone and dial a number with shaky fingers.

"Can I please speak to Mrs. Dee Ross? It . . . it's Amelia Mackenzie calling. Thank you." I wait, with an eye on the digital clock in the corner of my computer screen. Ten minutes go by. Then twelve. I'm thinking I'll wait three more minutes when someone finally picks up the receiver.

"Hello?"

"Mrs. Ross, I didn't think you'd answer."

"I didn't think you'd call." She does not sound happy. But resigned, maybe.

"Mrs. Ross, I am so sorry to dredge up the painful past like this. I really am. But at least four young men have killed themselves in your father's barn. One of them was my best friend. And a fifth who tried and failed was my brother Jack. I'm afraid it could happen again, and I want to try to stop it before it does." I pause, and when she doesn't say anything or hang up on me, I plunge ahead. "I need to find out why this is happening, and who's behind it. It could save lives. Does the name James Wallace mean anything to you? Jimmy Wallace?"

There's a very long pause. I work at being patient.

"Where did you get that name?" she whispers.

"I'm not sure you want to know." I wait for her to say something, but she doesn't. "There are five ghosts in the barn. One of them is your brother. I got the name Jimmy from him."

This time the silence lasts even longer. I wish she would say something. I try again.

"Do you remember a boy named Jimmy Wallace?"

Finally she begins to talk. Her voice is weak and shaking. "He was hired by my father to help out on the farm. Because Willy was going away to war. My father was going to need an extra hand, and he hired Jimmy."

"Jimmy Wallace?"

"Yes. Jimmy was from out west. He'd been staying with family in Meaford."

"Can you tell me what you remember about him?"

"Just that he was sick. He wasn't well. That's all. He wasn't right in the head. And . . . well, he killed himself. When he was only seventeen."

"He killed himself? In your barn?"

I can hear what sounds like gasping.

"He hanged himself in the barn. From the rafters." She adds, "Or that's what I was told. I wasn't there."

"Mrs. Ross, I know this isn't any of my business, but is it possible that Jimmy Wallace was in love with you?"

"He *thought* he was in love with me," she says, her voice trembling. "But it wasn't true love. It was more like an obsession. We . . . we went out a few times. Not real dates, you understand. I was waiting for Philip to come back from the front. That's all I cared about. I was just trying to be nice to Jimmy, but he took everything so seriously. He misunderstood everything. And he was so . . . so presumptuous. He started to get angry, to frighten me. But he was more vulnerable than we knew. It was all a big mistake."

"A mistake?"

"I confided in Willy. He was always so protective of me, and he was angry that Jimmy wouldn't leave me alone, with him about to go off to the war. He only wanted to teach him a lesson, he said. I regretted it soon enough . . . I've always regretted it. You have no idea."

"What happened? Did Willy do something to Jimmy?"

"You have to believe me. We didn't know. Nobody knew. Not until after, when it was too late."

I hear another shuddering breath. "I told Jimmy I'd meet him one evening in the barn. But it was a trap, and Willy was there instead. He told Jimmy to leave me alone. Said he was going to teach him a lesson. He tied him to one of the posts and left him there overnight. We didn't realize the harm it would do. A couple of Willy's friends heard about it and showed up at the barn later in the night to taunt him. Willy didn't know about that. It pushed Jimmy over the edge. The next morning Willy went in to untie him. I stood by the door, worried, already regretting it. When Jimmy saw me, he got hysterical. He was all wet with tears and urine, screaming for me to get out. *Get out!* I can still hear it." There's a long silence, broken only by the sound of her uneven breath.

"Did Jimmy call you Dot?"

A long pause. "Yes, he did. But why does it matter?"

"Because it's proof that there's a connection between him and the others who died in that barn. If he's the only one who ever called you by that name, that is."

"He's the only one." There's another pause. "Except once."

"Who was it, Mrs. Ross?"

"Willy. On the night he died." Her voice sounds so strained.

"Willy called you Dot?"

"Yes. Yes, Amelia, he did. Now I've told you everything."

"Can I just ask what he said to you when he called you Dot?"

"He said he wanted me to meet him later that night. In the barn. I can't tell you any more than that." There's another long pause, and then she starts to plead with me. "I've lived a very long life, Amelia. I was never blessed with children, but my marriage was a blessing. Fifty-five years with my beloved Philip. He was the love of my life. My only love. I'm an old woman now—I'm almost ninety—and I just want to live out my life in peace. Have some compassion, please."

"I am so sorry, Mrs. Ross. I really am. But I need to ask one last question: Did you meet your brother in the barn that night?"

"No, I didn't, and I wish I had." Her voice is breaking. "I've never been able to forgive myself for that."

"Why didn't you?"

"I'm sorry. I can't go on."

"Was it because he was talking like Jimmy?"

The line goes dead.

———

A tragedy that happened a long time ago has been repeating itself ever since. But how to stop it? What will it take? I know what I have to do, but I've got an hour of daylight, tops, to do it in.

Sneaking out of the house won't be easy. I check the backyard through my window, and sure enough, Joyce is out there with the horses. With my hand on my bedroom doorknob I try to compose myself, put on a casual face. I'm just going for a walk. I won't be long. Hopefully, no one will notice.

I open my door and there's Ethan standing on the landing, staring right at me. Like he was staring at my closed door before I even opened it.

"What's up, Ethan?" He continues to stare at me. "Played any video games with Jack today? I'm sure he's got time." I close my bedroom door behind me and walk by him. "If Joyce asks where I am, I'm going out for a bit," I say, heading downstairs. He says nothing. Jeez, he's really clammed up these last few days. Normally he's like a yappy dog. Maybe he's finally becoming a teenager or something. About time, I guess.

I grab my coat from the front hall closet and walk past Jack's bedroom door, which is shut. I give it a tap. "Just heading out for a walk, Jack," I yell through the closed door. I hear him say okay. "If anyone calls, I'll be back soon."

I need to talk to Matthew. But I also want to see if, with Matthew's help, I can talk to Jimmy Wallace. Find out what it will take to convince him to stop what he's been doing and go away. I mean, why assume you can't reason with a ghost? The little bit of experience I've had tells me ghosts aren't any more unreasonable than the rest of us. Just more stuck in their ways. And confused. Maybe Jimmy needs to have a few things clarified. Like the fact that a lot of years have passed since he died, and even though his life was horrible, he should really move on. Matthew says he can protect me. I'm counting on that.

Ten minutes later I'm approaching the crest of the hill, and I'm getting that familiar stomach ache. As much as I've come to hate the sight of it, the Telford barn is Matthew's home now. I don't know if he could exist outside of it. It may be the only life he has left in this world. If I don't watch out for him, who will?

In the barn everything is just as we left it, right down to the overturned wooden crate and the rope lying in a heap. I stand just inside the door and try to read the atmosphere. It's impossible, because I've brought so much tension along with me. I can't tell what's me and what's the barn. I stand perfectly still for, like, five minutes, trying to calm myself enough to sense something.

Finally, when I'm sure I'm not hearing or feeling anything, I take a few more steps inside and whisper Matthew's name. I stop again and listen. There are footsteps coming up behind me and I spin around. He's standing right there, where I just walked. As my eyes get more accustomed to the dim light, I can see his worried expression. For a change, he's the first to speak.

"Where have you been? Are you okay?"

"Me? Yes, I'm okay. My friend Kip, I think he's the one who's felt better."

Matthew doesn't say anything to that. He takes a slow step closer. "I did my best."

"Matthew, remember you said you could protect me?"

"You didn't get hurt, did you?"

"No, I guess not. I'm just saying that I'd like to count on you to protect me again."

"Of course. Forever. I've got no other plans."

"Well, let's take it a day at a time. Right now, I've come here to talk to Jimmy Wallace." I look around as I say the name, and then I say it louder, my voice filling the rafters. "Jimmy Wallace. That's his name. The boy who's responsible for all the bad stuff that's happened in this barn for decades. Four of his victims are in this barn. Am I right? The ghosts of four guys who killed themselves in horrible ways because they were possessed by Jimmy at the time. Where is he, Matthew? I want to talk to him."

I'm hyper-alert, bracing myself for anything. Oh my God, my legs feel weak!

"I haven't seen him lately," Matthew says simply.

"What?" I'm stumped. "Okay, fine. I'll just hang out with you for a while and see if he shows himself."

"Sure. Okay." Matthew perks up. "Make yourself comfortable. Pull yourself up here and relax." He gestures to the platform running along the side of the wall like it's his bachelor pad.

I take a look at it and shrug. Why not? I grab the wooden crate I used to help Kip when he was being strangled, and as I do, a flashback of cold fear hits me. I have to remind myself that Kip is all right. I pull the crate over to the side, get up on it and hoist myself onto the platform. It's made of boards covered in a thin layer of old straw. I crawl toward the back and lean along the wall, like I've seen Matthew do. He leans against the edge of the platform, his elbows on it, chin resting on his hands, facing me. He's smiling.

"I've been thinking," he says.

"Really? What about?"

"You know how everything happens for a reason?"

"Uh, not really." Wow, déjà vu. I feel for a second like I'm back in the library or the cafeteria, about to have a philosophical argument with him. It's a warm memory.

"You know how there's always a larger plan, even though we don't always know what that plan is?"

"Matthew, I feel like we've covered this ground before, and we didn't exactly come to an agreement last time. What's your point?"

"I've become a ghost, and you can see ghosts. Don't you think there's a larger reason for that?"

"Are you saying you became a ghost so I could see you? Or I can see ghosts so you could become one? Or what? Because I still think we were better off before."

"I'm saying it's destiny. We belong together."

It's kind of ironic, listening to him describe exactly what I felt before he died: that we belonged together. But I realize that something's changed, and it's not just him. I think maybe I've changed too.

"Matthew, where is Jimmy? Can't you look around for him or something? I don't have much time today."

"I don't know where he is. He's not here."

"What do you mean, he's not here? He's not in the barn?"

"He's not in the barn. At least, I don't think so."

"Well, where did he go? Did he just walk out?"

"I don't know." He sounds a little exasperated. "Amelia, do you love me? Do you still love me?"

"Of course I do, Matthew. What do you think?" He's looking at me so intently that it's hard to meet his eyes. "But seriously, what's happened to Jimmy? Has he ever just left the barn before? How come he can come and go, and you can't?"

"Because I love you, Amelia. I'm sorry I didn't tell you sooner."

Now I'm the one feeling exasperated. "Matthew, I'm sorry but I can't talk about this with you now. I need to find Jimmy. It's important. You have to tell me where he's gone."

Matthew shrugs. "I'm not sure," he says.

This is ruining my big plan, and I feel deflated. I'd had to screw up so much courage to walk back into this barn. I'm exhausted, and I find myself starting to let go. I shut my eyes for a moment. When I open them, Matthew is up on the platform with me, only a few feet away, leaning back against the wall and watching me.

"Is it that guy? The one who got strung up? Your new friend?"

"What? What about him?"

"Is he the one you're thinking about?"

"Kip?" I hear myself sigh. Do I think about Kip? Yes, too much. "I don't know. I don't know, Matthew." I feel so tired all of a sudden. "But no. I wasn't thinking about Kip just now. You are my best friend in the world."

"Forever?"

That catches me off guard. "Yes. I mean, if possible. I don't know . . . I mean, I'm afraid that eventually you may have to go somewhere else. Another world, even. It may not be something either of us can control."

Hearing myself say that, it sounds so unreal. Then I picture the barn getting destroyed. What effect might that have on Matthew?

"There's something you should know. Sooner or later, people are going to take this barn down. It could happen any day. Do you know what I mean? I'm just warning you."

"Who do you love more, me or Kip?"

It's like he's not even listening to me. "Matthew, I really don't have the energy to get into this with you. I'm so exhausted, I feel like I'm going to pass out. But I'm trying to tell you that when the time comes, you may have to move on. You may not have a choice."

"Why are you so exhausted?"

"Because I'm having trouble sleeping at night. Go figure!"

"Don't worry. Just rest for a while. I'll watch over you," he whispers. "You're safe."

I lie back. "I just want you to know that nobody could ever make me forget what you've meant to me these last few years. Your friendship saved me from total despair. If it weren't for you, I'd probably have quit school after grade ten. Or worse. Also, you were the first boy I ever lusted after. There's never going to be anyone else like you."

"You say that like it's all in the past."

I look at his face and I don't know how to respond. In my head I admit I've been having doubts. *I'm no longer sure it would have worked out between us, Matthew. Romantically, I mean. We never did see eye to eye, not really. Maybe we were always going to be better as best friends.* But these are thoughts I can't say out loud.

"Where is everyone else?" I ask. I'm slumping, half lying down on the straw platform, propping up my head in my hand.

"Around. They're around. Don't worry about them. You're tired, have a nap. I'll watch over you."

I guess five minutes can't hurt. I lie back in the straw, remembering Matthew in history class. I close my eyes, just for a minute, and picture his face as he answers a question, hopeful and confident. I remember the two of us sitting at the back of the library after school, giggling and bickering, me elbowing him when he teased me. I remember getting disapproving looks from a teacher when we laughed too loudly. I remember searching for him across a crowded school assembly, sharing a smile like there was no one else around.

I feel the gentle sensation of a cool wave wash over me. I'm slightly dizzy, like the barn is spinning slowly and I'm floating, breeze in my hair. There is movement all around me, something fluttering over me. The straw gets softer and softer, and I sink deeper into it. From the corner of my eye, I see the end of the rope slithering like a snake, uncoiling in the middle of the barn floor and gliding softly toward the platform. Then it's gone. When it reappears, it's on the platform, moving through the straw. Where is Matthew? It's getting closer and closer, until I can feel it moving against my thigh and wrapping tightly around my legs. In a spasm of kicking and screaming I wake up, scrambling to my hands and knees in a panic. I gasp for air, a sharp pain in my chest.

"Matthew!"

He's standing on the platform, looking down at me, four dark holes across his stomach, his shirt drenched in dark red blood. There's blood dripping from his nose and the side of his mouth; his face is as white as milk. I scream and scramble to the edge of the platform and over, falling hard onto the ground five feet below. When I look up at him again, the wounds are gone. The blood is gone. His hands are raised, palms toward me, like he's trying to calm me down.

"Oh jeez, Amelia. I'm so sorry. I don't know what happened there."

"I . . . I have to get out of here," I say, my voice shaking. I'm holding my shoulder, pulling myself up to my feet, feeling pain in my hip from where I fell. "It's not your fault, Matthew." I don't know what else to say.

I limp as quickly as I can for the door. But before I reach it, he appears in front of me again.

"Jeez, Matthew, are you trying to scare me on purpose?"

"Amelia, no. Don't be afraid of me. Please. Think about it. You'll probably be seeing ghosts your whole life. I can be useful to you. I can see ghosts now too."

"I hear you, Matthew. But right now, I just need to get out of here."

"I love you, Amelia," I hear him say as I run outside and head for the road.

30

I don't know how much of that was a dream and how much was a waking nightmare. But I do know I've been having nightmares ever since. It's not like I can tell Morris what happened. And Kip? Forget it. I'm aching to see him, though. I've phoned and left messages for him twice. Why won't he call? I've never felt so torn up inside.

Joyce is chopping red and green bell peppers for the Christmas Eve pizza—a tradition in our family. My mom started it when we were really young, and we won't let Joyce kill it. The pizza toppings have to be arranged in the shape of a tree, although Joyce always manages to make the star at the top look more like a crab or a lobster.

I have to hand it to her, though—she's really getting into the Christmas spirit this year. She even brought home a fresh-cut spruce and set it up in the front window of the living room. I'm putting handfuls of silver tinsel on the boughs, thinking about how it's been a while since I've felt any magic at Christmastime.

But when I see Kip through the branches, turning up the driveway in Morris's car, it feels like a Christmas miracle. My heart leaps and I literally run to the door, too excited to control myself. Talk about a mood change. I couldn't be more grateful.

He comes inside to admire the tree, says hi to Ethan and gets introduced to Jack, whom he hasn't met before. Then he pulls a wrapped Christmas present from one of the big pockets of his coat, holding it out for me to open. It's a CD of Bob Marley's greatest hits, the words *One Love* written across the cover. He kisses me on the forehead. "Merry Christmas." Damn, I wish I had something for him.

Kip says that after dinner tomorrow Morris is going to drive him down to Buffalo, where he'll catch the train to Chicago to have Christmas with his mom and stepdad. On Boxing Day he's catching a plane. Heading south for a week with friends, he says. Somewhere in Mexico. I don't register where. Which friends? I don't ask.

I pull on my coat and boots and we walk out back to see the horses. Glancing at his watch, Kip says he doesn't have much time. He needs to get back to have dinner with Morris. Not much time? Suddenly I can't think of what I want to say. I'm trying not to imagine him on a beach surrounded by girls in bikinis. Instead, I focus on the cool hat he's wearing. It's wine-coloured and made of wool, a cap with long flaps going down the sides, the kind they make in Peru. It suits his cheekbones. His shaggy gold hair is peeking out around it, and there's a shadow of a beard on his face. His eyes are so blue it hurts to look at them.

"I like your hat," I say.

"Morris has got a venison roast in the oven," he says. "Venison is his idea of a Grey County Christmas. In honour of all the deer in the manger."

"Yeah, right. We're doing the traditional turkey thing tomorrow. In honour of the turkeys."

"You know only two of the four Gospels mention Jesus's birth?"

"Let's not start that," I suggest.

"Yeah, and they're quite different."

"How's your rope burn?" I push down on his coat collar, leaning in for a quick peek at his neck. I touch the skin lightly, impulsively. "It looks pretty good," I say. Understatement.

He smiles at me. "One has shepherds and angels, the other has three kings." But then he looks down and the smile fades from his face. He leans against the paddock fence and Marley and Ponyboy saunter over to listen in. He stands there watching them. I have the feeling something's on his mind—he wants to say something—and I brace myself.

He clears his throat. "Actually, I came by to tell you that my mom's been bugging me to get back to school. Stop slacking off, as she puts it. So I've decided to register for a few winter-term classes. Back home." He turns away and starts stroking Ponyboy's nose.

"Classes? When?"

"January."

"Really?" *Oh my God.* "That's . . . soon."

"Yeah." He's still not looking at me. "I wanted to tell you in person."

I'm reeling. "So you're . . . you're moving back to Chicago? Like, right away? You're not coming back to Owen Sound after Christmas?"

He shakes his head, just barely. Wow. I feel crushed. *Are you just going to disappear?*

I feel like I'm going to cry, but I'm fighting it. "So soon Grey County will be a distant memory." I've got to stay cool. *Am I ever going to see you again?*

"Oh, I don't know about that. You underestimate the impact Grey County has had on me." And he touches his fingers to his lip, like it's still sore.

I think about that kiss. "I was hoping that was a memory you'd forget." *But I won't.* Then it slips out. "Is Serena going to Mexico too?"

Argh! I can't believe I said that out loud. What a jerk I am! As if I have a right to be jealous. He looks genuinely surprised. Confused, even. He's trying to form a word but nothing's coming out.

"I'm sorry," I say quickly. "I honestly don't know why I said that. I'm just feeling very, very . . . stupid today. I don't even know who Serena is." Okay, that just made it worse. "And I don't want to know either. It's absolutely none of my business." He looks close to saying something now, so I rush on. "Okay, okay. I admit it." I've got to explain. "I googled your name once and some Facebook pictures came up. That's all. Nothing more. I always knew you must have a girlfriend on the hook. Or two or three or whatever." Could this get more awkward? "So I really hope you have a good time. Wear sunscreen and a hat. Stay clear of sharks . . . and tap water. At least, that's what I hear. I've never been." He's looking at me with a sad smile. "But I'm . . . I'm sorry about the punch." *More than you know, Kip.* "I hope the girls in Chicago are less aggressive. I mean, I hope you find happiness." Oh God, I really *am* about to start crying. I can't believe how jealous I feel. Even the horses are gawking at me like they're watching a train wreck.

He reaches for my hand and I give it to him, surprised and grateful that he doesn't seem offended. He holds it for a moment, then lets go.

"No, I deserved the punch. In fact, I strongly recommend that's how you deal with *every* guy who tries to kiss you from now on. Promise?"

It's hard not to be amused at that, and for a moment we smile at each other. But then he looks away again. I have to say something. *Anything.*

"But what . . . what about your job?"

"I gave notice yesterday. I was going to take the next two weeks off anyway." He looks at his watch again and says he really should be on his way. We start walking toward the front of the house. I don't know what else to say. My thoughts are racing.

"Kip, this all feels so sudden. Is there something you're not telling me?" He stops, looking down at the ground, then shakes his head. "Is it because of what happened in the barn last week?"

I look into his face, searching. I see him swallow, see his eyes narrow. "No. That just makes this harder," he finally says.

"But is it something I did? Are you angry? At me?"

He shakes his head. "Look, I just think I'd better get back to school, that's all. Really, these last few months have been an experience I won't forget."

"But what about Morris? What does he say?"

"Believe me, Dad thinks it's for the best." He sounds a touch bitter.

"He does?" *What does that mean?* "I don't get it."

"It's not important."

We stop in the driveway. Standing side by side in silence, we stare out across 12th Line at the white fields and winter sunset. I'm trying to hold myself together. Then Kip turns and faces me. "Look, Amelia." He takes me by the arms, holding tight, and bends forward slightly to look at me at eye level. "Believe what you want about me, but I want you to remember one thing: you can count on me. If you ever need anything. A friend. A third brother. A sparring partner." He makes circles with his fists at me in a pretend boxing pose. One fist lands lightly on my chin and he gives it a little nudge. "Whatever.

You're the boss. If you ever need me, just call. Ten years from now, even. Okay?" My eyes are on his boots. They half turn away from me, then gently kick at the snow. "I care about what happens to you."

A third brother? Are you serious? I keep my head down so he can't see my face. *Ten years? You'll have a wife and kids by then!* A tear breaks free and trickles down the side of my nose, and I brush it away. And then it really hits me. *What a fool I am! I think I've fallen in love with you, Kip. How did it get this bad?*

He reaches down and takes hold of my hand again, but this time he brings it up to his lips, holding his mouth to my knuckles in a hard kiss. I realize the closest I'll ever come to Kip Dyson is that moment just before I punched him in the mouth. Then he lets me go again.

"I've gotta run," he mumbles, turning toward the car. "Be careful, Amelia," he says, looking beyond me, his eyes shiny and unfocused. I hold my breath. The pain builds in my throat, and before I can stop myself it overwhelms me and a tiny sob escapes, muffled by the sound of the car door slamming shut. The engine starts and the headlights cut into the dusk. He backs out onto 12th Line. I catch a small flicker of his hand at the car window and I lift mine, too late. He drives off. He's gone. He only came to say goodbye.

I walk back toward the paddock, straight up to the fence, where Marley stretches his head forward to console me. *Marley.* I've never thought about it before. I figured Joyce had named him after the ghost in *A Christmas Carol.* I wrap my arms around his huge neck and bury my face in his mane, crying into his warm coat.

What I meant to say, Kip, was, I'll never forget you.

I stay with the horses until the tears are no longer flowing. When I'm finally together enough to risk going inside, I can hear Bob Marley singing "No Woman No Cry."

"I hope you don't mind," Joyce yells from the kitchen. She means about playing my new CD. "It's been a while."

I can smell the Christmas pizza in the oven. Right now, though, I don't care about dinner. I head straight up to my room, feeling like somebody just turned up the dial on the earth's gravity. My knees give out and I fall heavily onto my bed.

After about ten minutes of me sitting there paralyzed and quietly weeping, my cellphone rings. I take a deep breath, then another, and answer it with a weak "Hello?" It's Jack, phoning from the land line downstairs.

"I'm in my room," he says. "Can we talk?"

"Sure. I'll be down in a few minutes."

I head for the washroom to rinse the tears from my face and check out my red eyes and nose in the mirror. *Who did you think Kip Dyson was, anyway? Your boyfriend? What an imagination!*

Feeling numb, I tap on Jack's bedroom door. I can see Ethan out of the corner of my eye, sitting in the living room in the dark with the Christmas lights on. Christmas blues, I guess. Jack tells me to come in and motions for me to close the door behind me.

"Are you okay?" he asks.

"Sure, fine. Just tired."

"Okay. You look kind of pale and sick or something." He's sitting in his wheelchair at his desk, and I take a seat on his bed. "I wanted to talk to you about something and I don't want Ethan to hear." He looks irritated and lowers his voice to a whisper. "He asked me about the barn earlier today. Asked me if I ever plan to go back in. It worried me the way he said it. Too interested. I have a feeling he's planning on going there himself."

He's picked up a large pencil from his desk and he's twirling it between his fingers. There's some kind of nervousness there that seems out of character for him. Like Joyce when she's wishing she could have a cigarette.

"Jack, is everything okay with you? I mean, are you settling back in? Are you feeling all right?"

"Gee, Amelia, let's see. I'm walking with braces and canes. I can barely go upstairs to use the washroom. It takes me forever to get dressed or anything. What do you think?"

"I'm sorry. You've handled this so much better than anyone else would, you almost make it look easy. But I know it's not."

"Don't mind me, I'm just grumpy. By the way, have you noticed any changes in Ethan lately? I mean, for one thing, he's not blinking and wincing anymore. It's like he's suddenly gotten over that whole facial tic phase."

"Now that you mention it, I thought something was different about him. He seems older. Maybe that experience last week had a psychological effect on him."

"So what do we do about the fascination he seems to have with the barn?"

"I don't know. Keep an eye on him? In case he has any ideas about going near it, I mean." And then it hits me. "There's no girlfriend who's dumped him lately, is there? Broken his heart? Anything like that?"

"Not a chance, I'd say. But there is a major attitude shift going on. He's not even interested in his video games this week."

There's a bang on the door that sends us both three inches off our seats. Only Joyce can knock like that.

"Christmas Eve pizza!" she yells. "Come and get it."

"Coming!" Jack yells back.

"Where the hell are my matches?" I hear her complaining as she heads back to the kitchen. I immediately think of Ethan. What's that little pyromaniac up to?

31

I've probably cried a little every day since Christmas Eve. Not a waterfall or anything, just a quiet trickle. It's like pressure keeps building and I have to release the valve. Afterwards I feel calmer. Or maybe more numb. Either way, it's better than the alternative, which would be a total flood. Between me moping around with a long face and Ethan acting like someone out of *Invasion of the Body Snatchers*, Joyce was happy when the holidays were done, that was obvious.

School has been the hardest part. In the hallways between classes, everyone seems to be talking to someone else, chatting or listening or poking someone with a pen. Everyone seems close and connected. Everyone but me. I keep on the lookout for Morgan, a friendly face, but she's always surrounded by other girls, especially Brittany, and I have to wonder if I sometimes get on her nerves. I know I kind of bring these feelings on myself, this sense of being a ghost among the living. It's an old habit, and it's hard to fight when there doesn't seem to be anything worth fighting for.

The other day in the cafeteria, Brittany decided to have some fun with me. She asked if I'd had any word from Kip lately, and I noticed that Morgan shot her an annoyed look. It was painful, especially coming from Brittany, because she so enjoys knowing how I screwed up with him. I had to say in front of everybody that he was back at university in Chicago and busy with new classes. *He has a really heavy workload*, I said with emphasis, trying to make the point that he had important stuff to attend to. It wasn't like he left town so he could hang out and do nothing somewhere else.

"I had him figured out," declared Brittany, seemingly uninterested in everything I had to say. "You could tell just looking at him how bored he was. He wasn't getting enough action. I mean, that's a guy who is used to having fun, you know?" She smiled at Morgan, a very smug look on her face. "Now, I would have got him to hang out here a little longer." A couple of the other girls at the table laughed and said things like "Oh, Brittany, you're *sooo* bad." Morgan smirked but then flicked a guilty glance my way.

"I don't know. I think there was more to Kip than that. Another side of him that maybe you didn't see." I was relieved that my voice didn't shake or crack.

"No, I'm pretty sure I checked out both sides thoroughly when you brought him to my place last fall. He was pretty hot from every angle." Everyone laughed at that. Who knew Brittany could be so witty?

The thing is, Morgan knows how I feel about Kip. I pretty much told her the truth when we went shopping at the mall last week. She was looking for January sales and I decided to buy some makeup. I'd been thinking that maybe I needed a new face—to give off less of a "weird sister" vibe—and she was thrilled to hear it. She insisted on taking control—comes from watching so many makeover shows on TV.

Morgan was suspicious about my timing, though. I tried to tell her that I was just bored with myself, which is true, but she didn't buy it. She asked if I was gearing up to make a move on Kip, and I had to tell her it was a little late for that. She thought that was tragic, of course.

"I got the feeling he was yours if you wanted him," she said. "He was waiting for you to give him a sign." She gave me a sympathetic smile when she saw my eyes filling up. "It isn't still Matthew, is it?" she asked. All I could do was shrug, like I didn't know. "That explains it." Then she told me all about what happened to her aunt after her uncle died in a boating accident. She never remarried, and Morgan's mom said it was because she could never let go of her first husband. No other guy could ever live up to the memory of him, and the older the memory got, the more perfect he became. "I know it sounds harsh," she told me, "but sooner or later you're going to have to let Matthew go. He's the one who died, not you. Don't let him keep you from having a life. Seriously."

In the end I kind of lost my nerve, so there was no big transformation. I only bought some lip gloss and mascara. Hardly enough for "before and after" photos. I told her I couldn't afford to spend more than that, but really I just felt crappy because I lose everyone I care about, sooner or later.

I haven't been back to the Telford barn since the rope dream. And even though Morris and I talk about once a week, we keep it short, and the only news he's passed on is that he spoke with Telford's daughter about knocking down the barn and she didn't take his advice very well. She said they couldn't afford to take it down unless it was done professionally, so they could recycle the old barnboard, and for that they would have to wait for better weather. He said she asked him to keep out of their business—nicely, of course.

I didn't say it to Morris, but I'm relieved the Telfords aren't in a rush. I still don't know what to do about Matthew, but I can't just abandon him to fate. And even if I don't know what it means on any realistic level, at least Matthew says he wants me. Kip only wants to be friends. But then again, Kip has so many more options than Matthew. Matthew only has me.

After Brittany said those things in the cafeteria, I was overwhelmed with sadness and regret about Kip. I kept asking myself if she was right, if things would have gone better if I'd acted differently. If I'd been more fun to be with. But then I'd remind myself that I would have embarrassed myself even more if I'd tried harder. Kip was always out of my league. End of story.

Morgan texted me after my run-in with Brittany. She said she felt bad for me and encouraged me to write to Kip. *Just send him a friendly little e-mail. What have you got to lose? Do it! Do it! DO IT!* Well, she had a point. Not much.

Dear Kip. I hope you are well. Sister Amelia.

I can't believe I just hit send. What a loser!

Ethan spends most of his time in his room now, and when he comes out he hardly talks. I think it's a weird puberty phase but Joyce has her eye on him, just in case. He'd better watch out. She's probably still got Dr. Krantz on speed-dial.

I thought about mentioning to Joyce that he's been stealing cigarettes and smoking out back, but why start a war with him? He's got plenty on me too. And he keeps giving me odd stares, like he knows even more than I think. It makes me want to booby-trap my room to see if he's been sneaking in and rifling through my stuff. Yesterday, apparently, he asked Jack if he knew what a Molotov cocktail was. Joyce overheard him and yelled, "Well, it's not something you drink."

I've been spending a lot more time out back with the horses. When Joyce isn't around, that is. It's because of something that happened the day Kip said goodbye. When I was stroking Marley's nose, I remembered how much I used to love horses when I was a little girl. I have a memory of my dad—and I don't remember much about him—hoisting me up on one of them when I was about four. That was when Joyce lived farther away, and we visited only once in a while. Soon after that, my dad had the car accident. Strange, but I don't remember anything about him at all but his big, strong hands lifting me up and setting me on the back of the horse. That's it. And I remember the horse, which was huge and gentle, standing perfectly still in Joyce's fenced field.

My problem with Joyce's horses came some years after that. I think it was when I was in grade six. Mom made me and Jack spend a few weeks on the farm one summer, and Joyce took us to work with her. It was brutal. I couldn't believe how many hours she spent each day taking care of those horses—cleaning up after them, grooming and all. It was like a slave camp, and I really resented it. That's when it first hit me how Joyce was such a drill sergeant. Jack didn't mind as much, 'cause he was a good rider, so he thought the work was worth it. But I fell off twice that summer, and I wasn't keen to feel that again, even though something was lost when I stopped riding. Some feeling I half remember when I see Joyce out back with Marley and Ponyboy. I guess, deep down, I do understand why she goes to so much trouble.

This afternoon I have coffee with Morris. His idea. He tells me he's got a dozen other ghost mysteries to investigate with my help, if I'm game for another adventure. "What do you say? Are you still interested?"

I feel less than enthusiastic. "It's just that I feel like we've got unfinished business in the Telford barn, so it's hard to think about moving on to another mystery."

"I get it, but I think we've gone as far as we can there. It's out of our hands now."

We talk a little longer. He says he's got a lot of ghost-tracking leads to follow up. Reported sightings in Grey County he'd love to investigate with me, to see if I can pick up anything supernatural. "No pressure," he says, "but it's what your mom and I started. I mean, we went on only a half-dozen outings or so before she decided she wasn't feeling up to it anymore. It was pretty amazing while it lasted, though. She was able to connect with a few ghosts and find out things I couldn't have uncovered in any other way."

Wow! I try to imagine Morris and my mom hanging out in haunted houses. It's so strange. Then he changes the subject, starts asking me about my long-term plans. Almost like he's my surrogate father or something.

"Like what?" I ask.

"Like university. You're intelligent, Amelia," he says. "You've got to start considering the next big phase of your life." And then he adds—a little cautiously, it seems—that I should probably be thinking about getting out of town, for a few years at least. Studying somewhere exotic and exciting. On an old university campus known for its ghosts, he suggests. In an old city.

I can't tell if he's serious. And I can't help wondering what the University of Chicago campus looks like.

I finally get up the nerve to ask him about Kip, trying to sound like a normal human being and not an emotional mess.

"You haven't heard from him?" He seems surprised. Then I remember that Kip said Morris thought it was a good idea for him to head back to Chicago.

"I hope you don't think I'm rude to ask, but did you encourage Kip to leave?" I swear he looks a little uncomfortable. He mumbles something about Kip getting in too deep. *Too deep?* I don't know what he means by that. Deep into what? The ghost thing? Or me? And what's wrong with deep, anyway?

As I sit upstairs this evening, wasting time on the Internet and enjoying some peace and quiet before Joyce gets home, the smoke alarm goes off again. This time, I run downstairs to see what's going on. I meet Jack in the hallway, moving fast in his leg braces and crutches toward the kitchen. When we get there, we stare in shock at Ethan, who's standing at the sink, facing the window curtains. They're on fire!

"Ethan! What the hell is going on?" We're both yelling. I run to the sink, elbowing him out of my way, and turn on the faucet, grabbing the hose attachment and spraying the curtains. The flames are out fast but the curtains are ruined. The hems are curled and black. With the smoke alarm still blaring, I turn on Ethan.

"Are you going completely mad?" He doesn't answer. "Joyce is going to kill you when she gets home. Psycho!"

He gives me this fixed stare. Almost makes me miss his facial tic.

"Really, Ethan," Jack says in this big-brother tone, "you can't go around acting careless like that. It's not like you. Snap out of it before something happens that you really regret." Ethan just smiles at him like he's some kind of stranger. He's lucky Jack's so kind-hearted. He could squash Ethan into the ground if he wanted to.

When I finally get back on my computer, I find an e-mail from Kip.

Hey kiddo. You around this weekend? I'm thinking of heading north for a little family reunion.

32

I manage to pull myself together, more or less, before he arrives. I'm wearing my new makeup and a new top Joyce got me for Christmas. I did some deep-breathing exercises to try to calm down. Waiting for him, looking out the living-room window, watching for his car in the driveway, the excitement is unbearable. At the sight of it I feel like I'm going to have a heart attack.

Ever since the e-mail, I've been thinking of nothing else but this weekend. The rest of the week was a writeoff. I just don't remember it. When I got home from school this afternoon, and Kip phoned to say he'd arrived and to ask if I wanted to go for a drive, I was so nervous I could barely breathe. He said he'd swing around in an hour or so. Just like that. For a minute after we hung up, I stood there by the phone holding my hands to my face, my mouth open like an idiot. Thank God no one was around to see me.

I've been trying so hard to hold it together this past month. To lower all my expectations and accept the hard reality that Kip was back with his friends in Chicago and had probably forgotten I ever existed. I knew I was lucky I'd even met him. Lucky he'd passed through my town—passed through my life—at all. But the hardest part was always the thought that I'd never see him again. I could never quite go there. Too painful.

When I finally open the door to his smiling face and those to-die-for baby blues, he gives me a big hug and a quick smack on the cheek. And this time I kiss him back. Kind of. I think I catch him off guard—maybe because I'm wearing lip gloss—but he covers it well and everything seems okay. I start to relax.

He always has made me feel more relaxed, somehow. There's something gentle and amusing about him, and it calms me, even though I realize he must be like that with all the girls. He just seems perfectly happy to be hanging out with me, after everything we've been through, and it makes me feel so lucky.

Anyway, he's never been to Inglis Falls, and it seems like the perfect place to go for a Sunday drive. I hope he likes it.

I've always had a thing for Inglis Falls in the winter. It's the most amazing waterfall in the county, but you have to see it when it's half-frozen. It's like an ice sculpture carved out of the water roaring down the rock face. And today is a brilliant winter day. The fields and trees have a fresh blanket of snow, and there's a bright blue sky. The snow-plows have been out and the roads are clear. Everything sparkles.

There's a little white skeleton dangling from Kip's rear-view mirror. A Mexican souvenir he brought back for Morris. He tells me he bought one for me too. Skeletons are very big in Mexico, apparently. I look across at him in the driver's seat of Morris's car and it feels like ages since I took in his face. He looks beautiful. He's still a bit tanned from his holiday, and he's chatty and in a good mood, full of stories about Mexico. He's switched his major to history, he says—almost like he's embarrassed to admit it—and while he doesn't know what he'll do with a history degree, he thinks it'll be interesting to study. I'm listening but I'm also looking at him.

"Morris must be pleased about that," I say.

Kip rolls his eyes at me, then says, "So what's going on with you? How have you been? How is everyone?"

"Everyone's okay. Joyce is the same. Jack's back at school full time. Still walking with his braces and canes, but moving faster now. It's still a shock to see him coming down the hall, I have to admit. I don't know if it will ever sink in, what happened to him. I'm just hoping he recovers so completely that it won't matter. And Ethan . . . well, Ethan's going through an anti-social phase. His teacher called Joyce to complain about him last week. And he's becoming a bit of a pyromaniac—oh, I'll tell you about all that later."

"And how about you?"

"Well, I'm . . . I'm okay. Surviving. Fine, actually. Right now I'm trying not to think too much about everything that happened this fall. I'm trying to think about the future."

Kip looks surprised. "That sounds very good," he says.

We drive for a while in silence. Maybe it's because Kip is only an arm's length from me, but I do have a rare feeling of hopefulness today, like I really have survived something after all. That's good. I don't ever want to go back to the way I used to be, especially after Mom died and before I met Morris. When I felt crazy. Matthew helped me endure those years, but when I think back, I know I was still miserable a lot of the time. Everything's a little different now. At least I don't feel like I suffer from hallucinations anymore—and that's huge, believe me.

I feel like I'm starting to accept a few things, as well. I understand now that the Matthew I used to know is never coming back. What happened to him was freakish and unjust and tragic, but it will never change. Things will never be the way they once were. Meanwhile, the farm is still up for sale, and I'm sure the barn will be torn down before any new owners move in. What happens to Matthew then is something I don't want to consider.

"For the first time, just about, I've been wondering what I should do after high school next year," I tell Kip. "Who knows? Maybe I'll go to university too." Not something I'd given any thought to before Morris mentioned it, but I've thought about it a lot ever since.

He laughs. "Dad'll have you doing a Ph.D. in paranormal activity. You're the protegée he always wanted."

We find an empty spot in the parking lot and get out of the car. I take hold of his arm and pull him toward the falls. Kip's face lights up when we get to the railing. The view is amazing, as always. The icy water is roaring over the limestone ledge, and the drop is wild; the waterfall is half-wrapped in a frozen blanket, a gravity-defying structure that juts out over the river below. The water crashes into a deep ravine cut into the sides of the escarpment, with pines and spruce trees leaning in along the slopes. I knew he'd like it. Everybody does.

"Impressive, eh?"

"Wow, that's very cool. And friggin' cold, I'll bet." We look in silence for a bit. Then he leans over and looks way down into the ravine. "Can we get down there?"

"Well, there is a trail—there are steps leading down to it over there—but I doubt people use them at this time of year. Slippery."

"What am I going to do with you?" He takes my hand and pulls me along the railing toward the steps. "You worry too much. I'm checking it out, and I think you should come too."

"Then watch your step. That's all I'm saying."

"You watch *your* step, Ms. Mackenzie," he says, mocking me.

When we get to the bottom, which is tricky because the stairs really are slippery, he stops and looks around. The trailhead is just in front of us, the trail cutting into the forest away from the river's edge. I have to admit that I'm starting to feel worried. I'd kind of imagined staying up top, overlooking that beautiful view, and I'm not sure how we ended up down here, surrounded by dark forest and staring up a bunch of snow-covered steps.

"Um, I'm not sure I'm up for a hike right now," I say, seeing him eyeing the trail. "The sun's going to go down in an hour or so, and I'm not really dressed for this. I mean, it's kind of cold, and"—I point to my head—"no hat."

He turns to me and puts an arm around my shoulder. "Homicidal ghosts you can handle, but cold ears, now that's scary."

"Well, I'm sorry I'm not much of an adventuress, like your big-city friends."

"You're lucky you're cute, that's all I can say, 'cause you're not much fun." He's standing close and tapping my chin. "You mean you want to climb back up all those steps so soon?"

"Okay, fine. Whatever." I pull away and head along the path into the forest. "Let's go for a hike."

He catches up to me, grinning. "Five minutes," he says, "then we can turn around, I promise. I'll have you home all snug and warm before dark."

We walk single file along the path, which is stamped with the tracks of hikers' boots and snowshoes from earlier in the day. But apart from the roar of the falls behind us, the forest is quiet. No one in sight. The trees grow thicker, the canopy of branches blocking out the sun. I trudge along, watching where I step, ducking the odd bough that reaches across the trail.

We've walked for about fifteen minutes when Kip, who's following close behind me, asks if I've had enough and would like to turn around.

"I don't want to push you too far or anything," he says teasingly.

We stop and listen to the forest for a moment, breathing deeply, looking through the trees on either side of the trail. That's something you can't do in the summer, when it's thick with bushes and leaves and undergrowth. Now I can see animal tracks in the snow thirty feet away. But apart from some birds overhead, everything is still. Heaven.

"We *are* alone, right?" he asks, watching me looking into the woods. "You'd tell me if there was an army of ghosts standing over there, wouldn't you?"

I laugh. "I'm not seeing any," I say lightly over my shoulder. "I guess we should head back. But this was nice. Thanks for pushing me. I mean it, thank you."

I turn around to head back the way we came, but Kip isn't moving and we stand face to face. His hands come up and rest on my shoulders.

"Will you do me a favour first?" he asks. "Make eye contact?"

Oh. This is embarrassing, but I force myself to look up at him, holding myself steady. We lock eyes and I feel such a surge of happiness being this close to him that I'm about to burst. "I'm so glad to see you," I finally whisper. Then I look away quickly, saying, "How was that?" and begin to push gently past him.

"Amelia." He seems about to add something, but then he doesn't. He drops one arm and wraps the other around my back, facing the two of us in the direction we came from, and we begin to walk back together, slowly.

I wish he would say something. Finally he breaks the silence. "Don't you find it odd that I've come back to see you so soon? Don't you wonder why? Aren't you even a tiny bit curious?"

"To be honest, I'm trying not to analyze it. I don't want to . . . um, expect anything."

He takes a deep breath. "It's because I wanted to see you again. Thinking about you practically ruined my vacation, you know."

"Really?" I can't believe this. I'm trying to keep my head clear, trying to stay on my feet. "The point is, you've moved back to Chicago. And I . . . I can't keep you here. And missing you sucks. You don't know . . ." He smiles. "I'm serious," I say, trying not to smile with him. "I've been trying to stop wanting to be with you so badly. It's worse than you know." Wow. I've admitted it.

"Do you always make decisions about what to feel and what not to feel?"

"If I possibly can. Yes."

"Ah."

"Besides, I can't compete with your Chicago girlfriends."

He laughs softly. "Ah yes, those imaginary Chicago girlfriends. Well, if I'm willing to compete with a bloody ghost, couldn't you at least give it a try?"

God, I'm suddenly feeling emotional. I will kill myself if I get teary.

"The problem is, I don't know how to compete. Happy now?"

I hear him let out a kind of sigh. We continue along the trail, his arm loosely around me. When we reach the steps leading up out of the ravine, he turns to me again.

"What am I going to do with you?" he asks. "You know you had me in the Bob Marley mask." And he wraps his arms around me and gives me a hug. With his face buried in my hair, he says, "Amelia, I . . . I tried to fight it, believe me, but I lost. I think I'm in love."

"You're not sure?"

"You know I am."

A shiver goes through me. "You're cold," he says, and starts undoing the buttons of his coat. Opening it up, he wraps both sides around me, pulling me close to him, my face against his shirt. "Warm up."

I slip my hands around his waist, wrap my arms tightly around his back, hold myself against his chest. He's holding the front of his coat closed around my back, enveloping me. I shut my eyes. I press closer.

"Warmer?"

I nod and shudder, but not from the cold.

"An old arctic tradition," he says. "Body heat." He pulls away and slowly slides down the zipper on my jacket from under my chin to the hem. I look up at him in surprise. "Trust me," he says, opening my jacket up and pulling me toward him, our clothing suddenly thin between us, our bodies together, hearts pounding. "Inuit science."

He kisses the top of my head and I feel his warm breath, the heat of his body pressing against me, the rough shadow of his beard moving against my cheek. Our lips touch and then our mouths press together, hot and moist in the cold air.

Whatever it is, Kip, it's working.

Miles away, I hear the muffled ring of my cellphone. *No, go away.* I'm reeling, light-headed. I look up at Kip, feeling flushed and over-whelmed and weak and happier than I've ever felt. It's still ringing. Keeping my eyes on his face, his chest, I struggle to remember how to answer my phone.

"Hello?"

"Amelia, where the hell are you? I've been trying to reach you for fifteen minutes." It's Jack, whispering hoarsely. He sounds angry, panicked.

"Jack? Sorry, my cellphone must have been out of range. What's wrong? Are you all right?"

"How fast can you get home? I'm here alone with Ethan. Joyce's gone out somewhere and she's not picking up her cellphone either. Ethan's lost it."

I try to catch my breath. "Lost what? What do you mean?"

"He's out of control. Listen, I've been doing the stairs for exercise. Just now, when I got to the top of the landing, I smelled something burning and peeked inside his bedroom. He was lighting matches and flicking them onto his bed. He's written stuff on his wall, too. I asked him what the hell he was doing and grabbed the matches off him, but he was all excited and happy. He said he's got to go meet someone. Someone special, he said."

"We can get there in about thirty minutes. But listen, has Ethan been back in the barn lately? Do you know?"

"No, no. Only that one time, when you guys were there. Before Christmas."

"He shouldn't leave the house. You know what I mean, right? Is he still in his room?"

"Yes, I left him in there to make this call."

"Can you wedge a chair under the doorknob? Or do something to keep him inside until we get there? Do whatever you can to stop him from leaving. We're on our way."

"You'd better hurry. He's acting totally psycho."

"What did he write on his wall?" I feel I have to ask, but I know what he's going to say.

"It looks like letters. Nothing that makes any sense. Just D-O-T."

33

Kip speeds along back roads while I dial Morris's home number on my cellphone, but there's no answer. I leave a message asking him to call me at once. "It's urgent!" I say. I turn to Kip. "He doesn't have a cellphone, does he?"

"Sorry, no," says Kip, eyes on the road.

"Any idea where he'd be?"

"Not really. The library, maybe, or a coffee shop. Or visiting someone. He could be anywhere."

I check my watch. "The library is closed by now."

We drive in a tense silence. I feel like I've been jerked back into a nightmare from a beautiful dream. I'm shivering, so I struggle with my zipper, closing my jacket, trying to think. How could this have happened to Ethan? "I don't get it. This doesn't make any sense. It doesn't fit the pattern."

Kip says grimly, "He must have a crush on some girl. Someone who dumped him, or somehow broke his heart."

I shake my head. "He's not interested in girls—or anyone else, for that matter." I think about Ethan all by himself, playing video games, watching TV. "What are we going to do?" Think, think. "Okay, what does this ghost want more than anything else?"

Kip heaves a sigh. "For Dot to finally show up at the barn?"

"Exactly."

He shoots a quick glance at me. "So what would happen if she did?"

"I don't know," I say. "Maybe she could convince him they weren't really meant for each other. Maybe she could tell him to get over it. Drop dead already." I look across at him, trying to read his thoughts. "What are you suggesting?" We're turning onto 12th Line.

"I don't know. Where's Joyce, do you think?"

"At the stables, probably." Then it occurs to me. "South on Highway 6. I mean, Williamsford would be on her way home."

He turns into our driveway. We race up the steps to the front porch just as Jack opens the door. He looks bad, like he's been in a fight. He's hopping on one leg, using his crutches. He's only wearing one brace, and he has a wet cloth wrapped around one hand. I can smell something awful, something burnt.

"Jeez, Jack, what happened to you?"

"Ethan pushed me down the stairs. I'm all right, except I think my finger's broken." He holds up his right index finger; it's blue and swollen. "And one of my braces is broken. But I was lucky."

"He pushed you down the stairs! Are you kidding?" I'm running down the hall, frantically looking into the living room and the kitchen, up the stairs. "Where is he?"

"He's gone. He wanted to leave his room, and I guess the chair I wedged under his doorknob wasn't strong enough. I could hear banging and I was halfway up the stairs when he busted out. I tried to stop him but he pushed by me, knocked me down. I don't know how but his bed was on fire."

"*What?*"

I run up the stairs with Kip close behind me. We stand at the entrance to Ethan's bedroom and look at the large letters in black marker on his closet door. They've been written with a strange, careful hand. Not Ethan's. There's a huge, burnt-out hole in the middle of his mattress. I can see the metal coils inside.

I suddenly remember that Matthew said Jimmy wasn't in the barn. That was almost a month ago. We run back down the stairs and I shout to Jack, who's standing in the hallway, "Did you hear from Joyce?"

"No, not yet. I haven't tried again. I didn't have a chance."

I grab the phone and dial her cell. No answer. I leave a message. "Joyce, call me as soon as you get this. Ethan's in danger!" I hang up and dial Morris's home number, getting his machine again. "Morris, when you get this message, please head to the barn right away. We need help. It looks like Ethan has 'gone Jimmy' on us—my younger brother, Ethan. He's left the house and he's . . . he's got to be headed for the barn. That's where we'll be. Please come. *Please!*"

As I hang up, I realize that Kip has the car. So how could Morris even get to the barn? I turn to Kip. "We have to go."

Just then, the phone goes. I answer on the first ring. It's Joyce.

"What the hell is going on?"

"Where are you, Joyce?"

"I'm at the stables. What's wrong with Ethan?" She sounds furious. I take a deep breath and lock eyes with Kip to keep myself steady.

"Joyce, I need you to go to the seniors' residence in Williamsford and find Mrs. Ross. Mrs. Dorothy Ross. She calls herself Dee. You remember who she is? I need you to tell her that Jimmy has Ethan. Can you tell her that? Just say, 'Jimmy has Ethan in the barn.' And tell her who Ethan is. You have to trust me on this. It's life or death." I've been talking too fast for her to say anything, but now she jumps in.

"Amelia, you're not making sense. What the hell is going on?"
Did she not hear anything I said?

"Ethan is headed to the Telfords' barn. He's acting just like Jack did the night he fell. The night he fell *on purpose*. You knew that, right? It wasn't an accident—it was attempted suicide. Mrs. Ross knows what's going on. Ethan is in terrible danger right now. I'm asking you to trust me, please!"

"What . . . ?"

"Please, Joyce! We'll be at the Telfords' barn. Just bring her there as fast as you can."

I hang up, then grab Kip by both arms. I'm terrified. We hold on to each other tightly, just for a second.

"Let's go," he says.

"I'm coming too." Jack hops to the door on his crutches. He beats us out and moves down the porch steps as fast as he can, swinging his braceless leg along.

"Fine," says Kip, "but you have to stay out of the barn. He got hold of you once and he can probably do it again. You'll stay at the car and wait for help."

The tires spray gravel as we race down the driveway in reverse and screech as we accelerate to full speed, racing south on 12th Line, Kip's little Mexican skeleton flying. As soon as we pull into the Telford driveway, we see footprints in the snow, leading along the side of the house to the big barn door. I feel cold with fear. I don't want to face this.

The car comes to a hard stop and Kip and I jump out. I turn to Jack in the back seat. "Stay here, Jack. Please. We're going to get Ethan out of there."

We run along Ethan's tracks toward the barn. Taking one last, desperate look at each other, we peek in. Ethan is deep inside, pacing back and forth across the centre of the floor. We brace ourselves and step in. He doesn't look up.

"Ethan?" I call to him like nothing's wrong. "Ethan, come out of here. Ethan?" He doesn't seem to hear me. I try a little louder. "Ethan?"

He's ignoring me. We take another step closer. He looks agitated but nothing more—thank goodness. It's like he's waiting for something and he's impatient. He's waiting for Dot.

We creep a little closer.

"Ethan, it's Amelia. Amelia and Kip. Jack's outside."

No response.

"Why don't you come out and see Jack? He thinks he broke his finger when you pushed him down the stairs. Maybe you should talk to him about that. He's pretty pissed off."

Ethan's still pacing, ignoring us. I look at Kip and whisper that I'm going to get nearer, and maybe he should stay behind me. He seems unsure. His eyes are on Ethan.

"Ethan?" I edge closer.

No response. I feel stuck, watching him pace like he's in his own little world. If this keeps up, at some point we'll need to jump him. Tackle him to the ground. Tie him up and drag him out. If only Jack could help. But even if Kip and I can handle Ethan ourselves, then what? Where do we go from here? To Emergency? To an exorcist?

Something moves off to my right. I turn quickly to look. It's Paul Telford, watching from a corner. He looks anxious. Great—even the ghosts are afraid. I look around some more. "Matthew?" On the left side, inside an open stall, I see a shadow sitting in the dark. When I look hard at him, the figure slowly stands up. From the shape of the cap on his head, I can tell that it's Willy. He's watching us too. Now my eyes dart between Ethan, still pacing, and the rafters above. I scan the dark corners of the barn. I feel that cool, cobwebby sensation again. I spin around. Kip, standing about fifteen feet behind me, gives a start.

"It's okay," I whisper, gesturing with one hand. I turn back slowly. This will be difficult.

"Matthew?" I keep my voice low. "Matthew?"

A dark shadow forms against the back wall and Matthew takes a step toward me. I can see his face. He's worried too.

"Matthew? Can you help? It's Ethan." I'm pleading now. "You've got to help us."

He opens his mouth slightly, like he's not sure what to say. He takes another step toward me. Toward Ethan. His eyes move from me to Ethan and back to me. Then I see him tilt his head. He's looking behind me, at Kip.

"Matthew! Can you help or what?"

He seems to heave a sigh. He takes another step closer, looking at Ethan, then stops as if unsure. Maybe he can't help. I turn to Ethan again.

"Ethan?" Nothing. I have to try something else. "Jimmy?"

Ethan turns his head, shoots me an angry look. He stops pacing for the first time since we arrived.

"Get out!" It's Jimmy talking.

That's all he says, and then he turns away. He seems distracted and confused, like we broke his concentration. He stops pacing, and in the dim light I can see that his features are strained and distorted, like he's going to cry. I back up slowly until I'm next to Kip.

"This isn't good."

"What's happening?"

"I don't know, but this is how I found Jack. I think this is the pattern. Like he's realizing that Dot's not going to show up. How long ago did I talk to Joyce?"

"I don't know. Twenty minutes? Maybe more?"

"Best just to keep an eye on him until he looks like he's going to do something stupid, then we'll tackle him."

Kip nods. "It's not like he's got a weapon."

Ethan starts making sobbing sounds, like his heart is breaking. I have a strong desire to comfort him, my little brother, and I leave Kip's side and walk toward him again. He's just standing in the middle of the barn, head down, shoulders shaking with his sobs. I'm about three feet from him when his head jerks up violently to face me. I have a heart-stopping flashback to the boy hanging by his neck.

"Get out!" he growls. "*Get out!*"

It gives me such a fright that I almost start crying myself. "Please don't hurt my brother. Please let him go." His eyes are blazing with hatred. I have to pull myself together. I back up to Kip's side again. He steps forward and grabs my arm, holding tightly.

"Look, it's going to be okay," he whispers. "We just need to kill some time. If I have to, I can take him." He tugs at my arm reassuringly. "Don't worry. I can handle it."

Ethan's sobs are getting louder. It's horrible. I don't know what to do but watch and wait. Then I remember Matthew, and try to find him again. All I can see are shadows—shadows of young men moving slowly in the darkest corners of the barn. I can make out Willy by his cap.

"Willy! Willy, you have to help us."

He comes closer. He's wringing his hands. He looks devastated.

"It was my fault," he says. "It was my idea, not hers. I made her tell him. Tell him she'd meet him in the barn. I had to teach him a lesson. I was going off to war, and I just wanted him to leave my sister alone."

Ethan is muttering between sobs now, but the words are impossible to make out. He sounds insane. He's working himself up into a rage. I feel like we're waiting for an explosion. There'll be no warning and nothing we can do.

"You met Jimmy in the barn. Your sister told us what you did."

He's shaking his head. Backing away again. "I didn't mean for it to end that way," I hear him say. "I didn't mean for that to happen."

"I know that, Willy. And Dorothy knows it too. You couldn't have guessed what Jimmy would do. But you have a chance now to put things right." I'm crying to him, pleading with him, but he's disappearing. "Don't go! Help us!"

I turn back to Ethan. "She's coming, Jimmy." Then I shout it out. God knows what effect that'll have, but I'm feeling desperate. "*Dot is coming!*"

"Where? Where is she?"

Have I just made things worse? I hold on to Kip as Ethan's rage escalates, his words echoing up through the rafters. And then he makes a move. He dives under the platform along the wall. Scrambling on hands and knees, he lunges for the pile of solvents I dumped from the crate last time we were here. He grabs a container of something and pulls off the cap, dousing himself in what smells like fuel, drenching his head, his clothes.

"You don't want to do that!" Kip shouts, diving under the platform toward him.

I'm frozen. I can only watch as Kip tackles Ethan, knocking him backwards into the straw. They wrestle under the platform, which is too low for either one to stand up. Kip is larger and stronger, and he's trying to drag Ethan back into the open barn. But Ethan is too wild and out of control; he's viciously kicking and throwing punches that Kip tries to block. He doesn't want to hurt Ethan, and they end up rolling in the damp straw until they're both covered in fuel.

Then Ethan grabs another metal container and whips it hard at Kip's face. There's a horrible clunking sound as it connects. Kip tries to pin him down and pull him out at the same time. Ethan rolls onto his back and kicks out his thick boots, landing a solid blow against Kip's chest. I hear the thud as Kip staggers back under the platform and hits his head hard on a wooden beam. He slumps forward to his knees. Ethan rolls over and crawls out from under the platform, scrambling to his feet. Kip staggers out behind him, weaving, facing Ethan with raised fists. He's bleeding from his forehead and cheek.

Ethan starts laughing. He has something in his hand, something orange that he's waving at Kip. It's Joyce's cigarette lighter! They're both covered in oily black fuel; the fumes fill the air.

"Ethan, NO! Please don't!" I scream. "Kip! You've got to get out!"

Kip staggers backwards a step but holds his ground. His eyes are on the lighter. I lunge at him from behind, grabbing two fistfuls of his open coat, pulling him away from Ethan and back toward the barn door. Blood runs down his forehead, the side of his face. Ethan keeps laughing, waving the lighter.

Just then, a voice behind us roars like thunder. "Ethan, what the HELL do you think you're doing?"

It's Joyce. She steps in front of Kip and me, turns to us and points us both toward the door.

Ethan sneers at her. "Get out!" he growls.

She looks at him, shocked. "Outside!" she yells, turning back to us. She helps me get Kip to the door.

I can see Jack outside, hopping on one crutch, petrified with fear. We stagger out and stand a few feet back from the door. Kip is dazed, blood dripping everywhere. Joyce looks down at his fuel-soaked clothes. She turns back and takes another hard look at Ethan. He's swaggering, smirking, her lighter in his hand. "Stay here. Keep him clear," she tells me, nodding at Kip. Then she turns to someone standing behind her.

"Mrs. Ross? Are you sure?"

34

rs. Ross steps around the corner of the barn, clutch-
ing her white cane. She looks tiny and terrified.

"Mrs. Ross?" I hold my hands out to her and she takes
them, squeezing tight. Behind her thick glasses, her eyes are full of
tears. I don't know what to say. "It's my baby brother, Ethan. Please
be careful."

"You take care of Pip," she says with a quivering smile, glancing
in Kip's direction, and she lets me go. She turns to face Joyce. "Yes,
I'm sure," she says, and leaving her cane leaning up against the barn,
she shuffles inside, alone.

I look at Joyce. "Hold on to Kip," I say.

"I'm okay. I'm okay." He's angry. "Amelia, don't!"

Joyce puts an arm around him as I turn toward the barn door.
"Amelia!" Her voice is severe.

"I have to go in. I'm the only one who can see them."

She opens her mouth to say something, but I'm already on my
way into the barn when I hear it: "Just like her mother."

Part of me wants to turn around and have it out with Joyce right there, but I need to focus on Mrs. Ross. She's taking baby steps, shuffling toward Ethan, who still stands in the middle of the barn, soaked in fuel, lighter in his raised hand. He's no longer smiling, though. He's trembling, his eyes growing wider as she approaches.

"Dot?" he whispers.

"Let that boy go, Jimmy. You let that poor boy go back to his family." She looks around the barn, then back at Ethan. I know she can barely see him.

He's still trembling. "Dot? Is that you?"

Mrs. Ross looks hard toward Ethan now. "Let him go, Jimmy. You've caused enough suffering. Let him go."

She walks to within about five feet of him. Ethan turns to her. His baby face, barely out of puberty, softens into an eager grin. He's covered in sweat and oily fuel and straw.

"I knew you'd come, Dot. I always knew it. I'm the one you love. I'm the one you're going to marry."

I can't believe this. Ethan, my baby brother. His eyes still glisten with tears, but he's brightening up. He keeps the plastic lighter held high.

"And I'll take good care of your daddy's farm. And we'll live here forever. And we'll be happy forever."

Mrs. Ross shakes her head. "It was never going to happen, Jimmy. I told you it was never going to happen. You wouldn't listen."

Ethan's expression changes. His features tighten. His mood is growing dark again. "Don't say that. Don't ever say that again! You said you'd come. You lied to me!"

"I was afraid of you. I wanted you to leave me alone."

"You loved me. You . . . you kissed me."

"Yes, I kissed you once. It was a mistake."

"You broke my heart. You humiliated me!"

I step closer. I see shadows moving in the background.

"I'm sorry, Jimmy. I'm so sorry. What we did . . . it was mean." Her voice is full of regret. "But that was a long time ago. Please let this boy go. He's done nothing to you."

"You were my girl."

"No. I was *never* your girl. I was Philip's girl. You know I was always Philip's girl."

"You said you'd come."

"I was afraid of you." Tears begin to trickle down her cheeks. "Willy said he'd fix it so you would leave me alone." And then she stiffens and raises her voice in accusation. "And then you killed Willy." She screams, "You killed Willy!"

"*Your* fault," he shouts back.

Crying hard, she raises her thin arms at him, her hands fisted.

Ethan's chin suddenly falls to his chest. The hand that holds the lighter slowly lowers, like he's exhausted. Then he raises his hand again, his thumb moving toward the cap of the lighter, his sad eyes on Mrs. Ross. His arms, head and shoulders are glistening with fuel.

"Don't!" she yells.

"*Your* fault." He whispers it this time. His thumb moves over the lighter.

"NO!" Two voices—mine and Joyce's, from somewhere behind me—scream in unison.

As we both lunge forward, I see Matthew appear from the shadows, his arm arcing, his hand swiping for the lighter. It flies out of Ethan's grasp, hitting the edge of the platform and falling to the ground. There's a spasm of shock on Ethan's face and his eyes blink hard in disbelief. Then he collapses to his knees on the dirt floor, shaking. He looks up with terrified eyes and a tear-streaked face.

"Mom?" he whimpers. "Mom?"

He's free. Jimmy has let my brother go. He's choking on tears, his shoulders shaking, his face full of pain. And in that one confusing instant, I realize it's Mom he's crying about.

Joyce and I both run to him. We throw our arms around him and half carry him out of the barn, and he falls in the snow, crying. He's okay. He's safe. On my knees, I hold him, rock him. I realize that when we lost our mother, Ethan's heart was broken. And to Jimmy, heartache is heartache.

"Everything's going to be okay, Ethan." He looks at me, his face twitching between sobs. Why didn't I get it before? "I'm sorry, Ethan. I'm so sorry. We love you."

Joyce has an arm around him, and I feel her hand on my shoulder as well. "We all miss her, Ethan," she whispers to him. "It's okay. We all miss her."

Then I hear Mrs. Ross's voice again, from deep inside the barn, and I pull away. I need to get her out. Kip steps into my path, trying to block me. We stand face to face, breathless, and I look up into his eyes.

"Get out of the way," I whisper. "And stay back. Don't be stupid."

"Don't *you* be stupid."

I push past him into the barn. I hear him step in behind me. "You're not doing this alone."

The sun is setting and it's getting harder to see, but I can just make out Mrs. Ross standing in the middle of the barn. Now the real Jimmy stands before her, his head resting sideways on his shoulder, his neck snapped. As his head slowly lifts up and straightens, blood gushes from his mouth.

"Mrs. Ross, it's time to get out of here."

She's not hearing me. Jimmy's stomach is drenched in blood. Holes in the pattern of a pitchfork ooze dark red across his abdomen.

"Go away, Jimmy!" She's shouting at shadows. "Never come back!" She can't see him, it seems, but she can feel him in the air. Her arms are folded. She's shivering. Her eyes dart in his direction— she must sense that he's circling her. Now the blood on his stomach is gone and I see yellow foam flowing from his nose and mouth, down his chin, to the ground. He's choking, gasping, bent at the waist, staggering in the straw. But his bulging eyes still watch her.

"Mrs. Ross!" I shout, but she doesn't look back.

"Leave us alone," she cries to Jimmy.

His arms now hang loose below the elbows, bone exposed, blood flowing heavily down his forearms, through his fingers.

"I'm sorry we hurt you," she cries, "but that didn't give you the right." She's gasping now, like she can't breathe.

With the side of his head blown away, Jimmy drops to his knees by the platform, where the orange lighter is lying in the straw. He looks up at her, his face torn and bloody. His movements are quick. I hear a click, see a flash.

"MRS. ROSS!" I scream.

It's too late. There's a blinding yellow explosion and the roar of fire. I spin around and push Kip toward the door. We look back to see flames spreading like fireballs under the platform where Ethan spilled the fuel, surging like a river along the platform, spreading up the beams, jumping across the rafters, racing along the straw-strewn floor. Mrs. Ross, kneeling in the middle of the barn, is on fire. Her arms are slightly raised, fingers held open. A wall of flame rises between her and us.

Outside, Joyce and Jack are screaming our names. We stagger backwards out of the barn and into the snow, which is glowing in the light from the flames. Smoke pours out of the doorway, and I can barely see Kip's fuel-covered clothes, his bleeding face.

"Kip, get up. Move!" I'm desperate to get him farther from the barn, which is now a monstrous roaring bonfire.

The fire lights up the cracks between the boards. Right up to the roof, the barn is leaking smoke and flashing orange light. Dry wood crackles and crashes. A dark cloud rises and fills the air, and we huddle well back—Jack and Joyce, Ethan, Kip and me, crying in disbelief.

I barely recognize the sound of the siren until the police car tears up the driveway. Morris and Detective Grierson run toward us as the entire right side of the barn collapses with a sound like thunder, filling the air with smoke, ash and flames.

Morris, his eyes wild with fright, sees Kip crouched beside Ethan in the snow, blood on his face, holding a red wad of tissue. He falls to his knees, hands on his son's shoulders.

"I'm okay," Kip says, before Morris can form the words. "But Mrs. Ross. She . . . she didn't get out."

Morris's eyes search for mine. Then he staggers to his feet, runs toward the barn door and shouts for Mrs. Ross.

Grierson has raced back to his car. He's on his radio. I can hear him reporting the fire, calling for an ambulance and police backup. Then he runs around the collapsed side of the barn. He and Morris circle the building, but they can't get close. They stand helplessly, watching the massive structure completely engulfed in flames, small explosions coming from deep inside.

Morris stares at the inferno. Then he walks back to us, head down, eyes brimming with tears.

"She was ready to die if that was what it took." Joyce is crouching beside Ethan, holding his hand. "She told me everything on the way over. She said she and her brother were cruel to Jimmy. And he paid them back."

I can't believe my ears. Is this my grandmother? Talking about a ghost?

Grierson walks toward us, his voice threatening. "What are we looking at here, people? Are you going to tell me this was an accident?" He glances from Ethan to Kip, takes in their clothes, damp and stained. "This isn't just arson. Someone is dead."

As he says that, the far wall of the barn collapses with a tremendous crash.

"Just a minute, Detective. Before you jump to any conclusions, hear me out." It's Joyce again, rising to her feet this time. "I gave your mother riding lessons, you know. She can vouch for the fact that I don't suffer fools much, and superstitious fools even less. But there are two things you need to know. First, Dorothy Ross was born and raised on this farm. And second, she came here tonight of her own free will, went inside that barn of her own free will. She had unfinished business, she said. And something else. I'm not saying these boys didn't get into a scuffle in the barn, spill some stuff. But when that fire ignited, it started inside, and we were all out here. Nobody here started that fire."

Grierson has been standing nose to nose with Joyce, his mouth open in surprise. Now he shuts it tight, looking grim.

"Nobody here?" he asks, looking her in the eye.

"No," she says. "I saw it all."

"Who started it, then? Are you saying Dorothy Ross started it?"

There's a long silence. Finally Joyce replies, "I'm just saying that nobody standing out here started the fire. How long would those two have lasted if either of them had lit a match?" She nods toward Kip and Ethan, both reeking of fuel.

While Joyce and Grierson are talking, I keep my eyes on the burning barn. I stare hard into the flames, through the smoke and the collapsing walls. Finally I see someone, and I get to my feet and step as close as I can bear to the heat. A young man is standing in the middle of the inferno. He has shoulder-length red hair and wire-rim glasses. He's facing me, and I see him lift one of his hands. He gives a small, awkward wave with his fingers, then turns and walks away, beyond the far end of burning barn, toward the road.

It's a wave goodbye.

Following him through the smoke and flames are Mrs. Ross and Willy in his army cap. Mrs. Ross stops to look back and I raise my hand. Tears and smoke cloud my eyes, but it looks like she's smiling. Brother and sister walk away from us, out of the burning barn, her arm on his. Farther behind, in the heap of burning boards, charred frames and supports and fallen rafters, I can make out two more figures following the others out of the fire. Jimmy and Paul, side by side. They all move together over the fallen back wall of the barn and, leaving no footprints, across the snowy field toward the road. *Matthew? Where are you?*

Through the billowing clouds of smoke, I finally see him. He's walking away too, his back to me. *Matthew?* He reaches the far edge of the flames. *Matthew, is this it?*

"What is it? What do you see?" Morris is standing at my side.

"They . . . they're all leaving."

Morris looks distraught. His eyes, red-rimmed, search desperately, but he looks right through the ghosts and on to the horizon.

Matthew? He stops, turns and faces me. I can barely see him. *Are you really leaving? We never said goodbye.* I strain to see him more clearly, frantic for any kind of sign. I hold up my hand but a cloud of smoke passes between us, obliterating him. As it clears, all I can see are ghostly shadows crossing the field on the far side of 12th Line. *Goodbye, Matthew. Goodbye!* And now I'm crying like my chest is cracking open. He's gone. This time, he's really gone.

I feel Kip's arms around me. He whispers in my ear, "It's over."

———

I've finally stopped crying. I'm exhausted, feeling numb but better.

Kip has been propping me up, holding me tight. The paramedics have bandaged his head and cheek, checked him for signs of concussion. They had him strip off his oily clothes to the waist, and now he's wearing one of their heavy jackets. Jack, Ethan and Joyce are warming up in one of the police vans. Ethan, head down and sleepy, is huddled under Joyce's arm, wrapped in a thick blanket. We've been told we can go home soon. Morris, looking haggard and distracted, has been standing apart, pacing and smoking a cigarette. A little earlier I saw Joyce watching him, and I decided to say something.

"Don't you think now would be a good time to kick the habit?" She looked at me, surprised. "You know, for your health."

Narrowing her eyes at me, she gave Ethan's head a rub and said, "We'll think about it."

I can't believe it's finally over. I rest my head on Kip's shoulder, my swollen eyes fixed on the collapsed barn. It's still burning like a colossal campfire in the snow, lighting up the evening sky. But suddenly I catch sight of something past Kip's shoulder, beyond the burning timbers, through the smoke. I pull back and tilt my head a little. Kip looks at me, leans in and kisses me on the forehead. He holds his lips there for a few moments, hard, and then I pull away. Look again.

Through the drifting grey smoke and the glow of flames, I can see a figure leaning against a tree. It's Matthew, with a half-smile on his face.

I can't move. I look up at Kip. I can't speak.

"Why do I get the feeling I'm about to get punched?" he whispers.

Matthew's smile widens. He raises his finger slowly to his lips, as if to say, *Shhh.*

ACKNOWLEDGMENTS

I am grateful to my first-draft readers, Don Gillmor, Shelley Ambrose and Susan Millican, for offering such generous encouragement to a natural-born coward.

I had a mountain of help in the editing of this book, chiefly from my agent, Jackie Kaiser. She guided me with patience and persistence, and whether she intended to or not, she has changed my life. I had the great good fortune to work with Janice Weaver of Doubleday Canada, with her sharp insight and kind touch. Thanks, also, are owed to Allyson Latta, for additional editing and her good counsel, and to my copy editor, Gena Gorrell, who, like Amelia's grandmother, doesn't mince words.

Finally, I'd like to express my gratitude to my husband, Michael Allder, for his love, strength and wise advice, and to my son, Ben Kotchie, for constant inspiration.

Turn the page
for a sneak peek

Amelia and Matthew's story continues in

A B S O L U T I O N

Coming in 2014
from Doubleday Canada

1

I walk up the driveway of the abandoned Telford farm, my legs feeling wobbly. I'm looking for Matthew, but do I even want to find him? I honestly don't know. Part of me hopes he's gone, only because I don't know how much more of him I can take. And that makes me feel terrible, because I still care for him. He was my first love.

Beyond the farmhouse, there's a heap of black where the barn burned down five days ago. The world's largest barbecue pit in a field of snow. It's still circled by yellow police tape. I guess they don't want anyone messing around in it. An old woman died in the fire, after all. Actually, over the years, a lot of people died in that barn, including Matthew. He's been dead for four months, but he's still hanging around.

So where is he now?

Not near the tree where I last saw him standing. Not near the barn ruins. Now what? I'm looking around and my eyes are starting to sting from the smoky stench still in the air. And they're beginning to go all blurry from tears. He's not here.

"Matthew?"

Maybe in the end he had second thoughts about staying behind and decided to take off with the other ghosts. Maybe he caught up with them across the far field. They were heading west on some kind of ghoulish pilgrimage. All the dead souls from the barn, including old Mrs. Ross, heading for a world beyond this one.

I rub my eyes and try to focus, squinting over what's left of the barn. I don't want to get too close to the charred and collapsed frame. The smell of smoke, an awful stink, is taking my breath away. It's hard to make out much in the wreckage. Mrs. Ross's body is gone—the police took it away in a bag. Everything's black like charcoal. But there are menacing bits of metal sticking out, old farm equipment mixed in with the burned barn boards that came crashing down.

"Matthew?"

Nothing.

It's hard to breathe. I feel dizzy and need to sit down. Walking over to the empty farmhouse, I flop down on the lowest step of the small porch at the side door. I pull my knees up and rest my eye sockets on them. I wrap my arms around my head to block out the edges of sunlight. I feel cold and empty inside.

That's when I feel Matthew's presence and look up. He's about twenty feet away—white face, black hair, across his abdomen four dark red holes dripping blood, blood trickling from his nose and smiling mouth. I jump up in fright and scream so loud that he disappears, but not before a look of worry comes over his face.

I'm bent over the porch railing, chest heaving and heart pounding, sobbing out loud, when I see him again. He's standing farther away, this time without the pitchfork wounds and blood.

I straighten, try to catch my breath. It's a struggle to speak. If I could hit him with a baseball bat, I would. I'm furious.

"I can't believe it!" I finally cry out.

"What can't you believe?" He moves a little closer, cautiously.

"I can't believe you're still here."

"You say that like it's a bad thing."

"What do you expect? Am I some kind of yo-yo you can just play with? You're gone, you're back, you're gone, you're back. Do you know how painful that is?" Now I'm yelling. "And what's with the pitchfork holes?"

He looks down at his shirt like he's embarrassed.

I sit down on the porch again, my head in my hands, elbows on my knees. I've got to calm down.

"I'm not sure. Sometimes that just happens. I think I have flashbacks—it really freaked me out at first. But why are you so angry? It's like you hate me or something. Was that not a good idea? Staying behind?" He pauses, waiting for me to answer. "It seemed like a brilliant one at the time."

I have to admit I *have* been feeling angry with him. I'm not sure why. Maybe it's because just when I thought I'd lost him for real, and was devastated, I also felt a bit of relief that's hard to explain. Like at least I could get on with my life.

"It's just so complicated," I finally say.

"Complicated by what?" he asks. "By Kip?" There's a hint of jealousy in his voice.

At the sound of the name, I set my jaw, shake my head quickly. "No. Not by Kip. Kip's not ... Kip's not even in the picture." Now I feel like hitting him again—I feel like hitting *anything*—because I'm lying and I know it. It's because of the horrible guilt I feel about falling so hard for Kip, and the pain of having to let him go.

"He's not?"

"No, he's not!" I look away, fighting to keep my eyes clear.

"Kip's not in the picture?"

"I just said that, didn't I? Are you deaf? Why are you so stupid these days?" I stop when I see his hurt expression. I would never have talked to him like this when he was alive. "Kip's got his own life to lead," I say, trying to calm down. Matthew looks at me, kind of perplexed. "Besides, he doesn't even live here anymore." Now I'm really depressed. "Matthew, I'm sorry. I don't hate you. I ... I've loved you since grade nine. Do you have any idea what it was like for me when you died? I just don't know how much more of this I can take, that's all. You, being a ghost. It's not easy."

"Like it is for *me*?" he shouts. Then his voice drops. "I'm sorry ..." He looks away, like he's forgotten something or lost something, and then I realize he's fading. I can see through him.

"Matthew, don't go. Don't disappear. Please? Just ... look, I'm sorry. I'm sorry for yelling at you. I'm not used to this new situation yet. But"—I nod as he gets a little clearer again—"but I'm getting more used to it all the time. I am. Just ... let's think for a minute. I mean, the barn is gone. What are your options? You can't just hang out in a friggin' field all day and night, can you?" I'm looking around. "Would you rather have a roof over your head? Would you rather have ... I don't know, privacy?"

"I don't know what I want," he says finally. "Nothing feels quite right. Everything feels a little strange. Sometimes I feel like I got a bad hit on the head. Like half my brain got stolen or something. I wish whoever stole it had taken the whole thing."

I think for a few moments. "Okay. I'm going to make a crazy suggestion: let's you and me break into this house and check it out. No one else is using it right now, so maybe you can hang out inside. That's better than wandering around out here where the barn used to be, don't you think? And that way, I can find you more easily. If I get this door open, do you think you could just go inside?"

I've noticed before that Matthew—ghost Matthew—seems limited in what he can do and where he can go. He was trapped in the barn. He seems stuck on the Telford property. It makes me think about Morris's theory of the geography of ghosts. How some places are more ghost-friendly than others.

"Do you think you could manage that? Just … hang out in there? You know—haunt the place. Like a proper ghost. Maybe learn some ghost tricks."

"You don't think I'm a proper ghost?" He sounds hurt, but then I see his eyes narrow like he's trying not to laugh.

"I'm just saying … I mean, who knows what you're capable of in your new state. You haven't really tested your … um, ghost powers, have you? I mean, we know what you're *not* capable of."

"Oh, like body contact, right?"

For an instant, I remember Kip's arms around me the night the barn burned down, and it's like Matthew has read my mind.

"I'm sorry. I shouldn't have said that," I say quickly, trying not to sound bitter.

"You know, you're way more heartless than you used to be."

"Well, you're way more brainless." I shouldn't have said that either. "So I guess the only thing missing here is a Cowardly Lion." Good. That made him smile. "And Dorothy," I add, and then immediately regret it. Not so funny. Dorothy was Mrs. Ross's name.

I get up to examine the door, trying the doorknob. Locked, of course, but a little wobbly, like there's a loose screw.

"Maybe we can take the knob off? A screwdriver would be good. Or should I just break the window and reach inside to unlock the door, like they would on TV? What do you think?"

I look over my shoulder for Matthew, but he's not there. I turn back to the door just as the curtain behind the glass flies up. Matthew's face on the other side of the window—mouthing "Boo!"—makes me jump. The doorknob turns and the door opens.

"You nearly gave me a heart attack!"

"You said I needed to learn some tricks."

"Not tricks on *me!*"

I don't even feel like going in now, but what choice do I have? I'm the reason Matthew's here. I'm the only one he's got. I bend down and take off my boots. I don't want some real estate agent to see footprints and think the house has been burgled. Taking a deep breath, I step inside, then shoot a threatening look at Matthew.

"I'm not hanging out with you if you're going to pull that kind of thing."

"Geez. All I did was walk through one wall. Maybe *you're* the Cowardly Lion."

I ignore that and look around. I'm standing in the middle of the kitchen, in my socks, and the floor is freezing.

"Okay, Matthew, will this do? Could you make yourself at home here? At least for a while?" A sudden thought makes me uneasy. "You don't think it's already occupied, do you? By another ghost, I mean. Can you tell?" I couldn't take another psycho ghost right now. I flash back to Jimmy, the killer ghost who haunted the Telford barn.

He looks at me and shrugs. "I don't think so."

"Okay. It feels empty to me too. So you can party, be a poltergeist. I'll try to sneak away to visit you as often as I can."

How tricky is this going to be? How risky? I mutter to myself, "I just hope I'm not going crazy."

"Like you're not *already* crazy?" He's smiling slightly.

"If I am, it's your fault." I head back to the kitchen. "But I meant what I said. What you do on your own time is your business, but just ... try not to be scary when you're with me. Understood?" He turns away from me, but not before I catch him breaking into a big grin. "I'm serious, Matthew. My nerves are bad," I say, trying to sound tough, like Joyce.

I pull on my boots at the kitchen door. "I'll sneak back in a few days. In the meantime, please be careful—and lie low." I try to give him a re-assuring smile and add, "Everything's going to be okay," but he doesn't respond. He's looking around the kitchen like he's suddenly feeling curious about his new digs. I step out the side door and close it behind me. Who am I kidding? This could be a disaster.